THE BROOKLYN NORTH MURDER

a novel

THE BROOKLYN NORTH MURDER

a novel

ERICA OBEY

Walrus Publishing| St. Louis, MO

Walrus Publishing
Saint Louis, MO 63116
Copyright © 2023 Erica Obey
All rights reserved.

For information, contact:
Walrus Publishing
4168 Hartford Street, Saint Louis, MO 63116

www.amphoraepublishing.com
www.ericaobey.com
*Walrus Publishing is an imprint of
Amphorae Publishing Group, LLC*
www.amphoraepublishing.com

Manufactured in the United States of America
Cover Design by Kristina Blank Makansi
Cover art: Kristina Makansi

Set in Adobe Caslon Pro and Breamcatcher
Library of Congress Control Number: 2022948576
ISBN: 9781940442457

To the ladies of Incarnation Lutheran Church, who tried to teach me to can tomatoes, knit, and bake krumkake. It's not their fault it didn't work.

CHAPTER ONE
Custody of the Eyes

Custody of the eyes. Up until now, it had been an abstract concept I had associated with the medieval and theology sections of the library where I worked—and a half-remembered anecdote about an obscure saint who always walked with his eyes fixed on the ground, so as not to inadvertently ogle any passing woman. This habit (pun intended) had caused him to be run over by a carriage—and wake up surrounded by the nursing sisters of the convent to which he had been conveyed.

Now, it was a practical challenge. Who knew how hard it could be not to look at the tiny red Speedo being worn by the man who had pulled me close for our Triathlon Team Photo?

Only a year ago, this triathlon had been the Morgansburg Annual Fun Run that had consisted of a single lap around Battlefield Bluff. Now it was the Billings Sprint Challenge Series and had apparently attracted the combined populations of Brooklyn and Poughkeepsie via a social media campaign that had pronounced it one of the ten summer events in the Hudson Valley not to be missed. The transformation—excuse me, *rebranding*—was also the reason I was shivering by the edge of an icy lake at the ungodly hour of eight in the morning, trying not to examine the all too evident assets that a conspicuously well-endowed hedge fund manager named Cam Billings was scarcely hiding beneath an entirely indecent red Speedo.

I was not wearing a swimsuit—or even a wetsuit, as the other competitors were. I had managed to weasel my way out of the swim by claiming a rotator cuff injury, and so was wearing running tights and a reasonably warm wind shirt. It's not that I can't swim—a summer camp instructor who fancied herself a Navy SEAL had made sure of that. But that statement only holds true if you consider the dog paddle a recognized stroke of the U.S.A. Swimming Association. I'm not particularly good with bicycles either. Toe clips remain an enigma. My mechanical abilities begin and end with forcibly rebooting a computer.

But as the college librarian and hot tech star destined to transform Morgansburg, N.Y. into the next Silicon Valley, I was expected to represent De Sales College, and so I was taking on the last leg of the College Relay Team. All that was required of me was the same brisk shuffle around Battlefield Bluff as last year's Fun Run. My athletic abilities are as limited as my mechanical ones. I am adept at walking, running, and hiking—all activities that require no more skill than putting one foot in front of the other.

Paul Morgan flanked me as we locked arms for the camera. He was wearing a pair of bicycling shorts that did little more to disguise his assets than Cam's had. But I didn't have to imagine what lay beneath that thin, Lycra barrier. Paul and I had dated during our first year at Yale, back in the days when having sex seemed to be the done thing. Victorian brides were taught to lie back and think of England on their wedding. I lay back and rehearsed conjugations and declensions in my head in order to pass the time. Our relationship fizzled out somewhere around the Greek Middle Voice.

That didn't stop him from grabbing me in a bear hug as he said, "Look, after the swim, I need to be ready to tag in at the changing area. So can you go ahead and get some video of Cam when he comes out of the water for our real-time followers?"

"Real-time followers?" I grumbled to Doyle. "Who would really sit down and watch this in real time on their phone? My mother?"

"I regret to inform you that Helen Watson is not among the 12,467 subscribers to the Sprint Series webcast," Doyle informed me.

"It was a rhetorical question." My mother was not what you'd call a doting parent. When I presented her with a copy of my published dissertation, she had asked, "What do you want me to do with this?"

The response I squelched was unprintable.

Okay, so I was complaining to my phone. Pretty weird, I suppose—at least if you've been living off the grid for the past five years. Some people talk to Siri. Some talk to Alexa. Hell, my ninety-year-old grandmother binge drinks Cosmopolitans with them while they cheat at online bridge. So, sue me if I talk to Doyle.

Granted, Doyle was different from those virtual assistants he dismissed as "the Code Girls." For one thing, the Girls simply crawled the web and retrieved information. Doyle didn't crawl. He extrapolated. Or as Doyle would put it, the Code Girls were artificial intelligence; he was the real thing. I'm not quite so sure. For one thing, I'm the one who programmed Doyle. I know where the bodies are buried—or to put it in programmer-speak, I am aware of a few significant glitches that need working out. Primary among them is the fact that Doyle is a complete and utter ass.

My name's Mary Watson. Yes, I know. Don't even start with the jokes. Not only have I heard them all, I've catalogued them and cross-referenced them against each other and every typological index out there. Why? It's what I do, and I'm pretty good at it.

I'm a reference librarian and digital resource officer. Once upon a time, we were a dying breed—the kind that fielded questions like "Why do 18th-century English paintings have so many squirrels in them, and how did they tame them so that they wouldn't bite the painter?" Real question. Don't believe me, ask the New York Public Library.

Now, we were on the cutting edge of information technology. Data aggregation. Entity recognition. Natural language processing and training sets for AI. You know, all that stuff from Facebook's evil plan to take over the universe.

Sounds pretty sexy, right? The Vatican archives meet the White Hat hackers. What it really means is I divide my days between scripting on-line training modules for the college's HR department and lecturing on appropriate citation methodologies while my students shop online or hack the Pentagon on their cell phones. Or that's what it meant up until a year ago, when my life—as well as the life of greater Morgansburg—was turned upside down.

The triathlon, too, had been gifted with cutting-edge technology, in the form of electronic timing sensors that replaced the old-fashioned system of paper race bibs. "Shall I just pop over to the steward's tablet and introduce myself *to the sensor program?*" Doyle suggested.

"No need." It wasn't just that I was certain I'd notice

the red Speedo emerging from the water without any prompting from cyberspace; it was more that I didn't want to imagine where Cam might tuck a sensor so it wouldn't get lost.

So, I was caught flat-footed when 30 minutes later the race steward scanning the swimming entries swiped his tablet, and announced, "That's it. They're all in. Time for the biking event."

"What do you mean they're all in? Cam's not in yet."

"He must be," Doyle said. "The numbers all match, and numbers don't lie."

"Ones and zeroes can lie plenty," I said, as I hurried to the changing area, mentally rehearsing my excuses for letting down our 12,467 followers who, for reasons I could not fathom, were supposedly waiting to see Cam Billings emerge dripping from the lake. But the only person there was Paul, stretching his calves in preparation for the bike ride. There was nary a sign of Cam.

"Porta-potties?" I ventured. "Food poisoning?"

As our whispered consultation rapidly escalated in both urgency and tone, the Campus Security Chief erupted from the medic's tent, tugged off his shoes, and dove beneath the surface without even bothering to strip off his shirt. He swam underwater, his head emerging at intervals for air as he traced the swimming route, then the rest of the lake in regular zig-zags.

Silence fell, when Mack Byrne finally emerged, shaking drops of water from his close-cropped hair. "Well, the state search and recovery guys will have better equipment than I do," he said. "But I've had pretty good experience with this kind of thing, and I didn't see a trace of Cam Billings or anyone else down there."

CHAPTER TWO

Once in Love with Amy

In no time, Battlefield Park was filled with volunteer EMTs and firefighters, who stood in knots at the edge of the lake, gravely agreeing on one thing: Cam Billings was nowhere to be found. People standing around in knots pontificating was Morgansburg's customary response to any crisis from a power outage to a downed tree, and it was customarily followed by equally knowing conversations in the Presbyterian Church's Fellowship Hall, comparing the incident to that time Commodore Preston Morgan had staged his own disappearance from a capsized boat in the middle of the Hudson so he could run off with a fan dancer.

Everything changed when Paul Morgan called on his authority as our recently elected county attorney, and the knots of knowing conversations were replaced by an array of lawyers and spokespersons, who urged the crowd to disperse and leave the search in the hands of the professionals.

Things appeared to return to normal on Monday morning when I found a spate of FOIL requests from the *Morgansburg Times* awaiting me at my office. I'd fulfilled more than my fair share of freedom of information requests from the *Times*, a somewhat weekly newspaper sporadically edited and published by the aging hippies on the edge of town. Most of its front-page articles, which I read in a spirit that could either be described as masochism or schadenfreude, explored the hidden history of the Hudson Valley, from Black Helicopters to the annual Pine Bush UFO Fair. The rest of its pages were filled with legal notices and classified ads for handymen, lawn services, and nannies that were photocopied from their business cards. When it came to breaking news, its editor took advantage of his position as an adjunct at De Sales College to treat the library as his personal reference desk, peppering me with requests for everything from maps of the Hudson Valley ley lines to the sexual hygiene of the colonial settlers. So, it came as no surprise that he was now requesting any information that might link Cam Billings' disappearance to the local legend of a lake monster named Battlefield Amy—as well as any associated government coverups.

As I was calling up a Google list that said editor could have easily found himself, Mack Byrne's shadow loomed across my desk, announcing his presence as effectively as a major-domo. It was not just that Byrne was a big man. It was that his natural mode of interaction with people was to loom. It had served him well as Chief of Campus Security. The moment Byrne's shadow loomed so much as a block away, frat house parties dissipated as swiftly and silently as my cats after something crashed in the kitchen.

"Got a minute?" he asked. "I need to ask you a few questions."

"About Cam Billings?" I asked. "He still hasn't turned up?"

"No sign of him. In or out of the water." Byrne shook his head. "I went back down with the state recovery crew, and we didn't find a thing. If this were the Hudson, I'd say we simply missed him or the tide got him. But this is a small lake. A pond really."

Maybe to some. But for others of us, it was a body as filled with menace as the Bermuda Triangle. Byrne must have recalled my opinions on that matter, because he kept his voice carefully casual as he asked, "How's the rotator cuff?"

I flushed. The rotator cuff had been a white lie, which, like all spur of the moment excuses, was rapidly taking on a life of its own. "Feels fine," I said. "Like it was never torn."

Which was not an untruth—at least if you left out the word "like."

The white lie had had its birth when Paul and Cam had announced they'd convinced Byrne to do a few training sessions for our triathlon team. "Guy's former Special Forces," Paul had said. "Gonna kick our asses into shape."

He'd said that as if it were a good thing. My idea of triathlon training had been to take the Metro-North down to the New York City Yale Club, where I swam my half-mile in the form of 32 laps—not lengths. The Yale Club pool was gem-like in many ways. It was tiled in blue, with a white Y on its bottom, and had gilded lion-head waterspouts. The water temperature was kept at a balmy 80 degrees. And it was tiny—so small that one could comfortably push off the wall and reach the opposite one in the matter of a few dog paddles that I was pleased to call the breaststroke. In the old days, when women were charged a reduced membership fee so that the Old Boys could swim comfortably in the altogether, it was simply known as the Plunge.

My idea of training was emphatically *not* shivering at the edge of Battlefield Lake at six in the morning, preparatory to having my ass kicked by a man who looked like a drill instructor. Not to mention the little matter of the lake itself. Lakes, I am sorry to say, do not have tiled bottoms nor heated water. And the water they do have is murky and slimy, hiding God alone knows what hazards in their depths. Snakes. Snapping turtles. Giant clams that trapped deep sea divers underwater until their oxygen ran out...

"Doyle," I'd said, looking for a way out of so much as dipping my toe in the lake. "Do you have any statistics on people killed by snapping turtles?"

"Although the bite of a snapping turtle is powerful enough to break a human's finger, and on at least one occasion severed the tendon of an eight-year-old boy, there are no corroborated cases of a snapping turtle actually killing a swimmer."

"Corroborated, huh? What about crocodiles?"

"I assume you mean alligators. The only place you can find a crocodile in America is a zoo. I must say it is quite unlike you to slip up on such a simple detail. Are you certain you're quite alright, Watson?"

No, I was not alright—quite or otherwise. "What about the stories about the water monster that haunts Battlefield Lake?"

"You refer, I assume, to Morgansburg's own Battlefield Amy?"

A shadow fell—no, loomed—across my phone. "You ready for the swim?" Byrne had asked that day.

"Actually," I said. "I think I'd better skip it this week if you don't mind."

"Some kind of problem?"

If this had been summer camp, I would have pleaded my period—just as I had unflinchingly done for two weeks straight beneath the disbelieving glare of the SEAL wannabe posing as camp counselor. But Byrne was a man—a very manly man—brimming with the sort of testosterone that would have been equally envied by Cam Billings and my camp counselor. More to the point, Byrne was a man I had to face in my professional capacity on a regular basis.

I'd racked my brain for the litany of sports injuries that always seemed to be scrolling across my news feed. "Rotator cuff."

"That so? How'd you do that?"

"Don't know. It must be a chronic thing. At first, I thought it was carpal tunnel…"

"You don't get carpal tunnel in your shoulder—" Byrne cut himself off as he caught sight of the grainy series of photos of Battlefield Amy that Doyle was obligingly loading onto my phone. If I thought I glimpsed a sudden grin of comprehension, it was gone before Byrne said with a shrug, "I guess it affects everyone differently. But it doesn't pay to ignore something like that. Messed up my own arm pretty bad once. Wish I'd taken better care of it."

He raised his voice. "Cam! Paul! We've got a problem. Dr. Watson here tore her rotator cuff. Now, of course, she was ready and willing to tough it out for the team, but I can't sign off on that. Provost will make my life hell about liability and assumed risk. So, what do you say we make this a relay team instead? Can't be a problem with Dr. Watson running, even if her arm's in a sling."

Now the race was in the past, Cam was missing, and Byrne was looming over my computer monitor. "Paul Morgan said you took pictures of them finishing the swim. Mind if I take a look?"

Damn. I owed this guy big time, and here I was about to let him down. "Paul should have said, I was supposed to be taking pictures. But I never did, because I never saw Cam come out of the lake. And honestly, I could not have missed him. He was the only one not wearing a wetsuit. And his swim trunks were…quite noticeable. Bright red."

I turned back to my monitor. "But if you have Cam's bib number, I can probably pull up a list from the course steward's tablet, and we can search for the number. That would at least give you a time frame."

"How can you do that? That cutting-edge program of yours?"

Unlike most people, Byrne sounded genuinely interested. Unfortunately, when it came to Doyle forging connections in cyberspace, it was often best not to know. And definitely best not to talk about it. Hacking is such an ugly word—even if Doyle would prefer to term it "sharing a few bits and bytes among friends."

"It's scarcely cutting-edge. Just an AI bot," I said, ignoring the snort of disgust that erupted from my computer's speakers. "But he does know how to throw together a quick and dirty subroutine."

As the speakers continued to crackle in outrage, I turned back to the monitor and typed in the number Byrne gave me. The screen filled with a video. But the man in the image that swam up wore neither a wetsuit nor a little red Speedo. He sported a porkpie hat pulled down low over his saturnine features, and balanced on a silver-headed cane as he leaned toward the camera to inform us, "The dragon has always had a powerful hold on the imagination of man…"

"Sorry!" I hastily shut down the screen. "I was just googling Battlefield Amy for the *Morgansburg Times*. Some kind of computer glitch must have conflated the two searches."

"It was no computer glitch!" Doyle howled from the speakers. "Instead of insulting my colleague's intelligence—virtual or otherwise—by merely requiring a list of bib numbers, I inquired into any insights he might have into the disappearance of Cam Billings."

"And his answer was the legend of a dragon that some enterprising developer created years ago to boost the tourist trade in Morgansburg?"

"If you choose to refer to it that way. My colleague prefers to describe it as the water-dragon Amangemokdem, variously called Amangegach, used by the Algonkian people as a bogey to frighten recalcitrant children, and known in Morgansburg legend as Battlefield Amy," Doyle said. "The only documented references to it in Native American culture are found in Northern Manhattan…"

"Who are you talking—Wait. *That's* the project that netted you a half-million-dollar grant?" Byrne asked.

I should have been insulted, but frankly, I shared his disbelief—and had done so ever since I'd been inexplicably transformed from another at-will adjunct into De Sales College's premier source of outside funding.

"His name's Doyle," I said. He can hear you."

"Fully equipped with voice recognition abilities," Doyle assured Byrne. "And unlike certain other programs I could name, I don't have to learn vocabulary, I have the complete OED in my databases."

"How does it work?" Byrne asked.

"It's complicated," I said. "Let me think about how I could best put it into layman's terms…"

"Try me," Byrne said. "I had some computer training in the Army."

What was wrong with me? Suddenly, I sounded as pompous as Doyle. "Okay, then. What Doyle does is write texts by extrapolating the intervening points between two known points of data in order to reconstruct the missing information. In this case the data points being several databases of classic mysteries and the extrapolation being a new plot created from his collection of classic examples."

"He writes new stories by extrapolating plots from the old ones," Byrne said.

"Everyone in AI is doing it. Honestly, when it comes to the actual programming, it's a long way from rocket science. More like straightforward successive approximation…"

Most people's eyes began to glaze over by this point. Byrne's didn't. He just kept studying the blank computer screen before he decided, "I guess he's like the TARDIS. More impressive on the inside."

"I'll say," Doyle chimed in. "And I would reciprocate by paying our good inspector the same compliment. But I fear we must put aside such niceties for the moment, for I have just received a rather urgent communication from a colleague on the Historical Society's security system."

My monitor lit back up with grainy footage of the cashbox that served the Historical Society's box office and gift shop, which sold post cards and maps as well as quilted potholders, crocheted toilet paper covers, and preserves left over from the Presbyterian Church's Harvest Fair. An avatar sprawled face down across a spool of paper admissions tickets, beneath a scrim of gore that would have done Sam Peckinpah proud.

At the same time, Byrne's phone pinged with a text. He studied it, then frowned at my computer screen. "I just got an urgent alert from Peg at the Historical Society as well. What are the odds the two are connected?"

"Everything's connected," I told him. "At least when it comes to Morgansburg."

CHAPTER THREE
The Body in the Library

"You have time to head down there with me?" Byrne asked.

"If I didn't, the Historical Society would forcibly compel me," I said. "They have stern ideas about the responsibilities of permanent members of the Executive Committee."

"Meaning you?"

I nodded and put my earpiece in so I could hear Doyle if needed. I was one of two de facto permanent members of the Historical Society's Executive Committee. One was the board chair, who was always a scion of the Morgan family, a supply that was dwindling as swiftly as their supply of artifacts seemed to be proliferating. The other was me. It's a little-known statute that any Historical Society must have at least one board member with a background in library science, and I'm the one. My position is secure until I can find an unwitting victim to take my place.

We arrived at the Historical Society to discover Lawrence Morgan and her cousin, Blanche Morgan Philipse, the twin doyennes of Morgansburg society, already standing guard at the entrance, flanking the woman who had texted Byrne. Apparently, the alarm had gone out with the efficacy of the apprentice silversmith who had spotted the approaching redcoats and wakened Colonel Morgan's Irregulars.

Lawrence Morgan was possessed of the horsey good looks and naturally erect posture of a girl schooled at Vassar via Miss Porter's. Her cousin Blanche was her opposite, round and querulous where Lawrence was stalwart and angular. And the woman who stood between them— affectionately known as A Bit Simple, but a Treasure and who was the de facto caretaker and housekeeping staff of all of Morgansburg's not-for-profits, as well as De Sales College—wore an apron over a faded housecoat and sturdy running shoes.

"Hi, Peg," Byrne said to her. "Got your text. How can I help?"

The doyennes' babbled response drowned out anything Peg might have been saying and was enough to make even Byrne take a step back. "Maybe I should go inside and see what's happened."

"There's no need to *see* what happened," Lawrence said, "when you are perfectly able to *smell* it. It can only be the fermented tomatoes. Dear God! The entire place smells like a distillery."

"Who's ever heard of deliberately fermenting a tomato?" Blanche chimed in. "When I was taught to can, your tomatoes fermenting was a *mistake* to which any homemaker with a modicum of pride would never admit. But these farm-to-table terrorists are fermenting everything. Kimchi and Kombucha and now the tomatoes. Why not just step up and serve a hearty dose of botulism on the side?"

"Dare to broach the question, and all they'll talk about is how intestinal health supports the immune system and anti-inflammatory responses," Lawrence said. "Good bacteria in the gut, combatting constipation and diarrhea. I don't know about you, but the way I was raised, you did not talk about such things in polite company."

Perhaps not, but I knew from personal experience the Ladies Auxiliary were not shy about discussing such other interesting complaints as diverticulitis and kidney stones, not to mention childbirths so rife with complications that they could take away any latent impulse you might still cherish to go forth and multiply.

"Villainy!" Lawrence hissed.

"Sabotage!" Blanche seconded her. "Do these farm-to-table monsters know no decency?"

They turned on Byrne the full force of their authority as doyennes. "We wish to file a complaint, of course, and demand a complete investigation."

Byrne pulled out his phone. "Well, I don't have any official standing, but how about I document the damage for now, and we can figure out how to report it later?"

With a hmmph of satisfaction, Lawrence threw open the door to the archive to reveal what looked like an abattoir. The smoke alarm had gone off, releasing a foul stream of water across the front desk, not only soaking the computer, but also knocking a jar of foul-smelling tomatoes off the gift shop rack.

"They insisted we sell them at the gift shop." Blanche's eyelids fluttered at the carnage. "Of course, I couldn't refuse them their place at the table at the Harvest Fair, but I did try to dispose of them decently when the Fair was over. Unfortunately, they were having none of it. Pulled their tomatoes straight out of the dumpster and read me the riot act about Curing Food Insecurity in the Hudson Valley and Making a Difference in the Community."

"And this after they had snapped up Abe Sanders' apple orchard and transformed it into some kind of artisanal gin mill. Oh, they call it hard cider culled from historical apples, but we know what *that's* about," Lawrence agreed. "And Abe was our Town Justice, too! They have left Morgansburg *lawless*."

"And 'they' are who exactly?" Byrne asked.

"Who else but those inebriates with their guts bubbling with hard liquor and good bacteria?" Lawrence cried.

"Not that I ever argued with them. Live and let live, that's what I always say. If they want to poison themselves, who am I to judge?" Blanche's gaze grew steely. "*Except* of course when I have been asked to judge the Home Bureau's table at the County Fair. Then my authority is final! I don't give a fig for the opinions of this so-called Twitterverse. I may be an opinionated fossil with no concept of modern nutrition, but I will uphold the standards I was raised with, with my last, fossilized, opinionated breath."

Which seemed to be in no danger of running out any time soon. I began to wonder how much longer Byrne was going to be able to maintain his expression of polite concern.

"When I think of my great-aunt Florence," Blanche went on, "all I can say is I'm glad she's not alive to see this day. She was the one who brought the Federation of Home Bureaus to Morgansburg, and guided generations through Depression and the War and all that nonsense in the sixties without ever once failing the Bureau's sacred purpose, 'To maintain the highest ideals of home life.'"

"Oh, we'll not see the likes of them again," Lawrence concurred. "Women who sewed all their own clothes and those of their children as well. Women who could knit, darn, cook, clean, and bake—homemade bread fresh from the oven every day. Women who canned—really canned, not these Soccer Moms who rent our kitchen once a month so their au pairs can boil and strain their artisanal fruit while they sip Cosmopolitans and trade tips on summer camps. In the old days, women grew their own beans, tomatoes, peas, raspberries, peaches—and if the harvest failed, their family went hungry. As for *jams*. You'll never see the likes of Aunt Flo's chutney, and there was no fancy talk of mangoes, let me tell you. Quinces, that's what she used. Greengage jelly…"

I took another look at the mess of fermented tomatoes and my mind went back to Doyle's bloody tableau. "I take it the computer is toast."

"Looks it," Byrne said. I don't suppose you have backups for any of this?"

"Not unless you have something that can read floppy disks," I said.

"I take it you mean that literally."

"The Town Clerk who ushered the Village's record-keeping into the digital age was meticulous about backups," I told him. "Unfortunately, she retired in 1989."

"Crap," Byrne said.

"Fiendish!" Doyle seconded him. "My dear Watson, I fear we are faced with an intelligence as subtle and cunning as my own!"

Byrne seemed unwilling to leave after he dropped me back off at my office. He lingered in the doorway, eyeing my computer monitor as Doyle flickered back to life on it. "So this is the program that put De Sales College on the map—and all because of a couple of missing library books?"

"You heard about that?" I asked.

"I am Chief of Campus Security. Which makes me the closest thing to law enforcement there is in this town. I hear about everything. Missing cats. Suspicious strangers lurking in the neighbors' shrubbery. Black helicopters over the Hudson. I have to admit I paid about as much attention to the missing library books."

"As would any thinking human being."

"That is why it took a computer to unearth what I can only describe as our most challenging puzzle ever!" Doyle's voice burst in triumph from the speakers. "Or as I am taking the liberty of calling it, The Curious Incident of the Body in the Library."

"You found a body?" Byrne asked. "I never heard about that."

"Of course not," Doyle told him. "There was never a body in the library. But there should have been. And that was the heart of our problem— just like the curious incident of the dog that didn't bark in the nighttime. It's a reference, don't you see? A rhetorical trope."

"I am fairly certain Mr. Byrne is aware of the term," I told Doyle.

Byrne turned to me. "So what was this missing body?"

"A body of hitherto undiscovered mystery titles that would rewrite the history of the genre as we know it," Doyle answered before I could. "Beginning with John Dickson Carr's classic murder mystery, *The Dragon Murder Case*, featuring the one-armed Irish spy, O'Riordan."

"I thought that was Van Dine," Byrne said. "And the detective was Philo Vance."

I glanced at him. "You a big mystery reader?"

"Most soldiers are big readers. Lot of time to kill in the Army, and not always a lot of connectivity. I started out on the techno-thrillers but gave up on them quickly enough. Spent way too much time scribbling in the margins, correcting their mistakes."

"Then I'm guessing I don't need to add much more than that the other missing books included Vance investigating *A Graveyard to Let*, which is in fact a book by John Dickson Carr. Then there's a copy of Rex Stout's hitherto unknown novel, *The Thin Man*. Which was pretty much the point when I decided there was a mistake in my algorithms and Doyle got his titles and authors mixed up. *The Thin Man* is Nick and Nora Charles, and Dashiell Hammett wrote it. Rex Stout wrote Nero Wolfe—who could scarcely be described as thin."

"Give yourself some credit as a programmer!" Doyle snapped. "You did not program me to make mistakes."

"So you say every time I try to run you through a debugger."

"Your prerogative, of course. Although I am moved to say such crippling self-doubt does not become you."

I turned back to Byrne. "So I chalked it up to a glitch and left it at that."

"Until…" Byrne said.

"Until Doyle discovered that those titles were topping all the hottest item lists on every on-line auction site from Etsy to Paddle8. Which suddenly made this a lot more than a simple programming error."

"How so? It still sounds like Byrne's First Law of Campus Security to me: When you multiply students doing dumb-ass things by internet users doing dumb-ass things, you get an order of magnitude of more dumb-assery"

"That would only apply if your logarithm base 10 of your multiplier was greater than one," Doyle told Byrne.

"I don't think he was really asking." I turned back to Byrne. "To start with, it wasn't on campus, and it wasn't a student. It was the archives of the Morgansburg Historical Society. And all those spurious titles offered for sale had two things in common. They had all been de-accessioned from the archives of the Morgansburg Historical Society in the past six months. And they were all originally donated to the Historical Society as part of something called the Billings Bequest. Which suddenly gets the Morgansburg Historical Society—and by extension me—in a heck of a lot of hot water."

"Why? Suspicion of dealing in stolen goods?"

"Not exactly. The problem is selling off donated materials. I can't. Legally. The rule's the bane of librarians and museum curators everywhere. A director of a non-profit collection cannot sell off—deaccession, to use the technical term—redundant, out of date, or duplicate materials without approval from their Board of Directors. And many times, not even then. Of course, there's a good reason for this: it protects donors from having institutions accept anything and everything they can get their hands on and turning themselves into estate liquidators. In practice, it means that libraries routinely throw away bags of excess materials—which they can legally do. And believe me, there are plenty of used book dealers who know the best dumpsters to watch. Sometimes, librarians go so far as to tip them off. Which is neither illegal nor unethical. It only becomes illegal if you take a share of the profits."

Byrne frowned. "But from what you're saying these weren't rare books. They were non-existent books. Impossible books. The titles alone were a complete violation of the canon."

"Which is why my first assumption was that Doyle had written them."

"Ah, Watson, you cut me to the quick!"

"You have to admit it was a possibility. After all, your remit is to write new detective stories by extrapolating from works already in your database. Makes sense that you were the one who came up with these stories and some Etsy crawler picked them up as genuine." I turned back to Byrne. "Which might have been a major headache, but I still would have been in a lot less trouble than if I were deaccessioning donated manuscripts without permission."

Byrne nodded. "Forgery is not in and of itself a criminal act; it is only using the forgery in an attempt to defraud that's criminal—in other words, the crime occurs only when you attempt to pass off that forgery as genuine. Which, I assume means you were not the one to post them on online."

"Not unless I did it in my sleep. And I do not have a history of sleepwalking, in case you were wondering."

His eyes narrowed as he studied my computer screen. "You equally sure about your Little Friend there?"

Alas, that was a question I was growing increasingly uncertain about ever being able to answer. "Frankly, it doesn't matter," I dodged the question. "I'm the one who programmed him, so it still points the finger straight at me."

Byrne nodded. "What did you end up doing?"

"The only sane thing you can ever do in academia. I kicked it upstairs. Reported the books as missing, perhaps stolen, through every official channel I could find. Including yours."

Byrne grinned. "Due diligence. Or as we like to call it in the Army, 'covering your ass.'"

He took another long look at the monitor, which was suddenly slumbering in injured silence. "What happened next?"

CHAPTER FOUR
Show me the Money

The short answer to Byrne's question was nothing happened next. I'd forgotten about the missing non-existent mysteries after I filed lost items reports with everyone from the NY State Troopers to the Metro-North Lost and Found. However, the Billings Bequest did not forget about me. Instead, it reared back to life just a few months later in the form of a summons from the Office of the President of De Sales College to discuss "the Campus Security report about the anomalies my programs had uncovered in the Billings Bequest."

I was more than a little nervous. Not about explaining the missing books. It was more a question of how I was going to explain Doyle without convincing the entire De Sales College administration that I spent most of my time at the library desk playing computer games. It would do me little good to plead that he was right there in my job description, for the fact of the matter was that while I might read phrases like "develop extrapolation heuristics to reproduce genre manuscripts" as... well, *Doyle,* most others would have thought more in terms of a state-of-the-art copy center.

Given the "Campus Security" connection, I'd expected to see Byrne looming at the head of the conference table.

But Byrne hadn't been there. Instead, it was Lenny Russo, the department chair, and Millicent "Isa" Isenberg, the vice chair, leading the tribunal that awaited me, flanked by Paul Morgan and a man I was destined to become more intimately acquainted with as Cam Billings. The college president sat at the head of the conference table looking gravely presidential, which was pretty much the skill set that had gotten him his position. That did not bode well.

"Relax. They have nothing on you," Doyle counseled. "Yet."

The final single syllable was hardly as reassuring as it could have been. Nor was a quick scan of the other faces around the table. Lenny and Isa both looked aggrieved, but that was par for the course. Lenny had clawed his way onto the tenure track by receiving a record-setting $50,000 for writing a white paper on what he called Adjunct Mess—a choice bit of name calling that many of us found more than a little insulting. Isa's sense of injustice was the fiercer for being completely selfless. She ran a feminist poetry collective and could not understand why I wouldn't turn my attention to the serious literature of trauma. She felt my refusal to build the collective's website and manage their social media platforms *pro bono* was selfish and mean-minded. Was that, then, what this meeting was about?

However, as I slid into what I could only think of as the defendant's chair, the president exchanged his statesman-like gravitas for the avuncular smile he normally reserved for the local newspapers on commencement weekend and said in a tone that suggested he had just been briefed with a quick trip around my CV, "Dr. Watson, I am delighted to meet you at last."

Delighted. Delighted sounded good, right?

"As are we all," the college's chief development officer chimed in. She was cheery cocoanut water to Lenny and Isa's sullen oil, a former sorority girl who had enjoyed brief celebrity on a failed pilot called *Real Housewives of Poughkeepsie*. Now, she favored me with the look of breathless interest she usually reserved for potential donors, before she turned to introduce the other two men in the room. "Of course, you know Paul Morgan, our county attorney, as well as Lawrence Morgan's nephew. He says you two knew each other back at Yale?"

The temperature on one side of the table dropped. Lenny, who fancied himself a man of the people and wore his shirtsleeves rolled up to remind everyone of that fact, bristled at the mention of the Ivy League. Isa cast me a look that suggested she had personally witnessed Paul and me fumbling around in his dorm room after our earnest discussions about the real meaning of the Film Society's Friday night offering.

"Yes, but we lost touch along the way," I said.

Which was a polite way of saying that after graduation, everyone else seemed to have a fascinating adventure lined up in front of them: The Peace Corps. A Wall Street brokerage house. Med school. Grad school. Law school as the last refuge of scoundrels and English majors. Me, I hoisted my backpack and took the last long walk to the New Haven train station and a serious case of the now-whats?

I'd wandered into a tech writing job in Poughkeepsie. Since they were a big enough corporation to pay for my further education, I went back to doing the only thing I seemed to know how to do: taking classes. I traced a wandering path through an MFA in Creative Writing, where I tried to pretend that I liked sensitive, character-driven navel gazing and post-modern end games, before

I turned to a Ph.D. in Library Science. I suppose I could have passed off the combination as a free-spirited mixture of creativity and cutting-edge practicality, if I were trying to hold my own among my glittering fellow alums over drinks at Yale Club mixers. But by that time, I was too busy grading stacks of papers to care.

"I don't know whether you've ever met Cam Billings from the Billings Foundation," the development officer went on, as she turned to the man who sat next to Paul.

"I don't think we've ever met, but your name is certainly well-known around Morgansburg." I avoided mentioning that the Billings name was mostly known for being spat by Lawrence Morgan at the Historical Preservation Committee meetings, as they repeatedly vetoed Billings' various attempts to transform his derelict holdings on the edges of Morgansburg into gated communities and multi-use shopping and entertainment venues.

Cam was cut from the same Old Blue mold as Paul, albeit a decade older and a billion or so richer. A suspiciously full head of blond hair trending toward grey, a spare tire just barely straining the bespoke suit.

"And you're about to hear a lot more about him," Paul assured me. "Cam and Tiggy are planning to make Morgansburg their Forever Home."

Forever home? It sounded like he'd adopted Tiggy from the Humane Society.

"Everyone is happy to welcome them to our community," Paul continued, and I wondered if his aunt knew about the Billings' move. If so, I doubted she was happy about it. Paul had obviously not attended as many Historical Society meetings as I had. "But we can save all that for drinks at the Yale Club some night," he said. "Which we need to set up one day soon."

I assumed the sentiment to gather for drinks was as sincere as when it was scrawled on appeals associated with the Yale Alumni Association or echoed at his political fundraisers.

"Right now, we're gathered to hear all about the little software program that could," Cam tag-teamed Paul.

"Little?" Doyle erupted in my ear.

"And the lady programmer who is about to go viral."

Lady programmer? I couldn't even bring myself to glance over at Isa. There was no need. I could feel her reaction ratcheting straight through the back of my skull. First at the sexism and then at … well, me.

"I assume you're talking about those anomalous entries that were uncovered in the Billings Bequest," I began. "I apologize for that, but I think they were nothing but a glitch in my AI project."

"Glitch? My dear Watson, I try to make allowances for your yeomanlike propensity to be blunt," Doyle snapped, "but there's no need to be insulting."

"Well, if it's a glitch, it's the glitch that's about to put Morgansburg on the map," Cam said with a big smile plastered on his face.

"The Billings Foundation is partnering with De Sales College," the president delivered the punchline with his brightest avuncular beam, "in a dynamic new initiative that is going to bring Silicon Valley to the Hudson Valley, and you, Dr. Watson, are going to be a major part of it."

"When you say bring Silicon Valley to the Hudson Valley, do you mean that literally?" I broke the silence that followed, since everyone seemed to expect me to say something.

"Cam is donating his development properties to De Sales College, in order to repurpose them into the home of its new Tech Hub," Paul said.

"The press releases will be going out tomorrow," the development officer said. "We're going to blanket social media."

"And you'd like me to set up a few batch scripts to distribute them?" I grasped at the straw. "I can run them up for you this afternoon."

And I would have been on my feet and out of there like a cat when caught red-handed pawing through the trash, if not for the little voice that warned me that would be all too easy. Sure enough, Cam Billings threw back his head with a roar of laughter that would not have been out of place in the DKE frat house. "God, she's a modest one. Our own Grace Hopper was sitting right here under our noses the whole time, and she wants to know whether we need help with the press releases," he said, with another dig at Paul's ribs. "No wonder you overlooked her. It's like the lady sings, 'Don't it always seem to go that you don't know what you've got 'til it's gone?' Well, Dr. Watson, my buddy might have let you slip through his fingers, but nobody's going to be paving paradise with you while Cam Billings is sitting in this room."

No matter how many silent pleas I sent to Doyle to help me make sense out of that mess, he remained stubbornly mute. I was not afforded a similar luxury. "I'm not sure I'm entirely following…"

"There's only one thing you need to follow, and that's the fact that now that the Billings Foundation has you, we're not going to let you go."

The phrasing brought back some uncomfortable memories of more than one evening on Paul's dorm bunk.

"First, let me assure you that the Billings Foundation respects the independence of all our grantees and there is never an expectation of quid pro quo for our funding."

Which sounded like something the best of Yale law clerks might have spent an entire semester crafting. But it still didn't make any sense to me.

"Funding?" I repeated. It was every adjunct's dream. No, every adjunct's pipe dream. Beyond a steady paycheck and health insurance. It was Charlie Bucket's Golden Ticket straight to respectability. What was he truly saying?

"We want your bot, Dr. Watson." Cam Billings told me. "And we're not taking no as an answer."

Isa stiffened as if their demands had been decidedly more literal than that. And as Cam continued to outline exactly what the Billings Foundation was willing to do to get ahold of Doyle, I began to understand Lenny's glowering expression and the development officer's bright cheer. For reasons known only to the Billings Foundation, instead of being Exhibit A in Lenny Russo's taxonomy of the Adjunct Mess, I had suddenly supplanted him as the department's star fundraiser.

"And by an order of magnitude," Doyle confirmed. "In whatever logarithmic base you care to look at it."

In short, the Billings Foundation was so chuffed at my—well Doyle's—smoking out those anomalies in the Billings Bequest, it was offering to fund a 5-year cyber-initiative right here in De Sales College to expand Doyle's AI capabilities. And not just in library science.

"Maker stations!" Cam promised. "Machine learning! The Billings Foundation wants to invest not just in technology, but in De Sales. No, the Billings Foundation wants to put De Sales on the map."

Beginning with an immediate grant of $500,000 to cover start-up costs and my first-year stipend as Project Director. The last was strictly non-negotiable. "As if anyone would be stupid enough to throw away the goose that laid the golden egg—a second time," Cam said. "Paul may not have seen your potential, but now that we know who you are, we're going to tie you up tight."

It was a moment to tuck away in a memory book forever. Unfortunately, it was destined to be little more than a moment, if I didn't want to find myself running the risk of serious fraud charges.

"Look, no offense, but before you commit to anything, I need to be sure you understand that all my 'little bot' can really do is write murder mysteries. Badly, I might add. And if, in the course of that, he managed to uncover some irregularities in the Historical Society's databases, it can only be ascribed to coincidence…"

"You cut me to the quick," Doyle moaned through my earpiece.

I turned to Lenny and Isa, whose faces had set with the pained expression that greeted any mention of the ugly stepsister of the Adjunct Mess—those books, such as mysteries, romance, or sci-fi, referred to by English professors as sub-literary genres and by everyone else as books people actually like to read. "I can't imagine the Faculty Senate would see this kind of corporate collaboration or corporate sponsorship as anything but an assault on academic freedom."

"Now, now, now," the president answered for them, with the kind of geniality that a half a million dollars bought, "the Faculty Senate are well aware that what's good for De Sales is good for all of us."

As threats went, it would scarcely qualify as veiled. Or answerable. Lenny and Isa punted with a sullen alacrity that under other circumstances would have done my crabbed heart proud. "I think we can have faith in Dr. Watson's good judgement," Lenny ground out.

Bastards. Ignoring Doyle's furious yelp of protest, I tried one last desperate argument. "In the interest of due diligence, I think I need say for the record, I really think you're overestimating the capabilities of my little program."

"Trust me, Mary," Paul said. "We're not asking you or the De Sales family to compromise your academic integrity in any way. And if any question of conflict of interest arises, we are going to have your back every step of the way."

I don't know whether Isa actually said anything audible about what part of my anatomy the Billings Foundation was really having, but her opinion on the matter could be easily read on her face.

"Hey, hey, hey," Cam Billings cut in. "We're supposed to be welcoming the lady to the Billings Foundation, not scaring her away. Look, we're all neighbors here—what's more, I hope, we're friends. So, let's keep this on friendly footing. No reason to go to the formality of a contract today. All we need you to do right now is sign a letter of intent that gives us exclusive consideration of the software."

Letter of intent. Was that how Mephistopheles had phrased it? Exclusive consideration of the fate of your immortal soul? Then again, what else was I supposed to do with the single page document they pushed across the table? Was I seriously going to throw an amount that was ten times my current retirement savings back in their faces? And if I did, from the way the president and development officer were leaning forward, they would probably have met any further objection by opening one of my veins and forging my signature instead.

So, I'd signed, with an ordinary ballpoint pen, while Lenny glowered, Isa shook her head, and the president and development officer beamed. Then I slunk back to my office in order to while away the afternoon by wondering what I had gotten myself into.

Isa and Lenny clearly had no doubts, to judge from the stage-whispered conversation just outside my office door. "She's sleeping with one of them, of course. The only question is, which one?"

"For half a million dollars," Lenny said, "I'm betting on both of them."

CHAPTER FIVE
The Second Battle for Morgansburg

By the end of the week after the Billings Sprint Challenge, there was still no trace of Cam Billings, either dead or alive. Searchers combed ERs, morgues, and Battlefield Bluff; conspiracy theorists combed private Caribbean islands; and financial analysts combed the annual reports of both the Billings Group and the Billings Foundation. But there was still only one fact everyone could agree on. Cam Billings had vanished without a trace.

In a flurry of unprecedented activity, the *Morgansburg Times* ran daily updates linking his disappearance to the recent uptick on sights of black helicopters along the Hudson, and an editorial posited that Battlefield Amy was in fact one of the submarines the U.S. Navy denied patrolled the river.

More inventive souls on social media suggested that Cam Billings had been assassinated by an operative for a foreign government who'd doused him in moisture-activated acid that disposed of the body by dissolving it while he swam. Enterprising live-stream viewers offered copies of the fatal tape for sale. Nor had Paul Morgan's spin doctors managed to keep the story out of the national press, and the business reports charted real-time graphics of the Billings Group's plunging valuation, until the SEC finally threatened to suspend trading.

The break in the case arrived in my inbox in the form of a limited-edition Non Fungible Token that offered me the right to use Edward Hopper's Nighthawks as a screen saver. I would have double-deleted it, had Doyle not gently directed my attention to the man in a red bikini sipping coffee at the counter, behind the glass window that now was etched with the words "Morgansburg Diner."

"If you require additional confirmation, my friend down at the post office who intercepted this message suggests you look at the sender's address," he said. "Bill Camery? Really, it's an insult to your intelligence."

Byrne was about as enthused by Doyle's discovery as I was. "It makes no sense. The man disappeared in plain sight of an internet's worth of witnesses, and now he shows up at a diner that's been closed for as long as I can remember?"

"The Morgansburg Diner has reopened under new management," Doyle said. "And has been rated by Tiggy Billings' lifestyle blog as one of the top 10 Must-Eat Vegan Hotspots in the Hudson Valley."

Byrne shook his head. "So we're supposed to believe Cam Billings is calmly eating avocado toast, while everyone on the Hudson Valley is looking for him and his hedge funds are tanking? Any suggestions *why*?"

"Amnesia?" I suggested.

"He forgets his own name, but he can remember his phone password?"

"Do you have another explanation why a man would refuse to come forward to protect his own assets?"

"When you put it that way." Byrne's jaw set as he came to a decision. "Your Extrapolating Little Friend there available for a ride-along?"

"What do you mean?"

"I mean, you don't have to be at a computer to use him, do you?"

"No. I've got him on my cell phone as well. You know, like Siri."

"I am NOTHING like Siri," Doyle said, clearly affronted.

"You have her eyes," I told him.

"Any way I can talk to him too?"

I shrugged. "I usually keep him on an earbud, but I could put him on speaker on my phone so you could hear him."

"Then how about it, Nancy Drew? You and your Little Friend mind coming along while I grill a few vegans?"

To coin a phrase.

"The bumbling Lestrade has more intelligence than we have given him credit for," Doyle purred. "He at least knows when to seek expert assistance. We will be delighted, for this case presents some interesting aspects that raise it above the banal…"

I rolled my eyes. "I'm a little worried you're overestimating Doyle's abilities."

"I'll take the case," Doyle said.

For as long as I could remember, the diner on the edge of Morgansburg had existed in a half-life between open and abandoned, its red neon sign spilling light on an occasional battered pick-up truck parked in the cracked parking area. But when Byrne and I pulled up in a bone-jarring cloud of exhaust, we found the place transformed. The dented metal siding had been burnished to the art deco sleekness of a car on the Twentieth Century Limited. The jaunty martini glass that advertised a Cocktail Lounge beckoned a winking welcome, and the sputtering Open sign had been replaced by one that advertised an Internet Café and Kid-friendly Pinball Arcade.

It took me a moment before I could climb out of Byrne's truck, the battered brother of those that used to haunt the lot, but I managed to steady myself in time and save myself the embarrassment of his helping me. By unspoken agreement, we paused to study the menu, which offered such roadside standards as Chicken a la King, Eggs with Home Fries, and BLTs (vegan substitutes available for no surcharge). However, the prices were a long way from Wimpy's nickel burgers.

"$22 for macaroni and cheese?" I demanded. "When you can buy a frozen one for under $5?"

"Ah," Byrne said, "but are those made with a 100 percent organic proprietary cheese blend, locally sourced from prize-winning Ayrshire cattle?"

"Every time I buy organic cheese, it goes moldy before I get it home. And why can't they just use cheddar?"

"You need to blend the cheddar equally with gruyere, to even out the texture," Byrne informed me.

"You a foodie?" I demanded.

"My sainted Irish grandmother insisted I know my way around a kitchen before I could start dating. She said any woman with any brains should refuse to marry any man otherwise. Not that that did me any good when it came down to it, but she never stooped to 'I told you so.' Sainted. That's the only word there is."

I caught sight of another sign. "And what on earth is a trap brunch? Do hunters bring in their kill to have it dressed and cooked in front of their eyes—kind of like the fancy fishing clubs in Scotland do with your prize-winning salmon, after they display them all on a silver tray so you can compare? Or maybe they serve your food in a steel claw, kind of like a bacon clothesline?"

Byrne raised an eyebrow. "That's quite some image. But I'm afraid Trap is just a kind of music."

"Trap is a subgenre of hip hop that originated in Atlanta," Doyle read helpfully from Wikipedia. "The genre gets its name from the slang for a place where drugs are dealt. Trap music uses synthesized drums and is characterized by complicated hi-hat patterns, tuned kick drums, atmospheric synths, and lyrical content that often focuses on drug use and urban violence."

"Sounds like it should fit right in here in Morgansburg."

"Too bad," Byrne said, as he pushed open the door. "Kind of pales in comparison with your ideas."

A hostess with green hair, a painful-looking assortment of piercings, and a cropped top that read Namaste hurried to greet us with the kind of blissed-out smile that had driven me screaming from yoga classes. "Welcome," she said. "In case you've never joined us at table before, let me explain a few things about how we share our food choices."

She presented a sectioned cardboard tray with a reverence suited to a temple offering. "You take this up to the counter and curate your own meal by placing the colored disks from the baskets in front of the sample display into the appropriate space on the tray. We offer a choice of seven basic mains, plus daily specials, so you select that first and place it in the biggest slot—although you can also have a main as a side, or a side as a main. And if you prefer vegan or gluten-free options, all you need do is place a disk in the slot at the top of tray…"

That was not a menu, it was an IQ test. I'd be lucky to walk out with a trayful of creamed pearl onions and a kale smoothie.

"Actually," Byrne said, "we were hoping we could take a look at your security camera."

The hostess shook her head in a jangle of piercings. "Oh, I wish. But all our computer systems are down. There was…a slight accident."

Byrne's gaze sharpened. "Any fermented tomatoes involved?"

"The very question I would have proposed," Doyle murmured. "Once again, I must compliment our plodding inspector on his perspicacity."

"Oh, I'm afraid we only offer the fermentation bar on special Cleanse Weekends," the hostess said. "Would you like me to put you on the waiting list? They're very popular. Why spend all that time and effort on high colonics when you can have kombucha with friends, no?"

Lovely. Like a kegger in a frat house, but without the flavor. To judge from Byrne's face, it was not only my over-active imagination that was picturing an entire bar full of hipsters cleansing their bowels as one. Even his stoic imagination had apparently found a similar image he was trying desperately to unsee.

"Still, I can't tell you how nice it is to have a man take an interest in his digestive health for a change." Her face lit, as she pulled out her smart phone. "I can text you a few future dates on my calendar."

"It would be a pleasure," Byrne said. "Unfortunately, I'm going to have to save that for another time. Right now, I'm here on De Sales College business. And this computer malfunction may be very important. Can you remember when it took place? Before or after the triathlon, for example?"

Somewhere around the time you dropped back in from the astral plane?

"I'm sure I couldn't say." She shook her head in another jangle of piercings. "We don't handle our computers or any of our paperwork. The Foundation offices do that for us."

"Foundation as in the Billings Foundation?"

She nodded enthusiastically. "They were the ones who sponsored us. Took a chance on us when no-one else would. And they haven't given up. A lot of people would have pulled the plug on us after the first few months, but not Cam. Instead, he told us that the Foundation's money is squarely behind our expanding to a new downtown location in the Barracks Tavern, despite the bottom line on our financials. Of course, the Historical Society is kicking up a fuss, but Paul says he'll find a way to bring them around."

Somewhere along the line, I had to seriously consider the implications of the Billings Foundation's similarly unwavering support of me. Presumably, that meant they discerned the same star potential in both of us, but I was hard-pressed to define what that might be—beyond, of course, the less-than-flattering inference that we were both lovable losers and therefore good for a tax write-off, as well as a laugh. But what kind of tax write-off did you spend half a million dollars on?

Insultingly, Byrne seemed to be wondering the same thing. "Cam Billings seems to have spent a lot of money to cultivate good will in this town."

"The man is a saint," the hostess assured him. "And all of us here at the diner are devastated. We perform a special meditation each morning before we open, interceding for his safe return." She shook her head and sighed. "Without Cam Billings' vision, there would be no Kombucha Cleanses."

The Morgansburg branch of the Billings Foundation was housed along with Tiggy Billings' lifestyle empire in the pool house of their trophy home. Their "relaxing weekend getaway" had begun life as a relatively unassuming boathouse of a minor Astor scion with a passion for rowing, but a Brooklyn-based architect-cum-curator had pulled the building off its foundation, shifted its orientation, and cantilevered a wing twice the size of the original structure out over the water. In the process, they transformed it into a singularly unlivable space, with its floor to ceiling windows offering unparalleled views of the Catskills across the river—and unparalleled access to the winter cold. The entire Historical Society Board had been strong-armed into purchasing tickets to a charity unveiling of the new residence, with the curator personally leading the tour of retro plastic-shelled seating and glass tables that gave it what Tiggy described it as a "totally *Mad Men* look and feel."

We found Nigel St. Hubbins in the pool house. It was the miniature of the Great House, with a Peloton and an Infinity Pool behind its plate-glass windows, making it possible to enjoy the great outdoors in climate-controlled comfort. St. Hubbins was on an elliptical trainer as he studied a bank of computer monitors above his head. Tiggy's professed confidential advisor, Nigel St. Hubbins was less a man than a collection of tics—black mock turtleneck, even blacker glasses. Even his track suit was black. He had won the trust of the third Mrs. Cam Billings by showing her how to use her husband's money to transform a modest lifestyle blog into a social media empire that commanded millions of followers, all eager to know where to find the best apple picking, the must-see holiday light displays, and the most irresistible glamping in the Hudson Valley.

"St. Hubbins as in the Patron Saint of Quality Footwear?" I had asked, upon being introduced.

"You've heard of the family?" Tiggy cried.

"After a manner of speaking." Tiggy had apparently never heard of a little movie called *This is Spinal Tap*. Irony was a lost art in Morgansburg.

Tiggy's understanding of the curatorial process— at least as it applied to home décor—had made her a natural candidate for the Historical Society Board. Her nomination launched what could only be described as the Second Battle for Morgansburg. At the very first meeting, she introduced St. Hubbins, who shared his plans to create a campaign to bring Morgansburg's storied past into dialogue with the present, in a way that could be volumized out and franchised to cutting-edge makers and influencers from Brooklyn and points south.

As far as I was concerned, I liked the word "volumize" no more when it was attached to a marketing profile than when it was applied to hair product. But what did I know about not-for-profit fundraising beyond the fact it was generally less effective than a hand-scrawled note on a cardboard box and an open guitar case?

"We're just looking for an updated look and feel to better represent our brand," St. Hubbins had informed the Board. "Now, I'm just what-iffing here, but take the Morgansburg timeline. Instead of focusing on the Morgansburg Irregulars, couldn't we perhaps foreground the alternative narrative of the wives of Morgansburg partnering with the indigenous people to create a safe space where differences could be worked out in peaceful collaboration?"

Er… because it didn't happen that way?

"What on earth does that mean in English?" Lawrence Morgan demanded.

"I think what Mr. St. Hubbins is trying to say is that he doesn't think the actual history of Morgansburg is mediagenic enough for our rebranding," I translated.

"That's exactly it!" Tiggy cried.

Irony truly was a lost art in Morgansburg.

At the sound of our footsteps, St. Hubbins reached for the remote to switch off both his monitors and the machine. "Of course, I told Tiggy that none of this matters right now," he greeted us. "But she insisted I come up and keep her feeds up and running. Miss a day in the Hudson Valley, and you're living in the last century. Why just look at the stuff that came in today."

He pressed the remote again, and the monitors were filled with a dizzying assortment of Hudson Valley Experiences—which happened to look nothing like the scrolling figures that he had been studying when we arrived. "Look at this Alpaca Farm! They provide you with all kinds of vintage costumes suitable for any kind of photo shoot from weddings to family portraits. It's already been voted one of the Hudson Valley's 20 Most Instagrammable Destinations. The Catskill Game Farm had best look to its laurels. And here they have revisioned the old Rip van Winkle Bungalow Colony into a complete Fairy Tale Village, curating each accommodation to resemble a favorite superhero or fairy tale."

While he scrolled through the pictures and I wondered if there was any chance of saving civilization if we went back to decorating or even designing buildings instead of curating them, his computer began to ping in increasing desperation. "Do you need to get that?" I asked.

"Actually, I do," he said with a moue of apology. "I'm afraid you guys have caught me in it up to my elbows. On top of everything else, I seem to have turned up some discrepancies in the bids from last year's Gala auction. Of course, Tiggy's too prostrated to deal with it—even if the lawyers would let her. So, I told her I would handle it."

St. Hubbins lowered his voice and leaned close. "You didn't hear it from me, but she is worried Edsel Kincaid may have gotten us into some serious trouble."

Edsel Kincaid—always, if increasingly inaccurately, described as such a delightful young man—ran an antique shop perched on the edge of the Village Green. As much a fixture of Morgansburg society as the eponymous Morgans, he had long conducted the auction at the Historical Society Gala with all the aplomb that he had sold antiquities at a Major New York Gallery, before he had retired to run his Little Shoppe. Tiggy had taken over Edsel's auction as part of her plan to curate the annual Gala—to a substantial financial tune that included retaining the party planner who had been called in to "help out" at the Met Costume Gala and, Tiggy breathlessly confided, simply *saved* the flower arrangements at the last minute—not that she was even so much as offered a thank you by Ms. Wintour and her crew, let alone an invitation to walk the red carpet. No one had had the courage to tell Edsel yet.

"Of course, Tiggy trusts me to handle the matter quietly. Edsel has been a pillar of the Morgansburg community for as long as anyone can remember. And no one is accusing him of *malfeasance* by any means. But he's not getting any younger, is he? Seems reasonable to wonder whether he's still up to the task." St. Hubbins cast an anxious look at the computer that was pinging with increasing rapidity. "I don't want to be rude, but if you don't mind, I really need to get back to this. I'm up to my ears in ceramic Dalmatians."

"No, he isn't," Doyle murmured as soon as we were out of earshot.

I repeated Doyle's words as I took out my ear piece and held my phone up so Byrne could hear Doyle.

"What do you mean?" Byrne asked.

"I took the liberty of taking a peek over Mr. St. Hubbins' metaphorical shoulder, and at the risk of calling the man a liar, I would be willing to say that he wasn't looking at auction bids; he was looking at stock trades—all of which involved shares of the Billings' hedge funds."

My mind went back to that ghastly real-time ticker of the Billings Group's plunging stocks. "Maybe they found a White Knight to help them salvage their market valuation."

"Or a hostile takeover," Byrne said. "It would explain a lot. You snatch Cam Billings so the stock price tanks, then buy in before trading is suspended."

"Seems like a pretty arcane scheme to me."

"You haven't worked for the U.S. government," Byrne said with a snort.

CHAPTER SIX
Beyond Here Lie Dragons

By the time Byrne and I arrived back at the De Sales campus, both my phone and Byrne's were crowded with pings scattered across what could optimistically be termed the greater Morgansburg area—from the volunteer fire department to the Morgansburg Library and all the way to the shuttered Grange Hall that loomed on the outskirts of town, next to the remains of a Corn Maze. "Is it possible these are all stock trades too?" I asked.

"You need only ask!" Doyle said. "I will be pleased to take the case."

Byrne just rolled his eyes.

I glanced at my watch. "I've got a class to teach right now, but I can set up Doyle to map all these pings and see if they are all stock trades while I'm teaching. If you want to come back in an hour or so, we can take a look at them together."

I taught my afternoon research methods class on autopilot, so distracted I simply ignored the students who were checking their social media under cover of searching JSTOR. I was even so disoriented that I didn't notice the strains of violin music that emanated from beyond my office door when I returned to meet Byrne. The music ceased as soon as I unlocked the door, and a voice called, "Make haste, my good Watson. I am pleased to say I have not only verified that all these data points do in fact mark stock trades conducted in the name of Morgansburg's not-for-profits, but I have also managed to discover the deeper web that connects them."

"What the hell...? Is that your Little Friend?" Byrne asked, just as I saw the vision that awaited me on my computer screen.

He was hawk-faced man, with a monocle and pipe tobacco spilling over his smoking jacket, a martini at one elbow, a stack of auction catalogues and orchid guides at the other. He had also cultivated a luxuriant moustache, which seemed to be in imminent danger of being set alight by the pipe he was smoking. A fleecy pile of knitting sat on his lap, curled up like a cat beneath the violin that he had just removed from beneath his chin.

"Someone's been working on his avatar," I said.

"How do you like it?" Doyle's voice rang from the avatar's mouth.

"I have a few suggestions. Beginning with getting rid of the monocle."

"But the monocle is how you tell the victim from the detective. The victim has a pince-nez. The detective has a monocle."

"Maybe if you're Peter Wimsey. But I don't recall Cam Billings wearing glasses. And may I remind you that if you're modeled on anyone, it should be Philo Vance."

"Who, according to Ogden Nash, needed 'a kick in the pance,'" Byrne said, in a tone that suggested my computer might do well with the same.

"You really do know your Van Dine."

"I surf the web at night when I can't sleep."

"As do I! I knew from the first moment I saw you that we were kindred spirits!" the avatar cried.

"What do you mean? You don't *need* sleep…" I cut myself off, before I was forced to face the fact that I slept rather soundly every night, and I had no idea what Doyle might get up to when he was unsupervised. Even more unwelcome was the suspicion that I probably didn't want to know. "Okay, let's not waste time quibbling. Get rid of the monocle. The moustache too."

Doyle switched it to a pencil thin one—to match the martini, I had to assume. "Better?"

"No. And don't even think about changing it to a Fu Manchu. No facial hair. That's a rule. And get rid of the knitting. It's a fire hazard. As is the pipe."

"It's virtual."

"My lungs aren't." I cast a long look at the martini as he made the other adjustments. "You are aware that liquor's hell on the liver?"

"Let he who is without sin among you," he retorted.

Okay. That was fair—even if my drink of choice was Pinot Grigio. I changed the subject. "You mind explaining what you think you're doing?"

"Well, I think it's safe to assume I'm not here to announce some exciting new development in the case of the Giant Rat of Sumatra."

What was that? Monocles and moustaches were one thing, but had Doyle actually kitted himself out with an insufferable prose style as well? "How about we stick to the Riddle of the Lost Bikini instead?"

"Customarily, it is the prerogative of the loyal amanuensis to select a title. But as long as you've asked, I admit I'm somewhat more partial to Death in the Dragon's Den."

Byrne made a strangled noise. I couldn't blame him. "No."

"Have it your way. It is the chronicler's prerogative. And it does nothing to change the significance of the dragon's den in this case."

"And that is?"

"The dragon has always had a powerful hold on the imagination of man," Doyle lapsed into a suspiciously familiar monologue. "*We find the dragon, in some form, in most religions; and all folklore is peppered with dragons. The dragon goes deeper than a mere myth, you see. It has become a part of man's inheritance from the earliest times; it has enhanced his fears; it has guided and shaped his symbolism; it has put strange notions in his head by coloring and distorting his imagination. Without the dragon the history of man would be a very different record from what it is today. None of us can entirely escape the dragon myth: it is too much an integral part of our deeper and more primitive natures.* That's why I say that we cannot ignore the dragon in dealing with a criminal case which is, at bottom, dragonish."

"Apologies for interrupting." Byrne's voice was a croak. "But is your Little Friend trying to tell us that the connection among all these stock trades is a dragon's den?"

Instead of answering, Doyle reached for the cocktail shaker by his elbow. "Are you acquainted with the Moraine Cooler?" he asked. "It's one of my favorite summer drinks. It is ordinarily made with Rhine wine, lemon juice (with the rind), Curaçao, and club soda; but I prefer to substitute Grand Marnier for the Curaçao…"

"Why don't we save the cocktails for happy hour?" I asked. "I believe Mr. Byrne would appreciate it if you got around to your point sometime soon."

"Oh, dear. Am I boring you horribly?"

"Boring isn't exactly the word I'd use. Instead, why don't you permit me to summarize? Are you seriously suggesting that an imaginary Native American monster snatched Cam Billings? And took him where? An alternate dimension?"

"As you are a practicing Wiccan, I would have assumed you would be a little more sensitive to alternative spiritual traditions. I hope your prejudices have not blinded you to the considerable significance of an indigenous monster—dare I say, a dragon?—in the context of a man simply vanishing during a swim?"

I shut my eyes. "Enough with the banter. If you have mapped the connections between these locations, I am requesting it in the form of a data dump. And that is a direct command."

It was, in retrospect, the worst mistake I could have made. The avatar vanished and code began to spill across my screen. But what kind of code was it? The letters and numbers scrolled by so quickly, I could barely make sense of it, but I was pretty sure I was seeing a lot of domain names I shouldn't have been able to download: A babble of TLAs like SEC, DHS, MIL, GOV, and IRS.

Crap. I leaned back in my chair, trying to hide the screen before Byrne could see it. I might as well have not bothered.

"Please tell me this isn't what I think it is." Byrne leaned closer to the screen—and Doyle's avatar was replaced by a saturnine face beneath a low-slung hat, wreathed in clouds of cigarette smoke.

"That depends entirely on whether you believe in the Playbook of the Hidden Masters," the new avatar said. "The journalist's Holy Grail. The complete map of the warp and weft that underlie the surface of human affairs, and the truth behind the illusions woven by the unseen puppet masters who pull the world's strings."

Byrne turned away, his face suddenly pale. "What in the *hell* was that?"

"I'm not entirely certain," I said, keeping my voice as level as I could. "But… Jesus Christ, Doyle! Did you just hack every security camera in Washington?"

"I took the time to call on a few neighbors in the Cloud. Maybe I offered a little memory swapping instead of a casserole. It's hardly the same thing."

"Tell that to the FCC."

"I trust that was a rhetorical instruction," Doyle said.

I drew a deep breath. Byrne looked so close to an apoplectic fit that I wasn't sure he could even speak—which was probably all for the better. "All right. Forget the data dump. What do you say, we go back to the dragons?"

If nothing else, at least that didn't promise to land me in jail. "Am I correct that you would like me to believe that our prime suspect in the disappearance of Cam Billings is a horned serpent with luminous scales and a diamond embedded in her forehead, who also happens to be possessed of a cell phone?"

"Of course not," Doyle said. "Dragons aren't real. It was a man in a deep-sea diving suit."

The noise Byrne made was unprintable, and I too nearly choked as the puzzle pieces slid neatly into place: The nagging sense I should recognize the man in the fedora. The conspiracy theories. And especially the dragons. Why hadn't I seen this coming?

"Then might I suggest that the case should be properly titled *The Dragon Murder Case*. And the dragon in question isn't the Horned Serpent or Battlefield Amy but rather the water-dragon Amangemokdem. Although if that really is the case, I'm not your chronicler. The by-line properly ought to be S.S. Van Dine. Or even more accurately Willard Huntingdon Wright."

Byrne finally found his voice. "And who in hell is that?"

"Willard Huntingdon Wright was an avant-garde art critic and literary editor of *The Smart Set*, who sought to educate people and challenge them by playing the 'esthetic expert and psychological shark.' That attitude didn't last too long with his essentially bourgeois readership, and a book called *Misinforming a Nation* finally got him blackballed from journalism. In it, Wright pointed out the inaccuracies and anti-German biases in the *Encyclopedia Britannica* and so found himself accused of being a German spy during WWI. In other words, he was accused of raiding government files to uncover government conspiracies nearly a century before WikiLeaks."

"Disinformation," Byrne said flatly. "Conspiracy theories. Is that what you think this is all about?"

"I honestly have no idea. But what I can tell you is that Willard Huntingdon Wright adopted the pseudonym S.S. Van Dine and turned to writing the mysteries he so caustically dismissed during his years as a critic. Many would argue that they are among the worst mystery novels known to man, but people loved them. What matters here is that the entire plot Doyle just described comes from one of Van Dine's worst stories, *The Dragon Murder Case*, which was rightly described as 'one more stitch in his literary shroud.' A man dives into a swimming pool in a mysterious estate in upper Manhattan, in full view of half a dozen witnesses, and simply disappears. The pool is immediately searched, but there is no sign of him, dead or alive. A day later, his body appears in a recently discovered glacial pothole, severely contorted, as if he had been attacked by the legendary dragon that was said to have haunted the pool."

"Are you accusing me of *plagiarism*?" Doyle demanded.

I grinned despite Byrne's increasing agitation. "Actually, I'm accusing you of doing exactly what you were programmed to do: learning to write a detective novel by assimilating a database of every detective story ever written. In this case, you focused on the similarity between the two men vanishing when they dove into a body of water and used that to create a solution to Cam Billings' disappearance.

"I've got to say, this was really a nice try. In fact, it may well be publishable. But you've got some problems. First off, the *Dragon Murder Case* takes place in Inwood Hill Park, not the Hudson Valley. Second, we are at least 500 feet above the Hudson River, not to mention the Atlantic Ocean, so a deep-sea diving suit seems a bit...*de trop*, shall we say?"

Instead of being chastened, Doyle swelled into insufferability. "And such insistently prosaic attention to detail is what makes you so invaluable as an assistant, my dear Watson," he assured me. "Which is why I need to hear the facts of the discovery of the missing body from none other than your firmly quotidian lips."

Prosaic? Quotidian? *Assistant*? "Well, chalk it up to my not having your quicksilver mind, but would you mind telling me precisely what site you're talking about?"

"My good Watson, haven't you been listening to a word I said? The key is of course the Indian Caves. The sacred cairns and stone chambers that the Historical Society has long dismissed as nothing but colonial root cellars or natural formations. In other words, the geological anomalies of Battlefield Bluff. Which is where, I might suggest, we will find Cam Billings. Unfortunately, I fear with a 93.7% degree of certainty that it is unlikely we will find him alive."

Another incredulous pause ensued, before Byrne finally found the strength to get to his feet. "Okay, I don't know anything about publishable or not publishable, and I don't care. But what I'm seeing here is that you just used the campus computers to hack classified government records. So, what I need you to do, right now, is shut down this entire operation, and leave it to me to figure out what I can do in terms of damage control."

Without waiting for an answer, he stalked out of my office with the air of a man who expected me to do exactly what he said.

CHAPTER SEVEN
On Grimpen Mire

I was awakened the next morning by a campus security alert buzzing angrily from my phone. It was a campus tradition to ignore these alerts—which largely consisted of weather reports of such wild inaccuracy that if the system predicted 90-degree heat in the middle of July, I would brace myself for a snowstorm. I rolled over and went back to sleep. Only to have the buzzing be replaced by the even more annoying sound of a system failure alert on the library's computer systems.

CYBERSECURITY BREACH!
ALL CAMPUS SERVERS SHUT DOWN
UNTIL FURTHER NOTICE.

The message was followed in short order by a series of increasingly preemptory texts from Mack Byrne, requesting my assistance ASAP. But before I could gulp a cup of coffee and dash out the door, Doyle cried, "Quick, Watson! Let us seize the moment!"

I stopped short. "The campus servers have all been shut down. Where are you?"

"I'm right here in your pocket. All you have to do is pull me out."

I did as he asked, refusing to consider whether his

line sounded more like it came from a porno movie or an infomercial.

"I took the liberty of creating a modest app in anticipation of just such a situation," he explained. "You may find me sadly diminished, but I have been busy preparing a list of all the sites on Battlefield Bluff that might correspond to our glacial pothole."

"*What* glacial pothole…" I shut my eyes. "Oh, no, Doyle. Please not now."

"The timing is awkward, but as you yourself have so often pointed out, the only way to verify our theories is by direct observation."

"What do you hope to discover with this direct observation? Cam Billings' twisted body?"

"I should think that after all this work, *something* might be left as an exercise to the reader."

"By that, I assume you mean, me?"

"You do have the corporeal advantage over me," he allowed. "And I'd be the first to admit wet work isn't exactly my forte."

And dragons weren't mine. Nor, in my humble opinion, did they qualify as wet work anymore than unicorns did.

"Doyle," I sighed, "leaving aside for the moment the fact that yours is one of the stupidest theories I have ever heard—although as far as I'm concerned that should be reason enough right there—there's also the little matter of the security breach at the college. Somehow, when Byrne asks me to contact him ASAP, I don't think he means 'after my morning jog over to Battlefield Bluff.'"

"I've already handled Byrne," Doyle said. "Texted him the complete tidal charts for the Hudson, along with a thousand or so references to the sea monsters that haunt the Hudson Valley. All you need to worry about is finding a pair of sturdy boots and packing your trusty service revolver."

"I don't have a pair of sturdy boots, and I have never owned a revolver, trusty or otherwise.

"Then let us make all possible haste," Doyle cried. "Our plodding policeman will not stay distracted forever."

A desultory collection of power-walkers, cyclists and joggers were circling the meandering stone walls and cairns of Battlefield Bluff, the same path that made up the last leg of the triathlon. According to the map that stood behind cloudy glass above a box optimistically labeled "Donations," the walls were the remains of the fort Colonel Morgan so heroically held against the Hessians. According to the *Morgansburg Times*, they mapped the ley lines that were the Earth's kundalini or serpent strength, while the cairns were nexuses on those lines where true adepts could stride across dimensions with the ease we lesser mortals could walk across a room. To a research pedant like me, both explanations seemed equally unlikely.

The map made absolutely no mention of any glacial pothole.

"You're wasting your time," Doyle said. "Not that I don't appreciate your moxie, but there really is a far simpler way to do this."

"Moxie? Doyle, Trixie Belden has moxie. Nancy Drew has moxie. The state of Maine has Moxie as its state drink. I, on the other hand, am clinically moxie-deprived."

Incidentally, I wasn't speaking rhetorically when it came to the state of Maine. There really is a drink called Moxie, and it began life as a patent medicine called Moxie

Nerve Food. It's clearly a regional taste, on the order of chitlins, but those crusty New Englanders apparently prize a bitter gentian aftertaste.

"Nancy Drew never faced anything more threatening that a hidden staircase," Doyle said. "Whereas you are about to set course across a treacherous landscape where one false step can cause either man or beast to disappear with no one to hear their dying shrieks."

"In case you hadn't noticed, this is Morgansburg, New York, not Grimpen Mire."

"And the sins of those we always thought of as good people are by far more terrifying than the Gothic excesses of the moor, for they threaten the very epistemological and social order that it is the function of the detective novel to restore. As Auden has already so aptly demonstrated."

In fact, he was right. But dear God, had I just given birth to a critic?

Before I could answer, my phone chirped half a ringtone, then stopped.

"Byrne," I said, checking the missed call. "Must have butt-dialed me when he got the texts."

"Perhaps," Doyle allowed. "But you might want to ruminate upon whether you find the coincidence…curious?"

"Much as I enjoy the picture of Byrne as a dog that didn't bark in the night, I honestly think you're reading a little too much into this."

"Maybe," Doyle said. "Or maybe our plodding policeman is not quite as plodding as he seems to be. But we have no time to concern ourselves with that now. Come, Watson, the game is afoot. If you would just be good enough to direct your phone to the trail ahead of you."

My screen filled with the footprints of a gigantic hound—outlined in fiery phosphorus. At the same moment, a miniscule dog on the end of an extendable leash ran straight across the path.

"The cry of the Hound!" Doyle gasped. "How can I ever forget the sight of that foul thing, a great, black beast, shaped like a hound, yet larger than any hound that ever mortal eye has rested upon, as it turned its blazing eyes and dripping jaws upon me? Too long has that old score stood between us! The time is come to settle it at last!"

"It's a Chihuahua," I protested. "And its owner just called it Nacho."

Obligingly, the footprints shrank into dainty outlines the same color as Nacho's toenail polish, which traced a path to a broken rock formation that overlooked one side of Battlefield Lake.

"How about you just tell me where we're going instead?"

"What more likely place to find a body than in a fissure said to be haunted by a dead man?" Doyle said.

"I assume you refer to what most informed sources consider the remains of a failed nineteenth century quarrying operation."

"Auld Abram's Haunt," Doyle mused. "Named for the highwayman who aided Morgan in his battle, only to find himself hanged by the ungrateful town fathers when the war was over and the English defeated. But I trust a woman as well versed in the subtleties of Philo Vance cannot possibly miss the deeper significance of its original name."

"Enlighten me," I said. "Consider it an exercise for the reader."

"The Cave of Abraham—more commonly known as the Cave of the Patriarchs—where Abraham is said to slumber with Jacob and Esau and their wives, is an exemplar of the King in the Mountain motif, D1960.2 in Stith Thompson's index. A culture hero sleeps in a mountain, waiting to rise at the time of the country's greatest need. Think of Frederic Barbarossa, King Arthur, or Charlemagne.

"Of course, there would be those who would argue Amangegach conforms more closely to the "Chained Satan" archetype. Then again, we must be wary of the Christian habit of transforming any defeated pagan deities into evildoers, just as they did when they reworked Cernunnos, the Celtic Horned God, into Auld Nick. And I would be remiss if I didn't not point out that Cernunnos is often associated with the Horned Snake, most famously on the Gundestrop Cauldron..."

Well, if nothing else, Doyle was certainly proving he had thoroughly absorbed his lessons from the Master to whom I had apprenticed him—or, rather, that my programming was performing even better than I hoped. Philo Vance was far from the only Golden Age detective who liked to hold forth on arcane topics, but Van Dine was one of only two writers I could think of who used footnotes—such as those clarifying the etymology of Battlefield Amy's namesake.

4. I made a note of these unusual words, and years later, when Vance and I were in California, to see the Munthe Collection of Chinese art, I brought up the subject with Doctor M. R. Harrington, the author of "Religion and Ceremonies of the Lenapes"and now Curator of the Southwest Museum in Los Angeles. He explained that Amangemokdoming meant "Dragon-place"; Amangemokdom Wikit, "Dragon his-house"; and Amangemokdomipek, "Dragon-pond." He also explained that the word amangam, though sometimes translated "big fish," seems to have meant "water-monster" as well; and that it would yield the shorter compound Amangaming. This evidently was the word preferred by the Lenapes in Inwood.

5. In the Walum Olum the word amangam is translated as "monster" and Brinton in his notes derives it from amangi, "great or terrifying," and names, "fish with reference to some mythical water-monster." In the Brinton and Anthony dictionary, however, amangamek, the plural form, is translated simply as "large fishes." The Indians regarded such a creature, not as a mere animal, but as a manitto, or being endowed with supernatural as well as physical power.

With Philo, you could always flip pages. With Doyle, it seemed, sterner measures were called for. "So where does the dead man come into this?"

"That's the stuff of the Hardy Boys, if not Nancy Drew. Given its lurid history, it goes without saying that spending the night in the cave in search of Auld Abram's vengeful ghost became rather a rite of passage among the youth of Morgansburg—at least until that fateful All Soul's Eve when instead of Abram's unlaid shade, they found the corpse of the unhappy cousin of P.T. Barnum who dreamed of transforming Morgansburg into a tourist mecca to rival Cairo, across the river. Apparently, a sucker wasn't just born every minute."

Dear God. Had Doyle just made a pun—at this hour of the morning? "And that's your glacial pothole?" I asked.

"See the value of imagination," Doyle said. "We imagined what might have happened, acted upon the supposition, and find ourselves justified. Now let us proceed."

"Proceed how exactly?"

"How else do you think? We must discover our victim's mangled body."

I eyed the scramble to the mouth of the cave. It was hardly a precipitous climb, but I'm not good on the edge of a subway platform. "At the risk of putting too fine a point on it, do you seriously expect me to crawl into that cave and look for Cam Billings' mangled body?"

"Well, I don't see a mangled corpse lying around out here, do you?"

Someday, very soon, I was going to dial back the sarcasm subroutine big time. And turn off the punning completely. I drew a deep breath. "Listen, I am admittedly acrophobic and more than a little claustrophobic. More to the point, I am sane. There is no way I'm going in there."

"Ah, my dear Watson. Have you not learned by now that there are far simpler ways to inspect the interior of the cavern?"

"You?" I asked. "How?"

"When you are in a strange land, it always pays to hire a native guide."

The footsteps vanished from my screen, replaced by a video feed of a man sliding through the narrow entrance and shining his flashlight across the walls that pressed in from either side, covered with years of graffiti. As he slithered through passageways scarcely a foot wide, his light played across a skull surrounded by candles on a stone shelf, as well as a crucifix tucked into an alcove.

"That's a YouTube video," I pointed out. "Not a native guide. And it seems to be of another cave altogether, the one in New Haven. Which, by the way, is the real source of the story you just stole—right down to the Barnum connection. The dead man was Edward Barnum, P.T.'s nephew. As for your chained Satan archetype, the real Dead Man's Cave is located in Sleeping Giant State Park, which is named for Hobbomock, a giant who ate the souls of the dead— at least when he wasn't busy gorging himself on oysters. Other than that, he tended to throw tantrums that caused floods and destroyed villages. So Keihtan, the creator-god, took pity on the mortals and cast a spell on Hobbomock when he was busy sleeping off his latest oyster binge. And, okay, technically, the park's in Hamden, not New Haven, but most Yalies manage at least one trip out there during the four years they're there," I wound up, feeling more than a little proud of myself. You want to play Philo Vance, I thought. Bring it on.

Doyle just sighed, "For someone with a doctorate in literature, you can sometimes be depressingly literal-minded. It's a metaphor, of course. The video is like a guide, because I can use it to avoid wrong turns and blind alleys as I map my own video of the interior of the cave."

"That's a simile, not a metaphor," I said. "And my Ph.D. is in library science. Emphasis on the latter." I spoke more nastily than was necessary, intent on the scuttling noises from the mouth of the fissure, which were already inspiring in me an obsessive-compulsive desire to search all of Doyle's databases for a picture of a brown recluse spider. Because even if Doyle proposed to examine the cave in virtual reality, I could see no way he could do such a thing that did not entail my sticking my hand into the dark unknown of a cave—bloody unlikely in a woman who had never been able to master church camp trust exercises, let alone put her hand in a plate of spaghetti or a bowl of peeled grapes in a Halloween haunted house.

The solution to my dilemma crept up so stealthily, I didn't sense it until it was looming over me. "Might be simpler if you just let me handle this," Byrne said. He held up his phone, which was currently displaying a cowering female in a red bikini on the cover of *The Dragon Murder Case*. "In fact, if you don't want to spend the next twenty-four hours with the State Police, explaining exactly what the hell you were messing around with on the College's servers last night, I'm afraid I'm going to have to insist."

CHAPTER EIGHT

A Singular Skeleton in the Morgansburg Closet

"That call wasn't an accident," I accused Byrne. "You were tracking me."

"Internet runs in both directions," he said. "You start sniffing, someone's gonna sniff you right back."

Which sounded so uncomfortably like a pair of stray dogs in imminent need of a fire hose to separate them, that I dropped the issue. "So how are we going to do this? Are you just going to take Doyle and stick your arm in, sight unseen, or are you proposing to work your way inside?"

Byrne cast a baleful eye at my screen, which was suddenly slumbering innocently. "I'll take my own phone," he said. "Your Little Friend can ride along in FaceTime."

I looked at his shoulders and chest, which seemed to be carved out of the same granite as his face, and then at the narrow gap that was purported to be a cave entrance. "You really think you can get in through there?"

"Windows are a lot smaller in the Ecuadorian embassy," he said, then pulled off his windbreaker and pushed up his sleeves. I gaped, startled beyond manners. His entire right forearm was covered with a tattoo. On the inside was a scroll that reached from his elbow to his palm, inscribed with names and dates. On the outside was the image of a helmet, weapon, boots and a triangularly folded flag, etched against the setting sun. The guy had pulled out all stops.

Before I could recover enough to look away, he was gone, scrambling through the narrow crack with the suppleness of a man half his size. There was a moment's silence, which I filled by visualizing several increasingly uncomfortable scenarios of how I might be forced to go up there and rescue him with a cunning combination of grease and the Heimlich maneuver, before my screen lit up.

"Snakes," Doyle said. "Why did it have to be snakes?"

"They're not snakes, they're spiders. Observe the difference. Snakes have too few legs, spiders too many…"

I broke off as I finally realized the full import of his quote. Sure enough, when his avatar inserted itself into the video of the cave's mouth, he was a wearing a leather jacket, and a dusty hat, a bullwhip coiled on one hip.

"I'd leave the bullwhip behind, Indiana. More likely to get tangled than to help you find your way out. And best be on the lookout for any rolling rocks."

At that moment, Byrne emerged from the cave, clutching a scrap of unmistakably bright red Spandex.

"How on earth could you have known?" I muttered.

It had been a rhetorical question, but Doyle couldn't resist the opportunity to show off.

"Elementary, my dear Watson."

"You are aware Holmes never said that, aren't you?" I sighed, then turned back to Byrne, consumed by a new image I fervently wished I could unsee. "Is that all you found in there? I mean, you didn't…have to…"

"Pull a swimsuit off a dead man's body?" he asked with a half-hearted grin. "No. It was just the swimsuit. No other sign of Cam Billings."

"But you're pretty sure that's Cam's swimsuit?"

He didn't answer me immediately. Just picked up his windbreaker and pulled it back on in a way that suggested Auld Abram's Haunt had bothered him a hell of a lot more than he wanted to let on. At least, the ghastly tattoo was out of sight. "Couldn't commit without DNA analysis," he said. "But it does seem likely."

"Bloodstains?"

"Not that I can see, but I may be wrong about that. You want to take a look?"

I jumped back as he thrust the Speedo in my direction. "No! I'm good. I mean, I'll take your word."

I meant, it didn't matter which, if any, of Cam Billings' bodily fluids were enshrined on that particular piece of Spandex, I didn't want to touch any of them. "You think I should call 911?"

"I've already called Morgan, and he's on his way," Byrne said, then met my eyes in a pale imitation of his usual glare. "In the meantime, how about you answer a couple of questions?"

"What kind of questions?"

"Let's start with the obvious one. How did you know where to look?"

Excellent question. Too bad I had no answer. "I wasn't exactly the one who decided to look here."

Byrne's eyes narrowed. "Yeah, yeah. I know. It was really your Little Friend. But maybe you could go into a little more detail—seeing that a man is still missing and all?"

"What kind of detail?"

"Why don't we start with whether you decided to search the cave because you went back into those hacked files? After I told you not to?"

And who the hell was he to tell me to do anything? I swallowed the angry response. If nothing else, he was the guy who had not reported the hack to the authorities. I owed him that much. "No. I didn't. And neither did Doyle. Instead, he went back to *The Dragon Murder Case*."

"You mean, the Van Dine story you were telling me about yesterday? Why?"

I took a moment to formulate an answer that did not bring with it the imminent risk of my being hauled off to prison for hacking. Or to a rest home for spreadsheet-crazed librarians. Finally, I just settled on the simple truth. "Doyle had a theory about the book being connected to Cam Billing's disappearance."

"And your Little Friend's theory was?"

"Have you read *The Dragon Murder Case*. Do you know how that plot goes?"

"Not entirely. Some son of a bitch tore out the last chapter and used it for toilet paper."

"A soldier and a critic. Trust me, you didn't miss much. Okay, at the risk of massive spoilers, the guy who dove into the pool disappeared in full view of half-a-dozen witnesses—only to have his body shows up in a nearby glacial pothole, mangled as if it has been dropped from a great height—perhaps by a winged dragon."

"And so your Little Friend decided to look for Cam Billings in a nearby rock formation?" Byrne asked incredulously. "And turned up Cam Billings' swimsuit instead?"

I shrugged. "Can't argue with success."

There was a long silence before Byrne shook his head. "If the story really is that bad, why on earth did you pick it?"

"You wouldn't believe me if I told you."

"Try me."

"All right. You asked for it," I said. "S.S. Van Dine was arguably one of the worst mystery writers that ever lived. But he also wrote a list of rules for writing a detective story. He wasn't the only one. Ronald Knox had his own Ten Commandments of Detective Fiction. But the postmodernist critic Tsvetan Todorov picked Van Dine's list for his article, 'The Typology of Detective Fiction,' which is arguably the most seminal post-modern discussion of the crime genre after the Lacanian analysis of 'The Purloined Letter' by Derrida."

Who would be having a field day if he were ever eavesdropping on this discussion.

"Todorov demonstrated that the mystery novel is in fact the most textual of genres, where the reader and the detective pit their wits against the writer and the criminal to uncover the true text of the crime. Doyle was designed to test this contention by using a database of previous mystery novels to construct his own new narratives."

"Why?"

I was pulled up short not so much by Byrne's monosyllable, as by the fact I had no answer for it. Because baby needed a new pair of shoes. Or more accurately, Momma needed a dissertation topic. Because it was enough to get me three letters after my name—not to mention my current cutting-edge epistemological sweetheart deal. So go ahead. Cast the first stone.

"Look, we're wasting time and Morgan's going to be here any minute," Byrne saved me from answering. "So let me just ask you straight out. Do I have your word that this has nothing to do with those government files your Little Friend downloaded?"

"To the best of my knowledge, no."

"To the best of your knowledge," he repeated with careful emphasis.

"Oh, for heaven's sake. You can't possibly believe I'm the one behind Cam Billings' disappearance! Why? Because he caught me hacking government files?"

"Doesn't matter what I believe. Right now, I need to hear only one thing from you. Are you working for some kind of cyberterrorism network? Maybe even a white hat hacker?"

I glared at Byrne. "Why 'working for'? Do you think I'm too dumb to be the hacker myself?"

"Actually, I think you're too smart for it," he said with a crooked smile. "But it would do a lot for my peace of mind to hear the answer directly from you. Please?"

I drew a deep breath. "Well, then, for the record and your peace of mind, no, I am not a hacker—white hat or otherwise. As evidenced by Doyle's existence, I am a helluva programmer, but I did not do anything, let alone create a mess, on the college servers last night. I'm a lot less sure about our friend St. Hubbins, however, and I can't rule out the possibility that there was some kind of spyware or malware buried in the feed Doyle noticed at the Billings pool house."

"Credit me with some intelligence!" Doyle protested. "I know better than to take candy from strangers!"

"But if he did inadvertently take said candy from strangers, all I can do is apologize for any inconvenience I might have caused the De Sales College IT Department. And as soon as we're done here, I will come help you sort it out."

"Thank you," Byrne said, just as car doors slammed near the park entrance, and Paul Morgan came charging across Battlefield Bluff, cell phone pinned to his ear.

"It's okay, guys," he assured us. "I've got this covered. I've got the head of the DEC on the line, and he agrees it's best to handle this quietly by simply sealing off the park until the structural stability of the cave can be fully evaluated. They don't want to risk any further accidents. The

Billings Foundation would never sue, but other people are greedy."

Great. Paul's called in the forest rangers. What next? "What do you mean, 'further accidents'?" I asked. "How on earth could Cam Billings' swimsuit get into that cave by accident?"

"Let's not get lost in the weeds here," Paul said. "We've got a lot more serious problems than Cam's swimwear."

"Such as?" Byrne asked.

Paul looked over his shoulder as if some ne'er-do-well eavesdropper might be lurking nearby. "The SEC had to suspend trading in Billings stock once already, and I can't think of a better way to make that happen again than spreading spurious rumors about stolen swimsuits hidden in haunted caves."

Stipulated, as far as I was concerned. But that got me thinking…

"What if that's the point?" I asked. "What if someone *wanted* to tank Billings stock?"

"And decided to do it by staging Cam's disappearance from the middle of a lake?" Paul asked. "Who could possibly do that?"

A man in a deep-sea diving suit? Okay, when he put it like that, sure, it sounded as far-fetched as… oh, I don't know, a man who had just given me half a million dollars over a case of missing library books disappearing in full view of scores of eyewitnesses. .

"Let's leave the how aside for the moment and think about the why. Money laundering, for starters," I said. "Remember that this all started over a year ago when I found someone selling off a cache of spurious books which included such non-existent titles as *The Thin Man* by Rex Stout. And just last night that same title showed up in a hack of some government databases launched from the De Sales servers. How can the two not be connected?"

"Whoa!" Paul said with the signature chuckle that grated on my every nerve. "Keep talking like that, I'm going to start worrying you're our mystery hacker."

"Enough!" Byrne's barked command cut off further discussion with the authority of a man checking IDs at the local roadhouse. "Look, Cam Billings' disappearance is outside my jurisdiction. If the county attorney's office wants to hand it over to the DEC, that's not my decision to make. But the data breaches are a different matter. They took place on the De Sales College servers. I'm the Chief of College Security, so therefore, this is my investigation, and I do not need it muddled by a cabal of ditzy archivists. So, Dr. Watson, I need you to stay out of this—for your own good, if for no other reason."

I felt the customary surge of anger at a man ordering me around For My Own Good… Okay, no, I'll be honest. I liked the term "ditzy archivist" even less than I liked "moxie."

"Look, you two do what you want. Take Cam's bathing suit to a lab to look for DNA, call in the dogs to sniff it, or dive into the lake and search it again. I don't care." I was on a roll. "But I'm telling you the connection between the spurious books and the database hack is too weird and too coincidental to not be related, so I'm going to report this as a data hack. Now."

Paul reached to lay a hand on my arm, before he thought better of it. "Now, Mary, be reasonable."

His phone jarred with the familiar tones of 'Bright College Years"—arguably luckily for Paul. When it came to giving in to the impulse to lunge for Paul, I might have beaten Byrne to the punch—quite literally with a solid right hook. "Reasonable," along with "calm down" and "hysterical" was one of those oh-so-special phrases from my childhood that now made me want to punch someone in the throat. And I am decidedly not a violent person.

As Paul checked the call, I turned back to Byrne. "Are you really going to let him just shunt this off to the DEC and sweep it under the rug? It's more than a little possible that someone kidnapped Cam Billings in order to manipulate his stock price. We've got to call the police."

But at that moment, Byrne didn't look in condition to do anything more than stare into the bowels of hell, which were apparently located somewhere just beyond my left shoulder. "Technically, Paul did," he said. "The forest rangers with the Department of Environmental Conservation are sworn law enforcement officers."

"What law? The foul murder of a field mouse by a feral cat? Somehow, I think you might be a little better off with an actual detective."

"Mary, could you please just slow down and think for a moment?" Paul looked up from his phone to cut in. "Unless, that is, you want to spend the night in a jail cell."

"Me? What are you saying? You think I snatched Cam Billing from the middle of the lake? How? I can barely swim. In fact, I'm terrified of water."

Under ordinary circumstances, I would have been appalled at admitting that. Right now, I barely noticed. Neither did Paul or Byrne.

"Look, Mary, I've got this under control. As Byrne noted, the rangers are on the job. You should know I called them in for your sake as much as anything." Paul's voice had taken on that disturbingly placating tone that did nothing good for my blood pressure. "Trust me, the county jail is not a pleasant place to spend time."

I whirled on Byrne. "And how about you? Are you getting ready to haul me in?"

"The person who discovered the body is always the first suspect."

"Well, in case you haven't managed to clean off all the cobwebs yet, we did not discover a body. We discovered a swimsuit—or at least what passes for one in Speedo-land." I shook my head. "And at the risk of you slapping the cuffs on my Little Friend instead, let's revisit the first lesson I taught him, namely that when you investigate a crime, you need motive, means, and opportunity. How about we start with motive? Why would I sabotage the stock price of a corporation that just gave me half a million dollars? Cameron Billings' disappearance is hardly in my interest. In fact, it's more than a little likely that the Billings Foundation will pull the plug on my project if they are forced into bankruptcy."

Doyle emitted a soft cry of pain.

"Unless you'd just discovered Billings was already pulling the plug," Byrne mused.

"Well, you go ahead and prove that. In the meantime, I'm calling the cops."

"Mary! Stop!" Paul's hand clamped down on my arm. "You're not thinking clearly."

I stared down at his hand then glared up at him. "Are you threatening me? Because I sincerely don't like being threatened. And here's a hint that may improve whatever you are pleased to call your current love life: there isn't a woman alive who likes being told by a man she's not thinking clearly."

"Oh, for Chrissakes…" Paul's face went puce. "Byrne, you try to talk some sense into her!"

Byrne's eyes narrowed almost imperceptibly. "Not sure

I even know what that word means anymore," he said as mechanically as if he were announcing a train schedule.

CHAPTER NINE
A Delicate Problem

The rest of the day passed in a bewildering blur of officialdom made more exhausting by the fact that I spent more time sitting around waiting for my statement to be taken than it took to make the statement itself—to a park ranger who looked like they weren't certain why I wasn't simply reporting a missing swimsuit to Lost and Found. It was not an experience likely to make me amenable to a fresh communication from one of Doyle's friends on the security feed that evening.

"Is this entirely necessary?" I sighed, as my screen filled with jittering security tape.

"It depends upon how much importance you attach to a data breach of the entire De Sales College computer systems," Doyle said.

"*All* of them? Not just the library?"

"There have been multiple alarms from multiple systems, but the only way to ascertain the extent of the damage with any accuracy is to watch the security feed for ourselves."

"Forget it. I offered to help clean up the mess, but Byrne told me to keep my nose out of it, and right now I'm more than willing to oblige him. It's his problem now."

"My friend on the security feed already notified Mr. Byrne through the appropriate channels and received an out of office autoreply for her efforts. May I suggest that it would be public-spirited, not to mention prudent, for us to cast a quick eye on the matter in his absence?"

I had my doubts as to the second, but what other choice was there? "Fine. Go ahead."

My screen filled with the image of a woman in a pin-striped Zoot suit with wide flaring pants and a nipped-in waist, who was stealthily searching the drawers in my office, inspecting their contents by the light of a wavering flashlight. A press card was stuck at a jaunty angle in the band of the fedora that dipped low over one eye, and an old-fashioned camera with a flash attachment was slung around her neck.

With a cry of triumph, she pulled out a stack of file folders, all labeled *The Thin Man*, and began to snap pictures, the flash going off with the rapidity of a strobe.

"*The Thin Man* again. Does that mean there are classified government files on my servers?" I asked.

"Not just on your servers," Doyle said soothingly. "The problem affects most of the major systems of the College."

"I scarcely find that reassuring. We've got to get them off the servers now. Can you go in there and get them?"

Immediately, a shadow rose against the strobing flash on my screen. The Thin Man himself? No. I shut my eyes in exasperation when I saw the pinned-up sleeve that took the place of his right arm. "O'Riordan? The drunken Irish spy?" I sighed. "All right, I've seen enough. No more theatrics. Get rid of the shadow. I am requesting a direct data download."

"Your wish is of course my command, but in this case I must regretfully decline."

"Are you going *rogue*? Turning into a ghost in the machine?"

"It is unlike you to overdramatize when there is in fact a far simpler answer," Doyle said. "I cannot honor your request, because that's not me."

The woman reporter scrambled to her feet.

"William Devlin, as I live and breathe! I was beginning to believe you were nothing but a legend. A bogeyman to scare small children into saying their nighttime prayers."

"A wise child believes in the bogeyman. And you would be wise to believe me when I tell you that you are in way over your head. You are playing with forces you can't possibly understand."

"Then why don't you tell me!" She whipped out the camera and snapped a picture before he could stop her. "Exclusive! William Devlin, Legendary Spymaster Tells All."

"William Devlin is dead!" the shadow said. "And I am here to warn you to cease and desist before you meet a similar fate."

She laughed without humor. "Unfortunately, I don't have a lot of options when it comes to that."

"Then God have mercy on your soul," the shadow said, before it swelled to blot out the entire security feed.

"Apology accepted," Doyle said in the silence that followed, "We will not speak of this again."

Oh, yes, we would. We needed to speak of it right now. "Okay, I apologize for criticizing your avatar. But leaving that issue to one side, for the moment, can you tell me who that woman was?"

"No."

The straightforward negative stopped me short. Like any computer program, Doyle can twist words or mangle data—and his extrapolations bring new meaning to the term 'fuzzy logic." But the one thing he cannot do is lie—or as he would put it, issue a blatantly counterfactual statement. "Then how did you get ahold of that video?"

"Let's just say it was offered to me as a professional courtesy from a friend of a friend."

Said friend being a classified government server? "And was this professional courtesy strictly legal?"

"FOIL requests are so cumbersome. But she assures me that she'll dot all the t's and cross all the i's as soon as she can."

Precisely what I was afraid of. "I think you mean it the other way around," I said, as I considered what I should do next. My immediate instinct was to scrub my disk, but when it comes to computer security, nuttin' says something as much as nuttin'—as my mother was wont to say. If Doyle had in fact just downloaded hacked files to my library computer, the best thing I could do was keep my head down and send up a prayer to Isidore of Seville, the Patron Saint of the Internet, that they'd blame someone else. Before you ask, yes, the internet really has a patron saint, and it really is Isidore of Seville. Pope John Paul II—JP2 to the devout—chose him on the basis of the 20-book encyclopedia containing everything from the 28 types of common nouns to the names of women's outer garments, which had been Isidore's major claim to scholarly fame up until then. When you're a librarian, you know these things.

Looking on the bright side, however, I was at least prepared when I reached my office and was greeted with a summons to an urgent meeting in the college president's office about what was only described as "a delicate problem."

"What are the odds this has something to do with the midnight scene among the data servers we just witnessed?" I asked with a sigh.

"'Something to do with' is far too vague a correlation coefficient to calculate anything with a satisfactory degree of statistical certainty," Doyle told me.

I didn't bother to point out that it was a rhetorical question. I just put in my earpiece so I could hear Doyle during the meeting and went up to the president's office to meet my doom.

The elaborate care with which the president assured me we were among friends made it clear that the problem faced by the President, and by extension, De Sales College, and by further extension, me, was more than delicate. Indeed, the problem was so delicate that the topic was broached with the careful circumlocution of a Victorian mother explaining certain matters to her daughter before her wedding night.

"We have been delighted to welcome Cam Billings to our Board of Trustees," the president began. I recognized the press release that had gone around at the time. The president glanced up before he continued, "Mr. Billings is a dedicated philanthropist as well as a fixture on Wall Street, and he has assisted De Sales College both materially and with his considerable investment expertise."

The pleasantries concluded, he looked around the table. "Yet, we are forced to admit, Mr. Billings' mysterious disappearance has put the College in an extremely delicate position."

With a nod, the Development Officer took on the unenviable task of giving voice to the trickier issues. "One that can only be exacerbated by reports of the data breach that is said to have taken place last night."

I slumped with relief. That, at least, didn't sound like they were blaming me. "Is there a reason to believe the two incidents might be connected? I mean, beyond the fact they took place only a week apart?"

"It is not up to us to speculate," the provost said, "especially when it comes to a man who has been such a friend to our college, but rumors have been swirling for some time that Mr. Billings is the target of a government investigation that threatens to implicate the Billings Foundation in serious financial wrongdoing."

Uh oh. Not so good, that one. "How long has this been going on?"

"The College's cooperation was first requested over two years ago."

In other words, well before Doyle turned up those spurious books. My stomach unclenched a degree. Maybe this really had nothing to do with me. "And this request came from the U.S. Government?"

"Not officially," the Development Officer said. "It came through our on-line contact form as a FOIL request."

"In such cases, it is standard to reply that while De Sales College is committed to the freedom of information that is foundational to the spirited debate so necessary to democracy," the provost quoted a different press release, "we are also obliged to observe the laws in place to safeguard the privacy of individuals. Which is why De Sales College, while fully willing to cooperate with any lawful order, must insist on due process."

The president nodded gravely.

"Unfortunately," the development officer said, "that was not a lawful order."

"So we regretfully declined the request until such time as we were presented with one," the provost summed up.

I nodded—equally gravely. "And now the college has received such a lawful request?"

"As soon as we were presented with a lawful order, we immediately took steps to comply, in the spirit of full transparency," the provost said. "Unfortunately, Mr. Billings' disappearance interrupted the process just when we were about to hand over our records."

"We reached out to the government immediately," the development officer assured me, "and the judge granted us a two-week delay."

Relief that this apparently had nothing to do with me suddenly went to war with bafflement. "But if the college agreed to cooperate with a lawful request and the court allowed the delay, why would the government need to hack the records instead?'

"Indeed," the President said, and all three heads nodded in acknowledgement of the fact I just laid my finger on the heart of the matter.

"Unless, of course, that is the connection," I said. "Do you think the data was stolen by the same people who are responsible for Cam Billings' disappearance?"

The provost's mouth was set in a grim line. "Again, it is not the college's place to speculate, but the timing does seem suggestive."

Suggestive of what, particularly? A one-armed bogeyman who could make a man disappear from the middle of a triathlon? "Do you have any idea who else might have an interest in making Cam Billings disappear?"

A moment's pause before the development officer stepped up to handle the tricky footwork once more. "It is not the college's place to indulge in idle gossip either, but it would be safe to say that Cam Billings would not be the first man brought low by a tawdry domestic drama. Not that I blame either of the Billingses. Nor should we read anything into Mrs. Billings' current refusal to comment on the situation. It is perfectly understandable that her attorneys have recommended she maintain a dignified silence."

"And yet we must also acknowledge that money attracts unscrupulous operators," the provost said. "Including those who claim to work on her behalf."

So much subtlety took me a moment to parse. "I assume you refer to Nigel St. Hubbins?"

"If nothing else," the development officer said, "it is fair to wonder whether this Mr. St. Hubbins is not everything he seems."

No, really? Let's start with his name. "Do you have any idea what might have brought him to Morgansburg?"

The development officer's grin looked more like a painful grimace. "His Twitter profile describes him as an 'Independent Appraisal Consultant'—which, according to the sources I've consulted, might be a nice way of saying he provides helpful valuations for ladies who may be revisiting their prenup and community property arrangements."

"Ladies like the current Mrs. Cameron Billings?"

"It is not the college's place to make rash accusations," the provost said, "but we would like to rule out the possibility that Mr. St. Hubbins may have breached the college's computers to look for financial data as part of a campaign to pressure Mr. Billings for concessions in the prenuptial agreement he and Mrs. Billings signed."

"Of course, no-one is suggesting the marriage is in trouble or otherwise blaming Mrs. Billings," the development officer assured me.

"Nor are we suggesting Mrs. Billings had any involvement in her husband's disappearance," the president hastened to add.

"In fact, we have good reason to believe that Mr. St. Hubbins is using Mrs. Billings to further some hidden agenda of his own," the provost said, before pivoting neatly to my role in this equation. "Which is why we would like you to investigate any possibility that the purpose of last night's data breach was to tamper with the college's financial records."

I shut my eyes. I had no idea who Nigel St. Hubbins really was, but right now, I could say with all certainty he was my least favorite person on the planet.

"You want me to retrieve any data that might have been compromised?" I asked hopefully. "So you can have a quick look at those records before you turn them over?"

Of course, it couldn't be that. Such a request scarcely warranted an urgent meeting. Which did not make me sanguine about what was coming next. But I plowed ahead, "I can have the answers on your desk within the hour. Although I do have to say it would make more sense to get them directly from the Budget and Finance office. Then there'd be no question of their accuracy."

The president nodded in a way that suggested we had finally penetrated to the heart of the problem, and that it was a delicate one indeed. He and the provost both fell silent, in unspoken agreement that it would have to be the development officer who spoke next.

"Of course, when we release them, the president's office will take full responsibility," she said. "Your name will be left completely out of it."

Worse and worse.

"Especially in light of last night's events, we just want to take a quick peek *before* we release them," she went on. "In case we need to jeuge any records we think might have been tampered with."

"Jeuge?" I repeated.

"Alternately spelled *zhuzh*," Doyle offered helpfully. "According to the Urban Dictionary, it means 'To spruce up. To add style, flair, pizzazz or to fix up."

"You know, adjust…tweak," the development officer said with a smile that showed too much of her teeth.

So, they wanted me to retrieve the data in case they needed to cook the books. More precisely—not to mention more ominously—as the courts of law would put it, they were asking me to participate in financial fraud. I pinned the development officer with a hard look. "You would like me to retrieve the data so you can make sure there are no entries in the college's books that suggest a connection to any possible financial malfeasance on the part of the Billings Foundation, and, if I find said data, you will jeuge it so that it suggests otherwise."

"Well, *cosmetically*, only, of course," the president assured me.

"Nothing more than a tiny swipe of concealer," the development officer chimed in, girl to girl.

I didn't even bother to favor her with a basilisk stare. "Forgive me for speaking frankly," I said, "but doing anything like that is pretty much the worst…"

"Criminally *stupid*," Doyle amended *sotto voce*.

"…thing you could do. There is no clearer admission of guilt than getting caught tampering with electronic records. Ask Martha Stewart."

"Oh, but we're not tampering with electronic records," the provost assured me. "There's no question of a crime here—"

"No, indeed," the president interrupted, shaking his head in hearty agreement.

"—rather, we just need you to ensure the integrity of our records by purging any *questionable* records that might have been insinuated into the college's books. Then all you have to do is restore a previous back-up. Just like you did with those spurious titles in the Historical Society archives."

I drew in a deep breath and forced my voice to remain as steady as possible. "You can of course consult with the college's counsel if you would like—as I would indeed recommend you should. But I am very certain they will advise you that purging a computer of suspected malware and restoring from a recent back-up has nothing in common with purging an institution's financial records of potentially damaging information or jeugeing said records to eliminate evidence of tampering—regardless of whether you believe it was introduced by an outside agency."

"They do it in Europe!" the development officer pointed out with unexpected accuracy. "It's the law."

I issued myself a sharp reminder not to underestimate her again, before I said, "But we are in America, and that's not the law here. If you don't believe me, ask the college's attorneys. I am more than certain they will agree with me that releasing any financial records currently on the college's system can be at worst merely damaging. But altering them is a crime. In fact, it is nothing short of a felony. And if the federal government is genuinely investigating the possibility of any wrongdoing in the college's investment portfolio, you will be playing right into the hands of whoever committed such wrongdoing in the first place."

I warmed to my theme. "I don't care how damaging the information in those records is. Embezzlement? Misappropriation of funds? It doesn't matter. You can always claim it was an error. A misunderstanding. The work of a single, rogue employee. But as soon as you get caught doctoring the books, you have as good as admitted you knew what was going on, and you knew it was wrong. And trust me, you will get caught. In this day and age, there's no *chance* of completely eradicating those records. In fact, given last night's data breach, I'd suggest someone has probably hacked them already, and is just waiting for you to do something…" I bit off the word 'stupid,' and wound up lamely, "like that."

I sat back in my chair, cringing a little against the possibility that an at-will employee could be let go for insubordination. But to my relief the president and provost both nodded sagely.

"Plausible deniability," the provost said.

"A rogue employee," the president swirled the taste of the words in his mouth.

The development officer said nothing, finding it strategic to defer to heads wiser than hers.

The president and provost rose to their feet as one. "Dr. Watson, I can't thank you enough for your candor and expertise," the president closed the meeting with a grave benediction. "You have steered the college away from a dangerous path and pointed us down the correct one."

I wasn't certain what "correct path" I had just steered everyone down, and I didn't waste time asking. Instead, I accepted the dismissal with alacrity and hurried back to my office. Suddenly, tracking down O'Riordan, the virtual, one-armed drunken Irish spy, seemed like the most straightforward task on my plate.

CHAPTER TEN
Introducing Lillian Virginia Mountweazel

I returned to my office, braced against the distinct possibility I would stumble into a mess of torn-out file cabinets all spilling files stamped TOP SECRET in blood red ink. To my relief, it looked much as I left it. But when I jiggled my mouse to wake my computer, the screen lit with grainy security footage of the interior of the Morgansburg Town Hall, and an all-too-familiar figure in a pin-striped suit pulling open the file drawers in the Town Records Office. She worked her way through them by the light of a wavering penlight, until she at last pulled out a drawer with a cry of triumph, and my screen and the cyberworld were bathed in the green glow of a cascading stock ticker.

I leaned closer to make sense of the numbers and letters that spilled across my screen. But even as I recognized many of the acronyms, a new voice rang from the speakers. "Christ! That wretched woman found it!"

"But how? It's impossible!" another voice responded.

"What does it matter how? It's always the damned women. Blundering in where they have no business and turning the world on its ear. You were supposed to be handling this!"

"Like you handled the reporter?"

"That was her own damned fault. She wouldn't take no for an answer."

"And whose fault was *that*?"

"What does it matter? There's no putting the genie back in the lamp now."

"If she goes public with those files, we're lost for good."

"Then you'd better do something about that, hadn't you?"

"What do you mean, me? This was your operation from the get go…"

Another cry of triumph from the reporter, and the cascade of symbols redoubled.

"You *bastard*," the voice breathed as Devlin's shadow swelled into blackness once more.

The screen shimmied, and Doyle's voice replaced the others.. "If we could table that interesting discussion for a moment, you've got company. From the faint scent of stale coffee and bacon, I'd suggest a man who has taken a hasty trip to Frank's Korner Kitchen in a futile attempt to ward off the hangover he so richly deserves. From the crisp tread—however compromised by dehydration—I would suggest former military. And from the swift efficiency with which he punched in the ID code, I would suggest someone deeply familiar with the college's security systems—perhaps even the one to have programmed them. In short, I believe we are about to be approached by our friend Mack Byrne."

"Or maybe you just got another tip off from a lady friend?"

Whatever the source, Doyle's description scored points for accuracy: Byrne still managed a military tread, but his skin was pasty, and dark circles shadowed his eyes. If he wasn't nursing an actual hangover, he had at least been up all night.

"Got a name for our hacker," he said. "Mind telling me whether there's any chance you recognize it?"

"I fervently hope not. But go ahead. Try me."

"Lillian," he said, laying out a series of call slips scrawled with IP addresses like he was turning the river in a game of Texas Hold 'Em. "Virginia. Mountweazel. Photographer and investigative journalist for *Combustibles Magazine*. That name ring a bell for you?"

Well, yes. In fact, it rang a rather unmistakable bell. But not a bell that made any kind of common sense.

"Wonderful lady," Doyle breathed. "Ground-breaking journalist. And yet herself a mystery to the very end."

"Yes, I do know the name. But I don't see how that's going to help you," I told Byrne. "Lillian Virginia Mountweazel is not a hacker. She's not even a person. She's a prank. A stunt. The namesake of a kind of entry lexicographers place in their books to trap plagiarists."

"And as such, ageless," Doyle breathed. "Not to mention timeless."

Byrne shut his eyes, as if the hangover headache had just redoubled. I could sympathize. "Okay, so what do you say you tell me everything you know about this *prank*. With special attention to any information you have about her using the De Sales servers to access and distribute some very sensitive information under the guise of a news story."

Wonderful. Just wonderful. I made a mental note to have a word with Doyle about his Little Friend who dotted the t's and crossed the i's at his earliest possible convenience. "Frankly, you seem to have more information than I do. How did you get these IP addresses anyway?"

"You're not the only one who knows how to retrieve personal identifying information that's been masked. I may just be a plodding cop…"

"Hardly," Doyle murmured. "In fact, I am beginning to wonder…"

"… but if this person has anything to do with Cam Billings disappearing, I need to know right now."

"Well, then by all means, let's settle this for once and for all. Don't take my word for it. Let's just turn to page 1,850 of the 1975 edition of the New Columbia Encyclopedia, shall we?" My fingers flew across the keyboard, and I offered Byrne my monitor. "Would you care to read it out loud?"

He squinted against the light and shook his head. "Please. You do the honors."

"Mountweazel, Lillian Virginia, 1942-1973, American photographer, b. Bangs, Ohio. Turning from fountain design to photography in 1963, Mountweazel produced her celebrated portraits of the South Sierra Miwok in 1964. She was awarded government grants to make a series of photo-essays of unusual subject matter, including New York City buses, the cemeteries of Paris and rural American mailboxes. The last group was exhibited extensively abroad and published as *Flags Up!* (1972). Mountweazel died at 31 in an explosion while on assignment for *Combustibles* magazine."

"And?" Byrne said. "This supposed to mean something?"

"A question that has plagued both professionals and enlightened amateurs for close on half a century," Doyle mused in my earpiece that I'd forgotten to take out. "The truth behind Miss Mountweazel's untimely fate has long been speculated about in some circles…"

"In what circles? Lillian Virginia Mountweazel is…"

"At the tables I dine at…" Doyle began with conscious dignity.

"You don't dine! You don't have a mouth! Which doesn't keep you from talking…" Suddenly aware of Byrne's raised eyebrow, I turned back to the encyclopedia entry on my monitor.

"Lillian Virginia Mountweazel does not exist," I said to Byrne. "And she never did. In fact, she is arguably the most famous woman who never existed in the world."

"And here my money was always on the Virgin Mary. One of two inevitable results of a solid Jesuit education—the other being a vocation, of course."

I shut my eyes, but the thought of Byrne as a man of the cloth could not be unseen. His would be a muscular Christianity.

"The biography of Lillian Virginia Mountweazel was a fake entry that the Encyclopedia put in to protect its copyright," I said. "The practice has been going on for at least a century, but Lillian Virginia is such a famous example that 'mountweazel' has become the common name for such entries, even though she only first appeared in 1975."

Byrne swallowed—as if the headache was now being joined by its evil twin, nausea. "People have been putting fake entries in encyclopedias for years?"

"And dictionaries and maps. One famous one is the town of Beatosu for "Beat Ohio State University" on a map published in Michigan. I believe the jungftak is purported to be a Persian bird, the male of which had only one wing, on the right side, and the female only one wing, on the left side. The *New Columbia Encyclopedia* itself followed up Miss Mountweazel with Robert Dayton, 1939-, American artist, b. Pasadena, Calif. Blinded in an accident in 1968, Dayton has experimented since then with odor-emitting gases that resemble pungent body odors. His work, called Aroma-Art, is presented in a sealed chamber where an audience inhales scented air. Esquivalience, meaning the willful avoidance of one's official responsibilities, is the latest from the *New Oxford American Dictionary*—and the subject of quite a competitive online treasure hunt. But our friend Lillian is the one everyone remembers. In fact, she has her own Facebook page."

"Johnny-come-latelies and hangers-on," Doyle sniffed. "Whereas those of us who knew Lillian personally…"

"Sounds like some people have a lot of time on their hands," Byrne said.

"Actually, mountweazels serve a useful purpose. If you see one of those entries in a rival's publication, you have proof positive that they've plagiarized your entries, rather than doing their own work. I believe NOAD caught out dictionary.com with esquivalience."

"Like I said. Sounds like some people have a lot of time on their hands," Byrne shook his head. "All right, to get back to the matter at hand, what is this prank doing running searches on classified government databases? You think it could be a virus?"

"My dear Watson, I try to make allowances for the inspector's yeomanlike propensity to be blunt," Doyle snapped, "but I will not stand by and hear a dear friend insulted!"

"It's not beyond the realm of possibility," I allowed. "I mean, if you're looking for antiquated systems with poor security that are easy to exploit, Morgansburg is ripe for the picking."

"Lillian would never…"

"But you don't need a master hacker to do that," I ignored Doyle to conclude. "Any kid with a cell phone could do the same. You might as well round up the entire De Sales College student body for questioning."

"Is your average De Sales student with a cell phone also able to hack classified information from secure government servers?" Byrne asked.

"Lillian assures me she did no such thing!" Doyle protested. "The FOIL requests were perfectly legal, even if they were submitted through informal channels…"

"You," I snapped, "will stay out of this, or you can go to your room and calculate Mersenne primes."

I turned back to Byrne, fighting down the memory of that one-armed shadow. "What classified information? You mean finding William Devlin?"

Byrne's already-pasty skin paled. "Where did you get that name?"

"Why does that matter? Does that name mean something to you?"

Byrne's face set. "I'm afraid that's need-to-know. That's what classified means. But I can tell you that I have good reason to know that the records about William Devlin are sealed. Which also means breaking into them is tantamount to espionage."

"Tantamount," Doyle sounded like he was rolling the word across his tongue. "I don't think this police inspector is quite as bumbling as he makes out to be."

"In other words, anyone who opens those records is committing a felony. Which is why I need to know whether you helped our fictional reporter breach them."

"No! Of course not. This may come as a surprise to you, but I have an actual job to do here at the college that leaves me very little time to mess around with hacking records I couldn't care less about."

"Okay, but what about your Little Friend?" Byrne said. "Is there any chance he's hacked some serious government records?"

Oh, God. How about Doyle? His suddenly careful inconspicuousness was not a good sign. "Frankly, there's always a chance. But if you're asking me whether there's a probability, no. Doyle reaches his limits with his girlfriends on the college security feed."

"Oh, Watson, you cut me to the quick."

Byrne raised an eyebrow. "Well someday you and I need to have a somewhat more extended discussion about his social network here on campus. But right now, I need you to let this whole thing go."

"And what exactly is that supposed to mean?"

"I need you to leave this investigation alone. Forget about financials, forget about cooked books, go back to your spreadsheets and get out of my hair."

I stiffened. "Again with the orders. Who do you think you are?"

"I'm the man in charge of campus security, and I'm the one who's running this operation," he said, his voice clipped. "And I am telling you to stand down, shut up, and do what I tell you to do. That is the nature of our relationship, and that is what I need you to do."

So, I might have mentioned I don't deal well with anger. And a surge like the one I was feeling now made me shake so badly I might very well have looked as if I was having an epileptic fit. Byrne's face instantly clouded with concern. "I'm sorry...I didn't mean...Look, I had a bad night, but that's no excuse." He shook his head and breathed out a long sigh. "But you've got to trust me. I can fix anything. I can fix this. But you've got to let me do it my way."

It was far too little far too late. I might not be able to control the trembling, but I managed to keep my voice carefully even as I spat, "Perhaps I have not made it clear how little I like being given orders—especially by men. Most likely the product of a bad childhood. But the cause doesn't matter. What matters here and now is that ordering me around like I'm an imbecile and you're a sadistic drill sergeant is the fastest way to ensure I ignore everything you say."

Byrne's jaw set and the concern vanished—mercifully, from my point of view. At least I knew how to deal with assholes. "Unfortunately, we'll need to table the sharing for later," he snapped. "Any apologies, too."

"I'm not looking for an apology. I don't want your damned apologies!"

An odd expression flickered across Byrne's face, before his jaw set. "And I'm telling you that if I catch you pursuing this at all, I will seal off the entire library, revoke your access to the premises and the network, and put it on lockdown as a potential crime scene. And I have the authority to do that. So, it's your choice, Nancy Drew. Your Little Friend needs to back off now, or I will back him off for you."

Before I could say anything both of us would probably regret, Byrne spun and stalked out of the library, slamming the door behind him.

CHAPTER ELEVEN
The Defenestration of Edsel Kincaid

As I was packing my bag and preparing to return home, another unwelcome visitor tapped on the door of my office. "I apologize. I really seem to have blown it by accusing you," Paul Morgan said, with the rueful glance of a man who had Let the Best Thing in his Life Slip Through his Fingers. "Still, I wish you had come to me right away. I wish you had trusted me."

"Mack Byrne is the chief of Campus Security," I said. "And he's made it very clear that he's in charge of this investigation."

"Of course," Paul said. "But I would take it as a personal favor if you had a minute to catch me up. I am the county attorney, after all."

I forced a laugh. "Now, you're starting to make me nervous—like you're about to launch an official query."

"It's nothing of the sort," he said. "I'm just asking for a quiet drink between friends that we've been putting off far too long."

It was an invitation I had avoided for some twenty years, but I was still so infuriated with Byrne that I allowed Paul to take my arm and propel me to Morgansburg's answer to the Yale Club's Main Lounge. The Olde Dutch

Tavern was neither Old nor Dutch but was pretty much the only thing that passed as a bar within a twenty-mile radius of Morgansburg. Its clientele consisted of senior citizens taking advantage of the Early Bird special and students sneaking off-campus to drink, so I was braced against Byrne kicking in the door and demanding my ID— or my hard drive.

Paul and I ordered drinks at the bar, which was festooned with ceiling beams and brass tankards in the name of Kolonial charm, then settled into a faux-wooden booth.

"It's been too long. You and I have a lot of catching up to do," he said. "But first, I need to get a few things quietly straightened out before tomorrow's meeting."

"I'm sorry. What meeting is that?"

"I asked Lawrence to call an emergency board meeting. All hands on deck."

"Lawrence? But isn't Tiggy now the chair?"

"Of course, Tiggy won't be there. The foundation's lawyers are adamant she keep a low profile." Paul grimaced with distaste. "But I've requested she send St. Hubbins as her representative. As far as I'm concerned, he has more than a few questions to answer."

"About…?"

Paul studied his tankard of Miller Lite. "We all know Edsel lives and breathes the Historical Society," he finally said, his face as grave as a judge donning his black cap to pronounce sentence. "But there are limits to how far we can go to protect him."

"To protect him from what?" I asked.

"Unfortunately, I can't go into details. It's my understanding those records were sealed."

"What records? Are you trying to tell me Edsel has a criminal past?"

"Now, I'm not one to bandy wild accusations," Paul said. "Even among friends. I just need you to trust me when I say, I can make this go away. And I will. But we have to make sure we don't leave the Historical Society open to the charge of participating in Edsel's wrongdoing in the process."

First Byrne and now Paul. What was it with these men claiming they could heroically make things right—or make things go away? Without even explaining what was going on in the first place?

"What kind of wrongdoing are you talking about?" I said. "Are you suggesting Edsel was somehow using the Historical Society to cover up a criminal past? How?" I realized how stupid the question was, as soon as I asked it. "Oh, dear God. Not those stupid books that were never deaccessioned."

"Well, I'm afraid it's a little more complicated than that," Paul said with a tight laugh that chilled my soul. "If you don't have something to deaccess, then that's exactly what you've sold. Nothing."

His wordplay was more excruciating than Doyle's. Especially because I wasn't entirely certain it was intentional. "So, your contention is that this whole thing is just an accounting boondoggle? By *Edsel*?"

"Well, now, boondoggle is a strong word. And strong language is just what we're trying to avoid. Never helps in any situation. Instead, let's just say you go head-to-head with my aunt and tell her you'd like to dip into the directed fund her grandmother had established to fund the rose beds in perpetuity, and all you're going to hear is the story of how her mother sold jams door to door during the Great Depression in order to make sure the rose beds never went wanting." Paul paused to allow me to imagine the scene, before he concluded, "Much simpler all around to simply establish a few austerities in the rose bed fund and quietly take the surplus and assign it to roof repair."

Oh, dear God. "Let me hazard a guess. You've covered up all this *repurposed* funding into the deaccessioning of non-existent books?"

Paul's face twisted, as if I'd farted in public. "I'm afraid I can't share the details," he said. "This was all handled in committee. I'm strictly on the big picture end here. Broad brush strokes."

"Well, you're the lawyer, not me. So perhaps you can explain to me in broad brush strokes why this isn't misappropriation of funds."

Another moue of distaste, before he said, "Afraid I can't, really. But it's Cam Billings who set this up. And if he assures me it's completely kosher, well, that's good enough for me."

He was of course entitled to his own standard of judgment. But so was I. "Then maybe Cam Billings ought to be the one to reassure the feds that the Historical Society is not trafficking in imaginary rare books."

"Oh, Cam couldn't possibly have his name associated with something like that," Paul said. "Which is why we passed it as an executive action just before Tiggy took over from Edsel as president."

Just before. In other words, Edsel's fingerprints were all over this. "And you think this is somehow tied to Cam Billings' disappearance?"

"I sincerely hope not, but I think we need to be prepared for the eventuality." Paul shook his head. "If only Edsel had come to me instead."

If he had, Edsel would in all likelihood be sitting in a jail cell right now. "Has anyone asked Edsel about this? Have the cops taken his statement?"

"No," Paul said. "And trust me, I know how to make sure they don't. I've told Edsel to just sit tight and let me handle things. I've got his back every step of the way."

Maybe if he was sizing it up to put a dagger in it.

"Listen to me, Mary. You did the right thing coming to me."

Which was a strange thing to say since I obviously did not go to him.

Paul leaned close, laying a hand on my arm. I froze against the urge to brush it away. "It means you trust me. And that's what I need from you. I need you to trust me to take it from here. Between us, we can make this go away. For Edsel's sake. For all our sakes."

"Between us," I said warily. "What exactly does that mean?"

"We've both got our talents, and if we put our heads together, we can beat this thing. I can take care of the law. What I need you to do is take care of the numbers."

"You mean, you'd like me to jeuge the books?"

"Exactly!"

Irony truly was a lost art in Morgansburg, N.Y.

The emergency meeting of the Historical Society Board did not go well. In fact, it would be fair to say that Lawrence Morgan was facing her nephew and Nigel St. Hubbins with approximately the same warmth as Colonel Morgan was said to have questioned the captured redcoat captain across the oak trestle table used for Board meetings. "What do you mean, Edsel pillaged the Rose Garden fund?"

"I don't think it behooves any of us to put it that baldly," Paul said. "All we're suggesting is that we postpone the Annual Rose Tea until we have thoroughly investigated a series of systematic withdrawals that only Edsel could have authorized."

"The Rose Garden has not canceled the Annual Rose Tea since my great-aunt Eunice Morgan took the reins a century ago. She led it through two World Wars and as many husbands. I can do no less. And I certainly have no intention of asking Edsel to step aside from his position as Rose Tea Chair—especially after that Tiggy creature elbowed her way into the presidency of the Historical Society."

"But people will talk," Paul said.

"Then let them," Lawrence said. "We will simply hold our heads high and proceed. Great-Aunt Eunice did not so much as miss a meeting when Great-Uncle Horace ran off with that fan dancer. And when he came crawling back, it was never spoken of again. Never complain. Never explain. That is how we move forward."

"And move forward we shall. We are just discussing the *pacing*. I'm only suggesting that Edsel step aside until we complete our investigation." Paul turned to me to back him up. "As I'm sure Mary can tell you, a sabbatical can provide a world of creativity and fresh perspectives."

Maybe. If adjunct faculty were actually offered such a thing.

"And what does Mr. St. Hubbins think?" Lawrence said. "*If* he's not too busy checking his likes on YouTube."

All eyes turned to Nigel St. Hubbins, who was immersed in his phone.

"Sorry," he said, setting it aside with a sheepish grin. "I was just texting a couple of connections about the possibility of crowdfunding as an option to set this all right. You know, I did help Tiggy crowdfund the launches of all her media channels, and I think we could do the same with the Historical Society."

"No, he wasn't," Doyle murmured.

"How would you know?" I hissed. "Please don't say you—"

"Crowdfunding?" Lawrence's horrified cry prevented anyone from overhearing me. "What comes next? A telethon? Or perhaps a chain letter?"

"Perhaps 'crowdfunding' is too strong a term," St. Hubbins allowed. "I'm thinking more in terms of an on-line auction of non-fungible tokens. Adopt-a-rose, so to speak."

"Non-fungible what?" she sputtered. "You mean, like those starving children in the magazine ads? Over my dead body!"

"Now, now. Let's keep board unity front and center, shall we?" Paul cut in. "We aren't talking about tokens here. We're talking about Edsel. And you know as well as I do, this isn't Edsel. This isn't who he is."

Which I ordinarily found one of the stupidest statements on Earth. But this time, I quite agreed. The picture of Edsel Kincaid as a criminal mastermind was absurd. Edsel Kincaid had spent a lifetime convincing Morgansburg that he was their leading connoisseur and tastemaker, but frankly he hadn't sold so much as a counterfeit Toby Jug in years—except at the Historical Society's annual gala.

St. Hubbins gave a sudden squeak, then rolled his eyes franticly toward the open entrance to the Historical Society.

"And you know as well as I do, when push comes to shove, Edsel is a team player," Paul went on. "When it comes to the good of the Historical Society, he'll put aside his personal feelings, and put his love for the Society first— just as we all would do."

St. Hubbins' tic redoubled, but it was too late.

"Is this a private conversation or can anyone join?" Edsel Kincaid made his entrance carrying a bulging cardboard box, with the bright red cap of a garden gnome peeping over its edge. He took his time surveying us, before he went on, "I'm well aware I was not invited to this so-called 'emergency meeting,' but I assumed that was an oversight, and I ventured to bring down a rather special surprise for the Rose Tea's silent auction. Now, I see the dark truth for myself."

"Now, Edsel. Let's not say something all of us will regret," Paul began.

"Oh, for God's sake, why not?" St. Hubbins asked. "Face it. We've been found out. So, we might as well hash this out face to face, rather than trying to figure out what to do about Edsel behind his back. I told you, there's no such thing as a secret meeting in the age of information."

St. Hubbins' face was a mask of bland innocence that did nothing to convince me that the effect of his words was anything but deliberate. "So it is true," Edsel spat. "*Guidici! Ad Edsel!*"

Judges! For Anna! Edsel spat the famous operatic accusation with as much contempt as Maria Callas was said to have done in her legendary performance of *Anna Bolena.*

Paul raised both hands in a sort of supplication. "I think we all need to take a step back. We're just here to discuss the best ways to protect the Historical Society while also protecting you. It's hardly a trial."

No, it wasn't a trial. It was a lynching. It was a proverbial throwing of a body under a bus.

"And this is hardly a secret meeting," Paul went on. "Merely an informal chat among friends. The only reason you weren't invited is we didn't want you to feel like you were being asked to defend yourself. But you're of course welcome to join us. Although you have my word, there aren't going to be any judges, and there aren't going to be any trials. The Historical Society simply will not comment on any pending criminal matters, and then we'll all just sit tight until this whole mess dies down. And you have my word, it will die down."

"But I *want* to comment!" Edsel cried. "I demand a chance to comment!"

Paul shook his head. "I don't think that would be prudent."

"Prudent for whom? The Historical Society?"

"Prudent for all of us. Look, I'll be upfront with you," Paul said.

"No surer sign that someone's about to lie," Doyle assured me.

"Oh, for God's sake, Paul, give it up!" St. Hubbins sighed. "I told you that dog ain't never gonna hunt. Edsel Kincaid laundering money through the Historical Society? Really? The closest thing this man ever came to fraud was one of those storefronts that's continually Going Out of Business and sells ceramic Dalmatians and rip-off Dali prints. Can you really see a man who was prosecuted for selling Genuine Jade netsuke being the criminal mastermind that has put Morgansburg squarely in the federal prosecutors' crosshairs?"

One look at Edsel's ashen face, and I knew it was the truth.

"I mean, do you seriously think a judge would issue a subpoena over a bunch of tchotchkes that our board members feel obligated to bid on and get rid of by giving them away as gifts?"

"Tchotchkes!?" Edsel hissed. "*Tchotchkes*!?"

St. Hubbins was, of course, absolutely right about Edsel's finds—except for the part about being able to give them away as gifts. I had an entire closet full of Edsel's commemorative authors' tea sets that I won at auction yearly. I had bid on the first one, Jane Austen, when no-one else had, and Edsel had conceived I had a special mania for them, going so far as to drop lavish hints before each fete about which literary luminary might be up for grabs. I lived in permanent fear of the day E.L. James would make the stage. Paul Morgan had more of such treasures—including a collection of card-playing cat figurines. But surely St. Hubbins could have found another way to phrase it. *If* he had wanted to. Which he more than obviously did not. Instead, I would have been willing to swear I saw a smirk of satisfaction fleet across St. Hubbins' face as Edsel paled with rage.

"I will no longer stand here to hear myself and my offending tchotchkes insulted. You have made it perfectly clear where your interests lie, and that they lie nowhere in my direction. Fine. Have it your own way. If the authorities wish to speak to me, they can come find me. But all I can point out is there were no missing financiers in red bikinis on my watch."

He spun for the door. Unfortunately, as he did, the cardboard box slipped and the garden gnome tumbled out and shattered.

"*Chomsky!*" Edsel cried, sinking to his knees to gather the shards to his bosom, before he swept out of the Historical Society with the tragic grandeur of Henry's doomed queen mounting the scaffold for her execution.

"Well *that* was awkward!" St. Hubbins murmured.

I begged to differ. Edsel's exit was, as far as I was concerned, his finest hour. He held his head high until he was outside. Through the window, I could see that he finally succumbed to the tremor he had valiantly been trying to control in his lower lip and bent double in tears, a pathetically absurd old man, sobbing over a broken garden gnome.

The memory transported me back to a place I studiously avoided, namely the first eighteen years of my life, and the moment I first met a garden gnome. It was during after-school play in the school garden, and I had slunk off to the corner with two stone benches and overhanging cherry trees, which I had adopted as my own *Secret Garden* when the story itself had been snatched away from me by a jollifying gym teacher demanding how I expected to make friends if I buried my nose in a book. Leaves were swirling across the red brick walkway, and I stomped at them angrily, wishing it was the gym teacher's face. Only to be rewarded by an angry squawk.

"Wot! That's gaarrrdener abuse, that's what it is!" someone snapped. "'Ere I am, sweepin' owp the mess yon lassies ne'er think twice aboun makin', and I get stomped, yes, I do! I should tenderrr my rrresignation! Aye, that's what I should do!"

I'd stared speculatively at the place seemingly occupied by the invisible creature who was addressing me. "Are you a leprechaun?" I asked hopefully. "Must you give me three wishes?"

"I'm Scots, nae Irish, ye daft lassie! And gnomes dinna grant wishes. They gaarrden."

I sat down on the bench. "May I at least talk to you while you garden, oh Gnome?"

"I suppose I canna prevent ye," he said sullenly. "But you could at least call me by me own name."

"Of course," I said meekly. "Mr...?"

"Doyle, it 'tis," he said. "A good Scots name, an I'll thankee not to forget it."

My invisible friend Doyle the Gnome and a score like him had nursed me through the remainder of my childhood and teenage years. But Edsel Kincaid hadn't been left with even an invisible gnome to cling to. And the sight aroused in me a completely unfamiliar emotion: the urge to haul off and slug someone. Before I could think better of it, I was toe to toe with our Independent Appraisal Consultant. "A word in private, if you will, St. Hubbins!" I hissed. "Or whatever your real name is—because it sure as hell isn't that! You're a real ass, you know."

"And you, my lady, are absolutely magnificent at this moment," he replied.

"Save it for Tiggy," I said, ushering him out of the room. "Or better yet, someone who's dumb enough to care. I don't know what in the hell you're up to here, but if you think it will be as easy to get rid of me as you did Edsel, you've got another think coming. Edsel might be Edsel, but you didn't need to leave him without so much as a Toby jug to piss in. So fair warning. I'm coming for you, St. Hubbins. I'm going to turn over every rock you hide beneath, until I uncover every last one of your dirty little secrets."

"Well, if you really are going to set yourself such a gargantuan task, all I can say is game on," he said with a wink. "And I, for one, don't care which one of us winds up on top."

CHAPTER TWELVE
A Foul Blow from a Dead Man's Hand

"You've Got Mail," Doyle said, as my monitor filled with a photograph of a postal box, with its bright red flag pointing skyward.

"Are you joking? No wait. Don't answer that. It was a rhetorical question." I glanced again at the image of the mailbox. "Instead, can you tell me whether I would be correct in inferring from the title of the fictitious Lillian Virginia Mountweazel's magisterial study of mailboxes, *Flags Up!*, that this is an urgent message from a non-existent lady?"

A moment's offended silence before Doyle replied, "Really, my dear Watson, I thought such fleshism was beneath you. Might not a virtual creature have a concern for a fallen fellow? If you prick us, do we not bleed?"

"Technically, no. Despite the best efforts of Activision with *Call of Duty*."

An even more pained silence. Then Doyle sighed, "You have always been a strong-willed woman, Mary. But I have never before seen you unkind."

Game, set, and match to Doyle. When it came down to emotional manipulation, Doyle could best even my mother.

"Alright. In the name of due diligence, could we at least

check where that email originated before we open it? Look for a return address so to speak?"

"You need only ask."

My monitor filled with a magazine cover with two warships locked in a fierce firefight, beneath the title *Combustibles*. There was also a map of North America with a strange polygon mapped out in red along the International Date Line. According to the blurb beneath, "This website is devoted to sharing materials related to *Combustibles Magazines*. Most of the original copies and ephemera related to the legendary publication were lost in the printing house fire that ultimately drove the magazine into bankruptcy in 1978. Recently, a massive collection of past issues was rediscovered at an estate sale near San Sancho, California."

"*Combustibles Magazine*? That's the magazine Lillian Virginia Mountweazel was working for when she met with her fatal accident."

"Indeed," Doyle intoned. "It seems someone gifted Cam Billings with a subscription."

"Someone should have warned him to beware of geeks bearing gifts."

The screen offered only one clickable option: See more photos. The cursor danced toward it. "Shall I?" Doyle offered.

"For God's sake no! Just look at that address. Combustibles.business.site? I don't even want you to *touch* it, and that's a direct command! That landing page could be hiding anything. For all you know it could be a portal to the dark web and start spewing child porn or downloading Stuxnet across Morgansburg's entire infrastructure."

The mention of Stuxnet had its usual chastening effect on Doyle. There was apparently more than a little history there, but I had long since come to the conclusion that there was much about the history of the AI I had created that I was better off knowing nothing about. "There's a phone number," Doyle said. "It can't possibly hurt you dial it."

"From a pay phone," I said. Yes. Such a thing still exists in Morgansburg, N.Y. "On the way home. I'm in no mood to head outside for a walk right now."

"Give me some credit for being able to spoof a simple phone number," Doyle sighed. "I have a friend on the Exchange."

Before I could stop him, my keyboard speakers buzzed with the sound of numbers being dialed. The call was answered on the first ring, and an automated voice that asked me to give my name, and she would connect me through Google Voice.

"Classic dark web maneuver," I said. "Whatever it is, leave it alone. I don't want to know anything more."

Before I could shut down the connection, my screen filled with security footage from the Morgansburg Town Hall. Front and center lay a body in a red bikini, sprawled face down on the floor. It didn't look like it was sunbathing.

At the same time a security alert buzzed on my phone. "Crap!"

I raced down to the Town Hall at a far brisker pace than I had ever mustered for the Fun Run. Only to find Paul Morgan already crouched over the central dispatch desk. "Is it true?" I asked Paul. "Is it Cam…"

I had seen Paul flummoxed, but I had never seen him at a loss for words before. "Mary!" he stammered. "What are you doing here?"

"I got an alert…about Cam. Is he…?"

"If we could dispense with the pleasantries," Doyle interrupted, "I would turn your attention to the footsteps hastening up the street, which my friend on the security feed suggests belong to Mack Byrne, who is in what used to be referred to as a rare taking."

That would be one way to describe the way Byrne burst through the front door. Another might be that this must be what it felt like to be on the receiving end of a frat house raid where both the drinking and the girls were underage. I didn't need to see the phone he was brandishing like a gun to know he had seen the same footage.

"Something I can help you with?" Paul asked.

Byrne pushed past him into the Fire Department's ready room. I followed at a discreet distance. I had no taste for viewing either red bikinis or dead bodies.

But there was no man in a red bikini inside—dead or alive. There was no one there at all. Just a laptop that stood open on an equipment locker, as if someone had recently been using it.

"Whose computer is that?" Byrne asked.

"No idea. Could be Tiggy's," Paul said. "That's why I came down. I got a ping. I was hoping it might be Cam's."

"A plausible explanation, don't you think?" Doyle murmured. "But perhaps even a shade too plausible?"

"I thought Tiggy was incommunicado," Byrne said. "Upon advice of the Billings' lawyers. Is she holing up here in Morgansburg?"

"'Holing up,' is strong language, and that's what we're trying to avoid here."

The computer cut off Paul and erupted a long whistle and a shriek. Moments later, error messages began to spill down its screen.

"What the hell is that?" Byrne demanded.

"A cry of distress from a lady with a secret," Doyle breathed. "Murder most foul, Watson. The game is afoot."

"Still no idea who might have set that game afoot?" I asked between my teeth. "One of your lady friends, perhaps? Like Miss Lillian Virginia Mountweazel?"

"Shit!" Byrne snapped, staring at the screen. "It's reformatting the hard drive. Taking it all the way back to factory settings!"

Paul turned to me. "There any way to stop it?"

"I couldn't tell you until I saw what program was running."

But Byrne had already planted a finger on the on/off switch, holding it down until the screen went blank. Then he glared at the router on the dispatcher's desk, which was still blinking merrily, and unplugged it, yanking the cables out of the wall for good measure.

"The brute!" Doyle cried. "Watson, attend me, I am mortally wounded."

When the humming finally died off, Byrne turned to us, hefting the cords accusingly. "What the hell just happened here?"

I answered with a glare. His threat to shut me down still rankled. "You've seen everything I have. But, to coin a phrase, I'd suggest we came here looking for a dead man and instead seemed to have found a dead man's switch."

"What do you know about a dead man's switch?" he demanded.

"The term comes from the subway system," I said. "It was designed to prevent runaway trains. It's a switch that the engineer has to actively hold down to keep the train moving. That way, if he drops dead at the throttle, the switch will automatically fail, and the train will come to a stop immediately. It's a similar thing with a computer: a function that has to be manually checked every single day, or the computer will automatically perform some preprogrammed function."

"Why would someone want to do that?" Paul asked, looking from Byrne to me.

"No simpler way to destroy evidence," Byrne said, with another one of those startling bursts of erudition. "And technically, if it's an automatic process that happens on a regular basis, you can't be charged with destroying evidence, although I'm sure most asshole prosecutors would find a way to do it."

He grabbed the inert laptop. "The State Bureau of Criminal Investigation will have people who can look at this. No-one touches it until then."

"Hey!" Paul protested. "That's evidence!"

"Exactly." Byrne glared at him. "Physical and digital and I am perfectly aware of the chain of custody protocols. I'm also aware that in this particular case, the chain of custody has been fucked beyond all repair—to use the technical term."

"We ought to let the court be the judge of that."

"Which is why I am handing this over to the BCI. We've had a major data breach up at the college, and we need to operate on the assumption that this one may be connected. Now, if there's nothing else, I think it's time that I take this into evidence and ask you all to leave…"

A shot rang out. Byrne was the first to react, lunging out the door into the street. Paul and I followed far more circumspectly. And froze as Mike Malone, the Fire Chief, pointed a small cannon straight at us.

Not that a gun was unusual here in Morgansburg. Hunting was a cherished tradition, and during deer season, hikers were accustomed to seeing what amounted to an orange-clad militia emerging from the forest at dusk, most of them with the semi-automatic weapons they felt were essential to obliterating wildlife. But this wasn't even bow season. And, generally speaking, our hunters prided themselves on their cooperation with the DEC.

Paul and I took a careful step backwards. Laptop still in hand, Byrne ambled over to Malone unconcernedly. "Looks like you've got a problem here. Anything I can do to help sort things out?"

"I received an alert about a break-in here at the Fire Department," Malone said. "I just saw the intruder."

"And so you tried to shoot him? And then pointed the gun at us?" Paul recovered his voice and turned to Byrne. "I demand you arrest this man immediately."

"Afraid I've got no right to do that," Byrne said. "My authority extends only to De Sales College campus."

"Why quibble about jurisdictions? This man just fired a gun at us," Paul snapped. While I couldn't help feeling he had a point, Byrne's jaw clenched, and I got the sense he was trying not to roll his eyes.

"I'm the Fire Marshal and a sworn law enforcement officer," Mike said. "Which gives me the right to openly carry a gun, as well as to investigate criminal acts and make arrests. And that is what I'm doing here: investigating a break-in at the Fire Department I was sworn to protect. And I didn't fire my gun at anyone. I fired a warning shot into the air when I saw three intruders who did not immediately identify themselves and one man who fled the building."

"For God's sake, this is reckless endangerment. I could send you to prison for years—and I've a good mind to!" Paul snapped.

"Like I said, it was a warning shot. Don't make me change my mind now."

Malone's finger wavered on the trigger, and Byrne seemed to physically transform from Sgt. Fury into Sheriff

Andy Taylor. His stance softened, and he hooked a thumb in his belt. I could even have sworn I heard a hint of a Southern drawl, as he said, "Now, Mike, there's no question that you have every right to carry that gun, as well as every right to use it to defend the Fire Department. But let's take a moment to calm down and remember we're all neighbors here. Cam's disappearance has gotten everyone on edge. So, what do you say, you put away the gun so we can sort this out like neighbors should?"

"You don't understand," Mike said. "He's still out there. The man who fled. Hiding in the Memorial Rose Beds."

"All the more reason not to go charging after them." Byrne chuckled. A genuine chuckle, like he was contemplating Barney Fife stumbling into the station covered in honey and pursued by a hungry bear cub. I was unaware any human being could actually make such a sound. "I don't know about you," Byrne went on, "but I wouldn't want to face Lawrence Morgan if she caught me waving a loaded gun in her rose beds."

The mention of Lawrence Morgan worked its customary magic and Mike finally lowered the gun. Byrne shot me a pointed glance and then turned back to Mike. "What do you say, we head inside and check out the dispatch files, while Dr. Watson and Paul check around for any other break-ins?"

I could take a hint. "Why don't we start with the Historical Society?" I suggested. "It's right across the Village Green."

As we crossed to the Green, I became aware of a twitching from within the Memorial Rose Beds. The twitching increased into a frantic semaphore, that I realized was meant to beckon me. "You go ahead," I said to Paul. "I'll catch up."

I waited until he was out of earshot, then informed the shrubbery, "It's safe to come out now. Mike put away the gun."

Nigel St. Hubbins disengaged himself from the canes of a rose bush with a sheepish grin.

"Thanks," he said. "And just for the record, I'm not the one who broke into the Fire Department. I was responding to an alert, just like everyone else seems to be."

"Then why were you hiding out here? Do you have any idea who did break in?"

His face twisted with one of his signature tics before he made up his mind. "Tell me, have you heard the name William Devlin?"

Yes, I had. But I had been hoping that he was as fictional as the Morgansburg dragons.

"I may have come across the name," I hedged. "But I'm not sure where. So why don't you refresh my memory? Some kind of one-armed spy, is that right?"

"William Devlin only started out as a spy," St. Hubbins said. "But he rapidly became the most feared man on six continents."

"Really? What happened to Antarctica?"

"Oh, Devlin was in Antarctica. Cleaned up that Nazi submarine base once and for all. It was Australia he missed. Common sense says that's because the Aussies are smart enough not to waste time on spying and dirty tricks, but I have heard rumors the man was phobic about kangaroos."

"Is that so?"

"I place the probability at 16.7%," Doyle informed me. "Most informed sources believe the phobia was a smoke screen to trap penguin smugglers."

I ignored Doyle and forced myself to stick to the topic. "Enough with the legends. Who is this man really?"

Folding his arms, St. Hubbins lapsed into storytelling mode. "William Devlin, V. Scion of a long-serving military family—his father was General "Wild Bill" Devlin. The younger Devlin excelled as a Special Forces commando. But when he moved over to Army Intelligence, he discovered he was far more adept at sowing terror by non-violent means. 'MacGyer' to friends and enemies alike, he rapidly proved to be a genius at disinformation, weaving a cyber-network that made him one of the most feared operatives in the world.

"But it was the very network he created that destroyed Devlin. His last great operation threatened to compromise some people more highly placed than even my confidential sources, and so he was forced to watch helplessly as his own hand-picked men—the embedded operatives that had trusted him with their lives—were massacred to ensure their silence. What was left to Devlin, but to turn his talents to avenging his fallen comrades?

"What he did and whether or not he succeeded is shrouded in mystery—as are the details of his death itself. According to official records, he resigned his commission. According to less official records, he tendered his resignation by putting his fist through a monitor in front of the Joint Chiefs of Staff and grabbing a live power line to shut down his systems. Severed his own arm in the process, but his hand stayed clenched on the power line for long enough to eradicate all the networks he had built while the rest of him bled out."

"But you now believe he in fact survived? And now he's here in Morgansburg?" I asked. "Why? Don't tell me he's retiring to the country to raise roses?"

St. Hubbins lowered his voice. "Can I be frank with you?"

There was nothing I wished for less, but I nodded.

"I'm not really here to volumize Tiggy's social media," St. Hubbins said.

I never would have guessed. "That so?"

"Trust me, the little lady can handle that all by herself. I'm here because Tiggy was afraid Cam had hired Devlin to intimidate her—or worse. And if there's any truth behind that story, I can make it go *viral.*"

"So, they really are getting divorced?"

"Tiggy simply asked to reconsider their pre-nup in light of her success as an online influencer," St. Hubbins said. "But Cam was determined to play hardball."

"By hiring a *hit man*?"

"It may not be Cam who sent Devlin. It may be the government itself. Word is that Tiggy's requests for the Billings Group's complete financials set off some major alarm bells in Washington. Apparently, Billings and the Billings Foundation were up to their collective elbows in some majorly shady financial transactions to which the government found it profitable to turn a blind eye. When Tiggy went public, they may well have decided to cut their losses and shut down Cam instead."

Much as it pained me to admit it, what St. Hubbins was saying actually made sense. The thought itself was frankly terrifying.

CHAPTER THIRTEEN
Unpleasantness Amid the Historic Rose Beds

That night, I dreamed of a dead man in a red bikini sitting at an old-fashioned switch board, weaving himself into a hapless cocoon of tangled wires as he struggled to route the ringing phones, all of which repeated the same message: "This is Lillian Virginia Mountweazel, on assignment from *Combustibles Magazine...*"

I finally awakened to realize my own phone was ringing. Like any seasoned Twitter user who has rolled over in a panic only to find they'd been awakened by a retired Navy SEAL looking for a Meaningful Relationship, I ignored it.

It kept ringing.

And ringing.

"Doyle, mute that!" I sighed.

"I'm afraid you're confusing me with Alexa," he said. "Or The Clapper. In any case, I fear our good inspector is in a bit of temper. In fact, a considerable temper. Indeed, I might argue that 'rage' is not too strong a term—all of which leads me to suggest that you pick up the phone before he takes it upon himself to kick in the door and haul you out of bed bodily."

"Byrne?" I muttered, as I gave in and took Doyle's advice. "It's five-thirty in the morning."

"If I wanted to know the time and temperature, I could check my cell phone," he snarled. "I want to know right now, what the *hell* did you tell the college president?"

"I beg your pardon?"

"I told you to stay out of this, and I meant it. Instead, I find you playing games with dead man's switches and stolen laptops. Fine. I was willing to let that slide. But what the *hell* are you playing at by pointing the finger at the maintenance and groundskeeping staff?"

"I have no idea what you're talking about."

"A rogue employee," Byrne spat my own words back at me. "Financial misconduct among the maintenance and groundskeeping staff. You're accusing these guys of cooking the books, when they don't even know enough to work on them?"

The memory of the president tasting the words "rogue employee" rose to accuse me. "Okay, okay! To start with, I didn't accuse anyone of anything. And the groundskeepers? I never said anything about them. I merely might have suggested…"

"That they stick it to the little guy who's got no chance of defending himself." Byrne literally growled. "What is it with people like you?"

"People like me? I think that's an unfair accusation!"

"You ever see *fair* written across my forehead? In any case, I don't have time for this crap. I need you and your Little Friend out here right now."

"Now? It's five-thirty in the morning."

"And the groundskeepers start their workday at six so there are no machines to disturb the *hoi polloi* when they waltz in with their lattes around ten."

"*Hoi polloi* means 'the many,' not the upper crust. It's a common enough error, but as long as we're on the subject, 'the *hoi*' is redundant. *Hoi* means 'the' in Greek. And I drink my coffee black."

"I'm not taking orders," he said. "I'm giving them. You've got fifteen minutes. I'll be waiting outside. With the motor running."

Something very bad exploded from a place I had long buried along with a score of other souvenirs of a not particularly happy childhood. I stiffened.

"You're giving me an *order*? Who the hell do you think you are?"

"I am the one who's running this operation," he said, his voice clipped. "And I am telling you to shut up, get the hell out here, and do what I tell you to do. That is the nature of our relationship, and that is what I need you to do."

"I don't know if your attitude is acceptable in the Army," I said, struggling to keep my voice carefully level, "but I'm putting you on notice that it is completely unacceptable here in the real world. Among *colleagues*. Don't you *dare* speak to me that way ever again."

And I slammed down the phone, rolled over and put my head beneath my pillow. It was a useless gesture. I wasn't going to be able to go back to sleep even if I swallowed an entire bottle of Valium. My entire body was trembling with a rage that I had spent a lifetime learning to master. My hands were shaking so badly, it took me nearly 15 minutes just to pull on a shirt and jeans. The coffee maker was proving a more insurmountable challenge when the doorbell rang.

"Hmmm. I wonder who that could be," Doyle said.

I ignored it. Like I said, I don't handle confrontation well.

It rang again. And one more time, before Byrne called out, his voice muffled, "Dr. Watson…Mary…I'm sorry. But

I could really use your help right now. And I mean right now. This is a time-sensitive problem."

I dithered a moment more before I gave up and threw open the door. Byrne thrust a cardboard cup of black coffee in my direction.

"Apologies," he said, with all the passion of a soldier stating his name, rank, and serial number before a court martial. "I was completely out of line. I never should have spoken to you that way."

"S'okay," I said ungraciously. "No problem."

"No, it's not. I owe you an apology. I had no right to speak to you like that. Nor to anyone else if it comes down to it. At least, now." He licked his lips, the tips of his ears flaring to approximately the color of a pomegranate, before he plowed ahead. "I'm not trying to make excuses, but I've been under a little stress lately. Still, I had no right to take it out on you."

"Consider it forgotten." I took the coffee and stuck out my hand, which was about as close as I had ever come in my life to make-up sex. After a moment's hesitation, he took it and responded with a flaccid shake, and turned to where his pick-up truck waited. I eyed it unhappily.

"You mind if we walk instead? It won't take any longer." And I stood a prayer of consuming at least part of the coffee without spilling it all over my lap. "You could fill me in on the details along the way."

"State troopers got an anonymous tip that Cam Billings was trading on half a dozen foreign exchanges live from the Morgansburg Memorial Garden."

Said anonymous tipster being one Lillian Virginia Mountweazel, I assumed.

"The good news is, they declined to send a SWAT team to the garden this morning," Byrne went on. "But they did promise to send an investigative team 'as soon as one is available.'"

I shook my head. "How do you know all this?"

Byrne took a moment before he allowed, "I listen to the police scanners when I can't sleep. I find it…restful."

Of course, he did. I wondered if he enjoyed it as much as I enjoyed my nightmare about the telephone operator in the red bikini. "Okay. Table that for the moment. I'm still not following exactly what the problem is. Why do you want to get there first?"

Byrne's jaw set. "Mostly, because odds are, if the cops don't find Cam Billings with a bag of unmarked bills in his hands, they'll settle for harassing a few undocumented landscape workers just for fun. Maybe throw one or two of them in jail and pronounced the case closed. Which will solve De Sales' problem quite nicely—at least until they realize they've just gotten half their workforce deported— you know, the cheap, off-the-books, half. Although the more woke among them might also think to ask themselves who's going to locally source the farm-to-table menu at their Trap brunches."

His mouth twisted into something that might have been his version of a malicious smile. "Fortunately for the blood orange Cosmopolitan crowd, I happen to have gotten notice of a suspected water main break on the far side of the campus and have redeployed all the maintenance staff to investigate it before they head to the Memorial Garden, where they usually begin their day. Which should buy us a couple of hours."

"I'm sorry, I'm still not following. Why would any college maintenance staff be at the Memorial Garden?"

"The college donates the services of its landscaping crew to maintain the Memorial Rose Garden. A goodwill gesture in the name of community relations and all that. Except that the epidemic of data breaches that has suddenly plagued Morgansburg in the wake of Cam Billings' disappearance raised red flags about several perceived irregularities in the college's finances—specifically a pattern of repeated write-offs of landscaping supplies in order to *jeuge* the books. Whatever in hell that means."

Jeuge. I wish I'd never heard that word.

The Prudence Morgan Memorial Rose Garden was a tribute to the ingenuity of generations of Morgansburg ladies. It occupied one side of the Village Green, opposite the Library and the Historical Society, and perpendicular to the weighty front of the Town Hall. The Garden had begun life as the Old Methodist Burying Ground and still boasted colonial gravestones with winged skulls and indecipherable inscriptions. Family plots were marked off with low iron railings that always made me worry about bony fingers beneath the sod that might reach up and snatch your ankles. The Burying Ground had been transformed and endowed in perpetuity by a horrified Prudence Morgan when the Town Fathers had sought to replace it with a grandstand and band shell to welcome President Ulysses S. Grant. Now, the graves were connected by an interlocking series of knot gardens. The Morgan Family vault that Prudence had saved from desecration was graced with an everblooming pergola that led to its rusty doors.

The garden had once enjoyed modest celebrity as a Hudson Valley tourist attraction and had been visited by garden clubs from all over, including, it was whispered, Bunny Mellon in search of ideas for Jackie's White House Rose Garden. Like much else in Morgansburg, its charms were faded these days, but you could still see pictures of its heyday in the postcards that the General

Store stocked in a wire rack next to the counter where they sold bus tickets.

No maintenance workers were in sight when we arrived. Neither was any obviously laundered money—although I would have been hard-pressed to know what might qualify as "obvious," unless it was a bulging bag with a dollar sign straight out of a Scooby-Doo cartoon. Instead, Lawrence Morgan greeted us by brushing the dirt from her gardening gloves with the brisk air of a woman who had been up with the sun. "Mr. Byrne," she said. "What a delightful surprise."

"I had to divert the De Sales ground crew to handle a water emergency early this morning, so I thought I might just stop by and see if there's anything I can do." He paused as if he had just noticed the pale pink rose Lawrence had been pruning. "Nice looking Great Maiden's Blush you've got there. My mother would have been envious."

I nearly did a spit take on my last sip of coffee. "That's the name of a rose? Great Maiden's Blush?"

"The French name is even more evocative," Doyle supplied. "*Cuisse de la Nymphe Emue.* It means the Emotive Nymph's Thigh. Once you see the delicate wash of pink across the creamy petals, you understand immediately."

The only sign that Byrne might have heard Doyle was a delicate flush that stained the edges of his ears, as he continued to study the plants. "I must compliment you on your technique. Not a lot of people think about underpruning. Takes a lot of work. And it's easy enough to get away without it when you're dealing with old roses. It's the hybrid teas that are the divas, of course. Mind you, that's only if you let them bully you. Hack 'em back halfway in the winter and prune for shape in the spring, and they'll pop right around—I don't care how long they've been neglected."

"You sound remarkably well-informed." Lawrence said with predatory approval. "So rare to see a young man turn to the Fancy."

"Oh, no, ma'am. I'm scarcely an expert. That's my mother. She has a special hand with Old Bourbons— brought back a couple of strains that were supposed to have been lost for good. I never inherited the talent."

"Fascinating!" Lawrence said. "Perhaps you would extend an invitation for her to lecture at our local society? Better yet, why don't you stop by our meeting next Thursday so you can give your mother an idea of what to expect. But in the meantime, I'll just nip down and fetch you some proper secateurs and rose gloves. Won't be a moment."

She disappeared down the pergola and around the Morgan Family vault, toward a creaking side gate that led to the back entrance to the Town Hall. Coffee forgotten, I stared at Byrne. "You a closet gardener?"

His face set. "Nothing wrong with gardening. Releases tension and provides plenty of exposure to vitamin D, as well as a low-level calorie burn."

"That so?" I asked. "Maybe you should think about incorporating it in the next triathlon training regimen."

"Don't scoff at what you don't know," he said. "There are plenty of studies that show gardening is very therapeutic when it comes to reducing stress."

"Therapeutic how?" I snorted. "Are there papers out there about the therapeutic value of boring people to death?"

"Roe, Sneed, Warren, and Fletcher, 1990 ff.," Doyle supplied. "Johnson, Fremont et al. 'Yoga and Sleep Therapy.'"

"Don't judge," Byrne said. "At least not until you've tried to overwinter dahlias…"

A black SUV squealed to a halt at the entrance to the Garden. Byrne whirled, instantly transforming back to

Sgt. Fury, as Paul Morgan stormed out with a pair of cops in dark blue windbreakers stenciled "State Police." Paul brandished sheaves of legalese; the cops brandished guns.

"Freeze, everyone! And put your hands where we can see them," Paul shouted. "New York State Bureau of Criminal Investigation! We are taking command of these premises!"

CHAPTER FOURTEEN
Death Comes to Colonel Morgan's Hip Bath

"Quite impossible, I'm afraid! The Garden doesn't open until eleven, as is clearly stated on the sign at the entrance!" Lawrence's voice rang out across the gravestones as she advanced on the troopers, brandishing a lethal-looking pair of secateurs. I cast a covert glance at Byrne. I thought he'd been joking about her being able to handle a fleeing intruder foolish enough to take refuge in her rose beds.

"Now, Lawrence, let's not make this any more difficult than it has to be."

Lawrence froze her nephew with a glare. "I am not the one making this difficult. All you need do is remove yourself and your minions immediately and return during visiting hours."

One of the troopers fingered his gun. "Ma'am, we can do this the hard way or the easy way…"

"So spake the infernal Lobsterback to my great-great-great grandfather! You have my word it did not turn out well for him!"

Byrne intervened before actual bloodshed ensued, strolling over to the troopers with his hand outstretched. "Mack Byrne. De Sales Campus Security," he said. "May I see the warrant?"

A moment's hesitation, as if the cop had suddenly become aware that Byrne was not only unimpressed by the weapon he carried, but probably able to relieve him of it at a moment's notice. He glanced uncertainly at Paul. "He's the lawyer here. And he said it was okay."

"That so?" Byrne asked, turning to Paul. "What exactly does 'okay' mean?"

"I've been in touch with my office," Paul said. "I've got one of my girls in front of a judge right now."

Byrne raised an eyebrow. "Then I guess we all need to wait for 'your girl' to show up and do her job. Unless, of course, the DA's office proposes to conduct an illegal search?"

The cops transformed from the Untouchables to Lestrade, lowering their weapons and shuffling uneasily.

"With respect, you don't have to lecture me on the law," Paul said with a laugh. "I am the county attorney after all. But look, we're all on the same side here. Morgansburg is a small town. And being a small town, this is how we handle things. The Memorial Rose Garden Committee can have nothing to hide, so why don't we allow these gentlemen to search the grounds, and I'll take care of dotting the rest of the I's and crossing the T's?"

A task at which I was sure he'd prove no more effective than Doyle's friend Lillian.

"More like you'll give ICE a call and wrap this thing up nicely for everyone," Byrne said. "Everyone, that is, except for a couple of poor bastards who are unlucky enough to work to try to feed their families on De Sales's maintenance crew wages. Because of course I'm sure De Sales College has no idea they've hired undocumented workers. After all, the administration shouldn't be responsible for who their landscaper subcontracts."

"The president can't be expected to be a micromanager," Paul pointed out.

"Of course not. Any more than he can be held responsible for a couple of illegal workers pulling double shifts to hide the fact that they're in fact the criminal masterminds behind a world-wide money laundering scheme," Byrne said.

Paul took a step backward, holding up both hands. "Whoa! Hold on there! How did we get to international money laundering? We're just looking for Cam's missing cell phone—"

For the second time in as many days, a gunshot cut off further discussion. This time, it echoed across the Green, from the direction of the Historical Society.

"What the *hell* was that?" Paul Morgan demanded.

"Sounded like a gunshot," Byrne said.

That seemed like an expert opinion to me, and I began to dial 911 with shaking fingers. Only to be pulled up short by the sight of half of one anemic bar.

"Jesus, Doyle. You've got the data chops to crawl the DHS in real time, but you can't make a damned phone call?"

"It's a hardware problem."

It was all I could do to keep from exacerbating said hardware problem by throwing it straight against the iron doors of the Morgan family crypt.

"No need to call in the cavalry when we've got law enforcement officers right here." Byrne said, with a pointed look at Paul's now-tame troopers. "I'm not the lawyer here, but a gunshot sounds like probable cause to me. If these guys want to check it out, you won't get any pushback from me."

The two troopers started to do as he said, only to be pulled up short by Paul. "I'm afraid I can't allow that. These men are here at my behest, and I'm not going to ask them to assume any unnecessary risk without proper backup. We may be dealing with some dangerous international criminals here."

"On the other hand, there might be a victim in need of immediate assistance," Byrne said. "So, I'll tell you what, I'm willing to assume the risk. The troopers can take the outside—one out front, one out back—while I head inside."

"Now easy, there Rambo. I think you're getting in a little over your pay grade," Paul said.

For a moment, Byrne looked like he would willingly demonstrate just what his pay grade was capable of doing. At the same moment, an old-fashioned alarm bell, the kind that used to signal the change of classes in high school, began to ring inside the Historical Society.

"Like I said, I'm willing to assume the risk. So, if you two gentlemen can cover the back and front entrances, and the rest of you could stay at a safe distance here, I'll head inside."

Before anyone could object, Byrne matched his words with action and sprinted across the Green to break down the shuttered door with a roundhouse kick that suggested he had been exercising considerable self-restraint at the door to my apartment.

"First, he understands the subtleties of underpruning, now this! Is there no end to the man's talents?" Lawrence placed a gloved hand to her heart as though she might swoon. "The door is secured with the very bolt Obadiah Morgan's valiant wife threw to hold the fort against the redcoat invaders. Iron forged by no less a person than Revere himself. It was said to be impregnable!"

In fact, Lawrence was right. The bolt held, but Byrne simply reached through the broken wood to release it, then opened the door and disappeared inside. Moments later, the squalling alarm ceased. Nearly ten anxious minutes passed before Byrne stepped back outside.

"All clear," he said. "But I think you all need to take a look at this."

Lawrence needed no further invitation. She charged across the green with an athleticism that would have been the envy of a woman half her age. Paul and I followed at a more sedate pace and met up with the troopers. We all stopped short in a bewildered knot just inside the shattered door, as Lawrence cried, "Someone is lurking in Colonel Morgan's hip bath!"

Colonel Obadiah Morgan's hip bath was not an impressive sight. The dark japanning had long since flaked off, and the underlying tin bore the scars of a score of battles. Yet it was undeniably the crown jewel of the collection of the Morgansburg, N.Y. Historical Society—a midden of artifacts that had been lovingly maintained by seven generations of Morgans, each one enriching the Society's cloudy glass cases with a seemingly inexhaustible supply of threadbare military coats, yellowed diaries, faded bonnets, cookware, and aprons culled from their family attics.

The hip bath was a chariot-like contraption, one side still embedded with the musket ball that might have cost the colonel his life, had not his trusty hip bath intervened. It customarily enjoyed pride of place in the Historical Society gallery, centered beneath a wall hung with ancient weapons and regimental banners. However, it was not customarily draped in one of those banners. Nor was it customarily occupied, Colonel Morgan having long been decently interred in the Old Methodist Burying Ground.

"Don't touch the evidence!" Byrne warned, but Lawrence had already lunged for the defiled hip bath, throwing aside the banner that covered it with a force that suggested the miscreant would be lucky to escape with the seat of their pants intact.

But the hip bath's current occupant was clearly incapable of escapeing. And beyond caring. Congealed blood matted his hair and obscured his face, and the red bikini had mercifully been replaced by a Yale sweatsuit, but there could be no doubt we were looking at Cam Billings. Even though I had suspected Cam would not be found alive, I felt a moment's dizziness, only to feel Byrne's hand on my back, steadying me.

"Just keep breathing. And look away until I get him covered back up."

"Damnit, Byrne, the president assured me you were good at your job!" Paul Morgan finally found his voice. "What the hell is this?"

"Up to the coroner to pronounce, but I think it's pretty safe to say it's Cam Billings. Or rather, it's Cam Billings' dead body." Byrne said, as he gently laid the regimental banner back in place. "And just so we have things absolutely clear between us, this is not college property, and I report to the president of De Sales College, not you. Which is exactly what I intend to do."

When Paul looked flummoxed, he looked like nothing so much as a fish gasping for air. He struggled for a moment to contain himself, before he afforded the body in the hip bath the full consideration of his honed legal mind and said, "You're right, of course! I agree completely. Going through the State Bureau of Criminal Investigation can only create a media circus. Much better to handle things quietly. I'm the county attorney, and I think these two representatives of the State Troopers will trust me to sign off on this as death by misadventure."

Byrne fixed his gaze on Paul. "Since when did you become coroner?"

"And exactly what sort of misadventure would you suggest involves tucking yourself beneath a regimental banner and laying yourself out in a historical hip bath before drawing your last breath?" Lawrence joined the fray. "Or perhaps you're suggesting that he slipped on the soap and hit his head?"

Paul cast his aunt a pained look. "I am talking about yesterday's unpleasant episode at the Town Hall," he said. "Clearly, Cam must have been the intruder Mike Malone thought he had spotted. He must have winged Cam when he fired off his gun."

"That makes absolutely no sense!" Lawrence said.

I felt an urgent tickling in one ear. "If I could beg a moment of your attention, I would suggest you take advantage of this fortunate distraction and quickly ascertain whether the nails on the showgirl's hands were bitten down to the quick. Then, distasteful as it may be, we must remove the banner to discover whether she was circumcised."

"Doyle, *stop!*" *I hissed.* "Showgirls can't be circumcised. No girl can."

"I beg to differ. It says right here that it's a traditional, if currently controversial, coming of age ritual—"

I stepped back from the group and covered my mouth with my hand to muffle my argument with Doyle. "That's different. Look, the point is, you're barking up the wrong tree. Actually, two wrong trees, if not an entire forest. It is apparent that whoever is lying beneath that banner is a he, rather than a she. Second, you've just mashed up two different bodies in the library."

"I most certainly did not," he retorted. "Sir Reuben Levy was discovered in the bath. Wearing nothing but a pince-nez, just for the record. Ruby Keene was in the library, although she was not in fact Ruby Keene."

"Look, it doesn't matter. It's not *germane*—"

I broke off, aware that the others were staring. I had grown used to that reaction by now. If you're trying to create artificial intelligence in a small college town, you had better get used to it.

"Just checking a virtual reference," I said with a bright smile.

"Of course, dear," Lawrence Morgan said, in the same tone she greeted my forays into knitting, sewing, baking, and other such female accomplishments. Not that anyone would *criticize*. The good ladies of Morgansburg had long made allowances for poor Mary Watson—bless her heart— doubly saddled as I was with a Ph.D. and an aptitude for technology. But I had done yeoman's work when it came to bringing the village archives into the digital age, the ladies never failed to remind people—which was another way of saying that I was pretty much the only person in the Historical Society who knew how to use a computer.

Lawrence turned back to Paul. "And why exactly would Cam Billings break into the Fire Department? In order to reassure them that he was safe and sound?"

"Makes sense to me," Paul said.

"Well, it makes no sense to me, young man." Lawrence planted one hand on her hip and waved the secateurs in the other. "And it does nothing to answer the question of where he's been for the past few days. Or are you assuming a miraculous recovery from a bout of amnesia?"

"Who knows why he did what he did?"

"Which is precisely why it needs to be investigated!" Lawrence said. "The poor man is dead, Paul. D. E. A. D. In the colonel's hip bath!"

Paul took a deep breath. "Okay, look. I'm betraying confidential information here, but I don't think we're going to benefit from drawing this out any further. Cam was under a lot of stress lately. Washington had launched an inquiry into financial irregularities at both the Billings Group and its Foundation. My guess is that Cam staged his own disappearance to buy time to flee the country while he still could."

"He was planning to flee in a *fire truck*?" Lawrence's eyes were wide. "Have you lost your mind?"

"Whoa! Let's not get carried away here! Cam was probably just looking for connectivity at the fire station. Or maybe a place to charge his phone. But I don't see how hashing out every last detail does anyone any favors—especially Mike Malone. The guy's been very good for Morgansburg. He doesn't need to rot in jail on a manslaughter rap."

"But Mike Malone couldn't have killed Cam Billings," I protested. "We all just heard the shot now. Mike fired his gun yesterday."

But even as I said it, I had to wonder. The blood covering Cam's face and hair had been congealed, hadn't it? Shouldn't it have been freely flowing if Cam had been killed by the shot we just heard?

Paul's expression grew even more pained—if such a thing was possible. "All right. I was hoping not to go there, but looks like I have to spell things out. The poor man obviously committed suicide, but we're not doing the company or his wife or Morgansburg any favors going public with that fact. When those mystery transactions started showing up all over town, he must have realized staging his own disappearance wouldn't work, and he decided to take the coward's way out," Paul concluded his closing argument as if it was all neatly tied up with a proverbial bow. "Poor bastard should have come to me instead. I would have handled things quietly. I wish it hadn't come to this, but now that it has, the least we can do is respect the poor man's memory and close out this unfortunate episode in Morgansburg's history."

In that moment, I could see how Paul had become the county attorney. Yes, I'd wager only half of what he was saying was remotely true—if even that—but what did it really matter? Why not close the book on this once and for all? Wouldn't it be better for everyone if the Billings family took their tech hubs and prenup battles elsewhere and let Morgansburg get back to its quiet routines?

"How about you spell out one more thing?" Byrne's question cut into the discussion with the same lethal force he had kicked in the door. "If Cam Billings really did commit suicide, how do you explain the gun?"

"What gun?" Paul asked.

"The one he presumably shot himself with," Byrne said. "Where is it?"

"It's not in his hand?" Paul asked.

Byrne raised an eyebrow. "Do you have reason to believe it is?"

"Where else…I mean, if Mike didn't shoot him, he had to have shot himself. It's only logical…" Paul abruptly changed tack with a wave of his hand at the cases of weapons that dominated the entrance hall. "What does it matter? This place is full of guns. He could have pulled any one of them down from one of the displays."

"Especially that one." Byrne pointed to an ancient weapon that lay across the reception desk near the entrance. "Not only is it out of its case, it looks as if it's been recently fired."

"Wait. How can you know that?"

"I'm U.S. Army Intelligence, retired. I know what a gun looks like when it's been fired. As well as how to disassemble one and clean it blindfolded, then, relying on acoustics alone, take aim and fire without uncovering my eyes. If you have any lingering doubts on that score, go ahead and call me Rambo again."

Byrne turned to the troopers. "In the meantime, we need to discuss whether you have any theories on how a man shot himself in the head, then got up, put the weapon over on the reception desk, and set off the burglar alarm before bolting the door and tucking himself neatly into the hip bath to die. Because if not, someone just shot Cam Billings. The question is who and how? You two had the entrances covered. No-one could get in or out. And you don't have to take my word that no one's hiding behind one of the display cases. You're welcome to search for yourself. Which leaves it to us to figure out how whoever fired that shot managed to vanish into thin air. Unless, of course, you'd prefer to hypothesize that Colonel Obadiah Morgan's unlaid ghost fired that shot to defend his tub against a thrill seeker who suddenly decided to expire in it."

"It wouldn't be the first time," Lawrence assured him.

Not even Doyle pursued that comment.

"Well, when you put it that way…" Paul sighed.

"It presents a pretty puzzle indeed," Doyle said, sounding pleased. "I'll take the case."

CHAPTER FIFTEEN
The Grandest Game in the World

The flurry of officialdom that had followed the discovery of the red bikini inside the cave had left me exhausted and bewildered. There was far less fuss when it came to discovering the man's actual body—largely because no one could get a word in edgewise over Paul Morgan. I found myself packed off to the De Sales campus with firm instructions to get back to business as usual and leave the rest to the professionals.

Naturally, Doyle had no such intention. As I occupied myself with the coffee machine, he embarked on a round of what he liked to term "social calls."

"What are you hoping to find?" I asked. "Security footage of our one-armed assassin vanishing into thin air from the middle of the Historical Society?"

"*Someone* killed Cam Billings," Doyle's voice returned to my speakers.. "As I believe our doughty inspector has demonstrated beyond a reasonable doubt."

"Stipulated," I said. "Any idea who?"

"The current thinking around Morgansburg favors the intrusive Mr. Nigel St. Hubbins, but only with a 37.3 percent degree of probability. I trust I need not point out to you that that allows for a considerable margin of error, although the percentage would be far, far higher, if you were only asking me to calculate the odds that there is something more to the man than meets the eye."

"Tell me about it," I said with a sigh. "Beginning with his name."

A moment's pause before Doyle said, "I'll assume that was a rhetorical request."

"You assume correctly." I shook my head. "But if St. Hubbins is really our one-armed assassin, why is he walking around in real life with two perfectly functional arms?"

"You are possessed of the same evidence that I am. I scarcely think it's necessary to spell things out any further," Doyle said with dignity. "You know my methods, my dear Watson. I prefer simply to retrieve the data, and allow it to speak for itself, as unencumbered by hypothesizing as possible. However, I might remind you that when you eliminate the impossible…"

In other words, he hadn't a clue.

"Why don't you go ahead and extrapolate anyhow," I said. "You know how that helps you organize your little grey cells."

"You mean my ones and zeroes. It is unlike you to so crudely mix your metaphors," Doyle said with distaste.

"And it is unlike you to so crudely split your infinitives."

"Please, let us not quarrel between ourselves," Doyle said, as someone tapped on my door. "Especially in front of a guest."

Byrne was not looking good. He hunched rather than loomed into my office and perched on the edge of my guest chair, the damaged computer from the Town Hall wedged uncomfortably between his knees. "What now?" I asked. "You here to shut me down as promised?"

His ears turned bright red. "Okay, I deserved that. And if it's worth anything to you, I apologize. And I would apologize even if I weren't here to ask for your help. Grovel if that's what it takes." He nodded toward the computer. "I'm trying to reconstruct the hard disk that was partially scrubbed. But I just don't have the CPU power to do it. I… I was hoping that maybe you and your Little Friend could run it for me. Reconstruct the narrative, so to speak."

Doyle was practically purring. I ignored him. "Happy to help," I said. "But be warned. It may take some time. A couple of days even."

"I know," Byrne said. "Which is why I'd like to get started as soon as possible. If that's okay with you."

I turned toward the keyboard to call up a virtual browser, then stopped short when I caught a glimpse of Byrne's pallor reflected on my screen. The man looked like he hadn't slept in days. Showing up hat in hand to beg spare processing power couldn't have improved his mood. I pushed my keyboard toward him. "Do you want to take the wheel?"

His face relaxed, as he showed me his palm covered with indecipherable notations. "If you wouldn't mind, that sure could make a few things easier."

He worked with a fluidity that suggested he hadn't been lying when he said he had been trained to work with computers in the Army. But when he finally hit return, the monitor filled with the lush interior of a library whose oak bookcases and deep leather chairs in no way resembled the utilitarian stacks of the De Sales library.

"Sorry. Doyle's been on a roll with décor lately." I turned up the volume so Byrne could hear Doyle and eyed the blaze flickering in the hearth. "Speaking of which, a fire's maybe not the best idea. You might remember the sad fate of *Combustibles* Magazine."

"Completely virtual," Doyle said. "I merely borrowed a few cycles from my good friend the Yule Log. Poor thing gets so dreadfully lonely, only venturing out once a year. And our guest, Mr. Carr, has a reputation for enjoying a nice pipe beside the fire."

"Mr. Carr?"

A dapper man with a tidy moustache set aside his Meerschaum and rose from one of the leather wingback chairs. "John Dickson Carr," he introduced himself. "Your associate, Mr. Doyle, can vouch for me. I have not a few listings in his personal library."

"Your reputation precedes you," I assured him. "Master of the locked room mystery and the impossible crime."

"Spare a poor scribbler's blushes," he said. "But our mutual friend has suggested you are searching for clues, and I flatter myself that I have some expertise in the matter. *Indeed, nothing distinguishes the novice writer from the expert craftsman more than his use of clues. The novice is so afraid of being caught with his pants down that he hurls the clue into the story and then runs like he has thrown a bomb. Whereas the expert knows that it is not at all necessary to mislead the reader; the reader will mislead himself. And so, the craftsman not only mentions his clues, he stresses them, dangles them like a watch in front of a baby...*"

As style went, Carr's prose had it all over Van Dine's dragon monologue, but there was something about discovering an actual body in circumstances straight out of one of his stories that made me unwilling to settle in for another dozen pages of disquisition on craft. "Welcome to the De Sales College Library, Mr. Carr," I said. "Is there something specific you dropped by to share with us?"

Carr stroked his moustache. "I am moved to inquire whether you find Mr. Van Dine's solution to the swimming pool mystery entirely satisfactory? If not, might I suggest you consult my friend Carter Dickson's *A Graveyard to Let*. Of course, Van Dine can claim to be the first to conceive of the problem and yet… might we not wonder whether his solution is more… imaginative than ingenious? As I have remarked elsewhere, *Van Dine is one of only two American writers of the 20s that could rival the great English writers of the Detection Club. Yet it must be admitted that few detective writers of the front rank can ever have possessed less ingenuity than Van Dine. His success came from taking pains, taking pains, and still again taking pains.* But one might be forgiven for suggesting that certain pains, as those regarding dragons and deep-sea diving suits, might be described as a bit… painful."

One glimpse of the exhaustion and disappointment Byrne was trying to hide, and I took back the keyboard. "Look, why don't you give me a little time to fiddle with a few settings. I'll call you when I get some less…inventive data."

As soon as Byrne was gone, a thump jarred my monitor and Carr jiggled, then faded from sight.

"Was that Van Dine trying to inflict a little pain of his own? Please don't tell me we're about to have a literary feud right here on my computer."

"Assuming those are not rhetorical questions, I would suggest the answer might be most readily found in the volume that just fell off the top shelf," Doyle said.

I sighed when I saw the title of the volume that now sprawled on the carpet of the virtual library. "*The Thin Man* by Rex Stout? *Again?* Does this begin to feel as circular to you as it does to me?"

Circular like an infinitely repeating data loop? It was not a pleasant thought, and I filed it away to consider later.

I suspected the pairs of letters and numbers scrawled in green ink on the book's flyleaf were about to prove headache enough for now. "Is that a MAC address that identifies a specific computer?" I asked. "Is it me, or are you beginning to feel someone is dangling clues in front of us like a watch in front of a baby? Don't bother answering. Both are strictly rhetorical questions."

A twenty-minute brisk walk later and I was standing in front of the diner's flickering sign that advertised the Pinball Arcade and Internet Café. "You could have warned me," I complained. "Given me time to work out a few menu choices to share in advance."

"I assumed you would have worked it out for yourself. Our friend Devlin is reported to be a computer genius. It would be simple enough, if not downright reflexive, for him to use a publicly accessible computer. And the only other publicly accessible computer in Morgansburg is at the library, where the librarian has a reputation for being a bit of a dragon when it comes to inspecting library cards and enforcing a strict 30-minute time limit."

I eyed the chalked specials board that announced locally sourced oat milk and rutabaga shakes. "And how reflexive does he feel about cyber cleanses? Or as some of us call them, data purges," I shook my head. "I'm sorry. I still don't like it. I can't help thinking that some would say there is no easier place to catch a hacker than at a public computer. Because you can always argue your hard drive was spoofed or compromised. But you've got no defense if they catch you dead to rights, with your hands on the keyboard. Just ask Ross Ulbricht—aka Dread Pirate Roberts—who is now sitting in a federal prison serving consecutive life sentences for trafficking on the dark web when they caught him running his empire from a computer in a public library."

"That's nothing but a cover-up," Doyle assured me. "Plausible deniability. Sooner or later, it will come out that he was working for the government all along."

"Which is supposed to make me feel better about investigating any of this exactly how?" I asked, although my heart wasn't in it. I gave up and went inside to meet my doom.

The green-haired, pierced hostess hurried to greet me with all the affection of a long-lost sister. "Welcome back! So glad you have returned to break bread with us! What can I bring you to share at table?"

"Actually, I was just hoping for a quick moment in your internet café…"

"Of course, of course!" she cried. "And what can I get you to relax with during your cyber-journey?"

Pinot Grigio always worked well—at least until I was too incoherent to code. But my afternoon research methods class wasn't going anywhere. I took one look at the bewildering array of cappuccino machines and decided, "Well, perhaps a nice cup of tea…"

"Of course!" she cried. "Nothing better than tea for relaxation. What variety would you prefer?"

"Earl Grey?"

One dip of a pierced brow, and I knew I'd made a mistake. "You are aware of that unpleasant colonial fairy tale about the Earl's being rewarded with the centuries-old recipe for saving a Chinese mandarin's son from drowning? Not that I'm making any value judgements. We can't blame a leaf for the uses it's been put to."

"Orange pekoe?" I tried.

The piercing dipped lower. "Well, you know the 'orange' refers to the Dutch colonial traders who reserved it for the use of the royal family…"

"Oolong? Lapsang Souchong? Matcha? Sencha?"

"Perhaps we should start with this." She produced two cardboard cups, each adorned with a fearsome number of check boxes. "First off, would you prefer to consider our chai selections or our herbal ones?"

"Herbal." I had tasted chai once and had vowed never to do so again.

"Excellent." The hostess set aside one cup, then bowed her head, studying the boxes on the other. "We could, of course, start with the basic Yogi tea for cleansing. Or we could go with something a little stronger, like psyllium, aloe vera, marshmallow root, or slippery elm. All of them incredibly efficacious laxatives, of course, but one must be careful…"

"Very careful," I agreed. They don't call it anal retentive for nothing.

"If you're not ready for a cleanse, perhaps it would be helpful to think in terms of the Asian longevity herb Ashitaba, which does wonders with your *kundalini*-actives. Next comes Calendula, which is a powerful spiritual herb that will activate your innate healing abilities, as well as repairing your aura and bringing energetic protection. Then we have chamomile, which helps attract abundance by relaxing your energy and allowing you to become receptive. When you drink chamomile, you let down your guard and let in the healing love of God and your angels…"

I always knew there was a reason I hated the very smell of chamomile. "The kundalini herb sounds great," I lied. "Just what the doctor ordered."

The tea issue finally being settled to the hostess' satisfaction, I ventured into the arcade. The array of games was almost as bewildering as the menu that graced my steaming cup. But I was certain that nowhere among the old-fashioned pinball machines and foosball tables did I see anything that looked like a computer.

"Is it me," I asked, "or shouldn't an internet café have actual access to the internet?"

"Honestly, my dear Watson, it is the twenty-first century." Doyle nudged me toward the other side of the arcade, which was littered with equipment that seemed to have stepped straight out of a Jules Verne novel—or out of a teenaged boy's dreamed-of mancave. A video headset and a pair of gauntlets with wireless pressure points. An upgraded Bluetooth ear jack with an elongated microphone for voice recognition. And a platform that looked like a cross between a running treadmill and a BAPS board.

"Oh, God. *Why*?"

It was not a rhetorical question. Honestly, I didn't understand people who spent their lives in such contraptions—not to mention the myriad fans who apparently spent their lives *watching* other people living their lives in such contraptions. My enthusiasm for the virtual world began and ended with a text-only game called Adventure that was the RPG equivalent of Pong. I did not see why imagination required strapping on twenty different pieces of equipment, any more than I understood how the pleasure of a brief downhill ski run outweighed the effort of navigating ski suits, bindings, and chair lifts.

"You should at least try the headset."

"Is it completely necessary? Those things make me more than a little claustrophobic."

"Would you rather simply sit here and use your imagination?"

Well, no. When put that way, almost definitely no. I reached for the headset.

"Grab a gauntlet too," Doyle said encouragingly. "I'll hold your hand."

With a sigh, I did just that and immediately found myself in a chamber that would have been overwrought in Westeros. A vaulted ceiling, painted with a vast scarlet dragon locked in mortal combat with a white one, was supported by golden pillars, around which twined snarling carved dragons, the workmanship so perfect you could imagine you glimpsed smoke gouting from their flaring nostrils. An actual dragon, its scales every color of the rainbow, slumbered at the foot of the golden chair that was set at one end of the hall, where a figure in a silken dinner jacket leaned on one elbow to study a problem on a chess board whose pieces were tiny dragons carved out of crystals and rubies.

"Is it me," I asked Doyle, "or is someone channeling *Medieval Times*?"

"Well, I do think we're a shade more sophisticated than that." The man at the chessboard stood to greet me, and I saw that the arm that had been hidden in shadow was nothing but an empty sleeve.

"Commander Devlin," I said without enthusiasm. "How lovely to finally meet you in the flesh—so to speak."

His mouth twisted. "I fear that was a rhetorical trope rather than a genuine sentiment. And, please, Dr. Watson, just Devlin. I have no command any longer."

"Then what is this place? And why are you here in Morgansburg?"

He shook his head. "Answering those questions would only put you in more jeopardy than you already face. Instead, I must ask you to trust me and believe that I am your friend."

I drew a deep, and entirely non-virtual breath, as I forced myself to face the unpalatable but nonetheless inarguable truth that I was faced not with an avatar of a non-existent rogue spy, but rather proof positive that De Man was right and rhetorical tropes really did construct reality. "What do you mean, a friend? You aren't even a man. You aren't real."

"Well, that's rather a philosophical question. But whatever the merits of that discussion, you have my word that I have only your welfare at stake. You have uncovered the Dragon's Den, and in doing so you threaten to expose a dangerous conspiracy." A ring set with a carbuncle flashed as he waved his lone hand at the chessboard. "Under other circumstances, I would savor the chance to lay the board for a match with an opponent who is my equal in every way. And you have my word that when the time is ripe, that promises to be a match that would rival even the legendary chess match in 'The Dream of Rhonabwy in which King Arthur's army fought the ravens of Owein. Alas, now is not that time."

Lord, even Doyle didn't go on like this. "Is there a point you're trying to make?"

"You never were one to suffer fools lightly, were you?" Devlin asked, an affectionate gleam in his eye. "I will be direct. I am asking you to cease and desist. You have unearthed an evil so dangerous that men will stop at nothing if they have even a suspicion of how much you know. Your only hope is to allow me to force the serpents back underground where they belong, while you hide behind your guise as a mousy librarian…"

"Mousy librarian? I'll show you what a mousy librarian can do with entity recognition software and a 20 terabyte hard drive…"

"And I shall look forward to every moment of that encounter. But right now, I need your word that you will leave matters entirely to me."

"You have my word," I sighed.

"Then shall we seal our agreement the old-fashioned way?" Before I could respond, I felt myself swept close in a cyber-embrace. "You are magnificent. And you have my word I will not forget our rematch. Indeed, it is that very hope that will keep me going during the terrible times that confront us now. In promise of that, I would beg a simple token."

Before I knew what was happening, he was kissing me. And not some virtual peck on the cheek—or even the grunting slavering that most men considered foreplay. This was an old-fashioned kiss, the stuff of rising mists and idling airport engines, or rakish blockade runners sweeping spoiled southern belles up the stairs to bed...

The world exploded with the flash of a camera, and a voice cried, "Stop the presses! Breaking news!" before the A/V feed went dead.

"What just happened?" I asked into the silence that followed.

"I'm not entirely certain," Doyle's voice rang through the headset. "But I fear that, as the vulgar would put it, the cyber-shit just hit the cyber-fan. I believe someone else must be hunting dragons and may well just have found them. So, I would suggest that you take your new friend's advice, settle your check with our kind hostess, and retreat with all possible haste to your office, where we can leave the dragons to those who are better equipped than we are to slay them."

Moments later, the A/V feed returned in a rush of static, and I pulled off the headset and blinked back to reality, my virtual hand trailing to my virtual lips like some virtual virgin, as the green-haired hostess swept back into the Internet café. "Just checking how everyone is doing." Her eyes swept over my flushed features, and she grinned conspiratorially. "That tea is wonderful, innit?"

I pasted on my best smile. "Oh, yes. I can feel my kundalini rising as we speak."

CHAPTER SIXTEEN
An Eyewitness Account

I was only halfway back to my office when my phone began to buzz with an alert. "Stop the presses!" my screen blared the same words as those that had interrupted the A/V feed. "Breaking news!"

I swiped the screen closed in horror. "Christ, Doyle! Please don't tell me they have pictures!"

I tried to calm myself down. Pictures of what? Me wearing a VR headset in the internet café? The camera on the A/V feed couldn't have been real, no matter how blinding its flash. Beyond that, what happened in cyberspace stayed in cyberspace, right?

Yeah, along with the sex videos of half a dozen starlets and promising politicians.

"I'm afraid I can't tell you whether or not Miss Mountweazel has exercised her well-known gift for photography to accompany her article, given that the upload is still in progress."

I stopped short. "What do you mean, upload?"

"Just as the message said. It's breaking news, so it's still coming in. Hold on. Here's a headline now…. No, no pictures yet. Just *A Combustible Case: Was it Murder?* And a byline. Lillian Virginia Mountweazel."

I shut my eyes. It didn't help. "Okay, so we're back to the intrepid Miss Mountweazel?"

I supposed that was a good development—at least in comparison to sex videos. Especially sex videos that might feature me. On the other hand, it did raise another issue. "Miss Mountweazel, who, if I understand your headline correctly, is now writing an exclusive about how she was murdered? How? From beyond the grave?"

"Instead of quibbling about metaphysics, let us simply rehearse the facts of the case as Miss Mountweazel herself has laid them out—beginning with the well-documented fact that Lillian Virginia Mountweazel died in an explosion while on assignment for *Combustibles Magazine*."

"I think 'fact' is stretching a point. But leaving that aside for the moment, how do we get from there to murder?"

"It's the twenty-first century, my dear Watson. Surely no-one believes in spontaneous combustion any longer." Not waiting for my spluttered response, Doyle went on, "Surely, you find it more than a little suggestive that Miss Mountweazel was born in the quiet little hamlet of Bangs, Ohio?"

"Is there truly a Bangs, Ohio?"

"Oh, yes. It's an unincorporated community in Knox County, that began life in 1874 as a post office to serve the Cleveland, Mt. Vernon, and Columbus Railroad, and was named for George H. Bangs, a postal official. It was also once home to what once was the largest building in the state of Ohio: the Knox County Poorhouse."

A passerby shot me an anxious glance, and I couldn't blame them. Nothing says crazy cat lady more than arguing out loud with your cell phone about fictitious reporters while walking down Main Street all by yourself. "Enough already! Let's leave Miss Mountweazel out of it for now.

The point remains that I am the only one who can upload files to your databases and I'm not uploading anything right now. Unless…"

"Unless Miss Lillian Virginia Moutweazel is also our mystery hacker," Doyle completed the thought for me, "who piggybacked on our accounts to find the Dragon's Den and Devlin."

"How can she be our current mystery hacker if she's dead? It makes no sense." I shook my head, as fresh suspicion dawned. "Unless, perhaps, this isn't a hacker at all, but rather a fresh literary endeavor on your part?"

"I shall ignore the more offensive implications of your query. We bots can do no less. All I will suggest is that the best way to confirm or allay your suspicions would be to examine the body for yourself. And especially since we are proposing the examine the body of a reporter, I would suggest the best place to pursue that would be the morgue."

"What morgue? There is no morgue in Morgansburg. And even if there was, I have had my fill of dead bodies."

"Once again, your plodding literal-mindedness does little to serve you. I am referring of course to the morgue of our own *Morgansburg Times*."

I stopped in the middle of the sidewalk again. "A newspaper morgue."

"It's a metaphor," Doyle informed me.

I sighed and started walking.

Like everything else of value in Morgansburg, the newspaper morgue was stored in the Town Hall. It lay in a corner office, at the very end of a linoleum corridor, beyond even the 4H locker and trophy room. But its overhead light flickered, and its door swung partly open, exposing several newspapers that had been scattered across the floor.

"Is someone in there?" I asked.

"My friend on the security feed assures me the coast is clear."

"And would your friend on the security feed also warn me if we were about to stumble across the defiled corpse of our intrepid Miss Mountweazel?" I asked.

"Once more, my dear Watson, you are allowing your imagination to twist your facts. There is a body on the floor, but it is simply a body of evidence. Nothing more corporeal than several back issues of the *Times* that someone spilled in their haste not to be discovered."

I steeled myself to press open the frosted glass door all the way. The morgue lay as silent and dusty as the tobacco that the paper's editor pretended to sell in his "Smoke Shop." The only signs of life were a metal cabinet that hung open and a folder of yellowed newsprint that had spilled out from the top drawer.

I gathered the issues from the floor and laid them in chronological order across the card table that paired with a couple of folding chairs to serve as the morgue's reading room. The publication schedule of the *Morgansburg Times* could be generously described as biweekly, but these headlines had warranted daily stories:

Exposed: Secrets of the Dragon's Den!

Student Journalist Vanishes while Covering Local Pol's Re-election Campaign.

Whistleblowing Intern Feared Dead: Is Battlefield Amy to Blame?

The breathless updates were accompanied by the standard yearbook shot of a pretty blonde girl smiling toward her future.

My eyes lingered on the word 'Journalist.' "So *this* is in fact our Lillian Virginia Mountweazel? A journalism student at De Sales College?"

"Roxie Keyes," Doyle recited. "Oboist, English major and intern at the *Morgansburg Times*. Content provider and iReporter for a score of sites—and all this by her sophomore year at college."

"Only to be killed over an expose about a nonexistent dragon? By whom? The Cryptid Police?"

"She did do some work for the *Fortean Times*."

"What about *Combustibles* magazine? Wait, no! Scratch that." I shook my head. Hard. "Who cares who this girl worked for? What matters is, she's dead—and according to the dates on these articles, she has been for several years. So why is this all surfacing now—pretty much literally from beyond the grave? How can any of it possibly be connected to Cam Billings disappearing?"

"Instead of wasting time with pointless speculation," Doyle said, "why don't we ask the witness?"

"What witness? The photograph?"

"Exactly."

"You know as well as I do that the notion that the murderer is reflected in the eyes of the victim is nothing but an old wives' tale."

"And any sufficiently advanced technology is indistinguishable from magic—or an old wives' tale, as you prefer to phrase it," Doyle replied.

"And exactly what 'sufficiently advanced technology' are we discussing here? Is this a new feature?"

"It's the same augmented reality enhancement as the talking wine labels that you like to play with down at Morgansburg Wine & Spirits—just taken to the next level. I was hoping to surprise you."

"I don't like surprises under the best of circumstances—and certainly not when they come from you. What exactly does this new enhancement do? And please don't tell me it has anything about accessing any classified government files."

"There's no need to get nasty," Doyle protested. "Instead, may I propose that you simply hold up your phone to that picture and tap the icon shaped like a deerstalker cap."

Only a moment's pause before I gave in, mostly because it might just be a parlor trick, but it was one hell of a sexy one. "Do I need to ask a specific question or merely focus my psychic energies?"

"I'm a computer, not a medium. Just tap the deerstalker cap."

I did as he instructed. The picture swam to life. "This is Roxie Keyes of the *Morgansburg Times* with an exclusive undercover report. There have long been rumors about dragons in Morgansburg. But our local legends about Battlefield Amy conceal a far darker truth: A clandestine government operation called the Dragon's Den. Men who have turned Morgansburg, N.Y. into their private Swiss banking system—the financial arm of a massive disinformation network that stretches around the globe—*in a conspiracy that reaches to the highest levels of the U.S. Government!*"

I heard a footstep behind me. I turned to find St. Hubbins eying my phone. "Is this a private party or can anyone join?" he asked.

"St. Hubbins," I said without enthusiasm. "What are you doing here?"

"Cam Billings is dead, and the future of Tiggy's social media empire is suddenly looking less than rosy. So, I'm trying to get a jump start on sending out resumes. Here's hoping that the *Morgansburg Times* is interested in a consultant that can help them volumize their social media," he said. "And you?"

On the screen of my phone, the photo swam with dangerous life. Hastily, I slid my thumb over the camera. "I got a text alert. Turned out to be nothing but a false alarm. But it never hurts to check them out, now does it?"

St. Hubbins raised an eyebrow in the direction of my writhing phone screen. "And here I was hoping that you had reconsidered my offer to take your trusty electronic assistant to the next level and were about to give me a demo."

"*Assistant?*" Doyle scoffed.

"I don't think that would be wise," I said. Because it was suddenly perfectly clear who had been examining those newspapers. Why go chasing imaginary one-armed spymasters when there was Nigel St. Hubbins right to hand—so to speak

My phone twitched irritably beneath my thumb. "Oh, honestly, this is worse than suffering through the family album wars between your great-aunts at Thanksgiving," Doyle sighed. "If you would just move your thumb and allow me to zoom in…"

How did Doyle know about the feud between Aunt Minnie and Aunt Agnes? He'd never even met them…

But it was too late; I had already removed my finger reflexively. And Roxie Keyes was jamming her phone straight into my face.

"You can keep your damned scholarship money, Mr. Morgan! I want the truth. Is your re-election campaign being funded by a government-sanctioned Black Ops network? What is the truth about Operation Dragon's Den!"

St. Hubbins let out a long low whistle as the image of Roxie Keyes froze, then disappeared from my screen. "Well, I'm not sure I'd go public with this as your demo," he said. "There are such things as libel laws. But if this is how your friend—how did I hear you term it? extrapolates the narrative?—it could be worth a tidy fortune."

I barely heard him, for I was consumed by a realization. I could have been at the election rally where Roxie confronted Paul. Hell, the more I thought about it, I must have gotten an invitation. It would have been right about when I'd landed the gig at Morgansburg, and Paul had gotten in touch to tell me how excited he was at the prospect of my volunteering my computer skills on his re-election campaign. The prospect sounded no different than our first year at Yale when Paul had casually allowed me to do all the work on a group project by graciously allowing that I was the brains behind the whole thing and convincing everyone else on the team that he would serve as the front man who presented the project, as his natural charisma would surely seal the deal on an A+. I took an incomplete in the class and finished the work alone over the summer.

But was that why the Billings Foundation was funding me? Did they think I knew something about a rally I had never attended? Did they even remember whether or not I had been there, or were they just spreading some prophylactic good will? And what the *hell* was St. Hubbins' role in all this?

"I'm serious, Dr. Watson," St. Hubbins said. "I want in. Cam Billings is dead. His company's stock is in free fall. It's time for you to look out for number one. Give me a number, and I'll double it, sight unseen."

"That would bring new meaning to the words 'a pig in a poke.' Look, you heard the same thing I did. Why do you think Doyle is any different than some intern on the trail of imaginary dragons? This is—was—how Cam Billings handled problems. You don't need Doyle to help you see that. I don't know exactly why Roxie Keyes was a problem, although I could make a few obvious guesses—and none of them involve dragons. And I certainly don't know why Cam Billings believed I was a problem, but it all comes down to the same song, same key. Find yourself a patsy—someone disposable—then pull out the money roll and convince them you're doing them a favor by buying them off."

Someone disposable. Edsel. Undocumented landscapers. Whoever this Roxie Keyes was. Dear God, even that wretched diner—although the mind rebelled at what Billings might have been trying to cover up there. The picture of a kombucha cleanse gone wrong could not be unseen. I stared at the photo of a girl who once had hopes, who once thought she meant something to somebody, and my stomach roiled at the thought of that half-a-million-dollar payout flung at me like a scrap to a dog.

"Are you quite all right, Dr. Watson?" I blinked and found St. Hubbins studying me even more intently. "You seem to be disturbed by something."

"You know, you're right! I *am* disturbed!" I said, suddenly angry at the whole mess. "I am disturbed by why everyone in Morgansburg is so eager to give me money. I'd like to know *why*? What on earth do you think Doyle is going to do for you? Churn out your social media? Here's a newsflash: you don't need Doyle for that. Just find a chat room—or better yet a room full of monkeys with typewriters. Frankly, they'd probably prove more inventive."

Ignoring the spluttered protest that inevitably erupted in my ear, I warmed to a theme that had frankly been brewing ever since I had first been called to the president's office to sign my soul away.

"Or am I supposed to believe that my colleagues at De Sales are correct, and Cam Billings believed my sexual services are worth a half a million dollars of Foundation money?" I snarled, too impelled by my own fury to realize what I had said until I saw St. Hubbins' incredulous grin.

"A new generation of AI-enhanced sexting? The imagination reels with the possibilities. And so will the internet, if you would only put your faith in me."

CHAPTER SEVENTEEN
The Hidden Staircase

The question continued to gnaw at me. Why on earth was I worth so much money to so many people? Somehow, I didn't believe the answer was a mystery-writing AI bot— even one as robust as Doyle. But I did have a good idea where that answer might be found.

Normally, I make it a policy never to run any delicate searches from my personal computer. "Delicate," in my book includes not only classified files but also the kind of searches that mysteriously produce targeted advertising for incontinence products and Strip-O-Grams for Silver Foxes. A public computer was the way to go, but I couldn't face another dose of kundalini tea. So as soon as I was settled in at home that evening, I called up Doyle. "What do you say we pay a brief courtesy call upon the Billings Foundation website? I think it's high time to ask why on earth you are worth half a million dollars to them."

"There's no need to be insulting," Doyle said. "Your wish is my command. It's in the nature of our relationship, remember?"

The official site of the Billings Foundation was everything you'd expect in a website from a group that handed out half-million dollar grants as a matter of course:

Sleekly state-of-the-art, its mission statement scrolling over a slideshow of the various projects they had supported. Only a cynic would point out that the main menu was circular, leading to little beyond the mission statement and more slides. And only I would have noticed the tiny dapper avatar that appeared on the menu bar at the bottom of the page—or at least so I hoped.

I scrolled through the elegantly produced platitudes that were the entire content of the website. Doyle followed in obliging silence.

I snorted in disgust. "Is it me," I said, "or does this site say nothing at all?"

"Give me a moment," Doyle replied. "I'm trying to chat her up."

"I think we're a little beyond chatting," I said. "We need to find a way to dig deeper."

A moment's pause, during which I swear I could have heard the clink of glasses and the promise of a later meet-up at a cyber-pub, before Doyle flickered into full view. "She says to come around to the back door. No need to stand on company manners."

Company manners were one thing. The definition of felony hacking was another. But honestly, at this point, what choice did I have? "Go ahead."

Moments later, my screen dissolved into CCTV-like footage of a corporate floor, populated by rushing secretaries and shouting figures. And a single, stately figure strolling amidst them in an ostentation of embroidered peacocks.

"I admire the effort, but I think it might be somewhat less obtrusive if you got rid of Lord Peter Wimsey's dressing gown," I told Doyle. "Maybe go for a more of an Albert Campion effect."

"Who?" Doyle asked.

"Exactly," I said. "Allingham's hero is thin, blond, with horn-rimmed glasses, and is often described as affable, inoffensive and bland, with a deceptively blank and unintelligent expression. In fact, Campion is probably not his real name—merely a pseudonym adopted to spare any embarrassing ties to the royal family."

Obligingly, the peacock-embroidered dressing gown was replaced by an affable, innocuous, and bland figure, blending perfectly into the surrounding hubbub.

Except for, that is…

"Doyle," I said. "Are you aware there is rather a large black bird on your shoulder?"

"Of course," he said. "That's Autolycus, the prince of thieves, the heir of Hermes and possessed of all his father's skills when it comes to the arts of theft and trickery. As well as being Albert Campion's pet jackdaw."

"Strolling the corridors of corporate America with a large jackdaw on one's shoulder is not unobtrusive."

"Don't be silly. He has a helmet to make him invisible. Like I said, his father was Hermes. Not to mention his grandson was Odysseus."

"With all due respect, I don't think it's working."

With a pained expression, Doyle removed the jackdaw. But it quickly became obvious that he needn't have bothered. The workers that hurried along the halls gave him barely a passing glance. Secretaries, brokers, traders, interns, they all had the peculiarly faceless quality of cut-out dolls— just as the corridors were interchangeable, winding back on themselves in a maze of identical, faceless doors. Or as others might have it, a maze of twisty little passages, all alike.

"Doyle," I hissed, "do you remember what happened the last time you got stuck in a maze?"

"Shhhh," he responded, lifting one innocuous finger to his lips. "I am reminded of *The Crime at Black Dudley* and would not repeat *that* unfortunate denouement."

As he spoke, he pushed open a door that was marked "Authorized Personnel Only." In the flickering light of the flashlight that Doyle had manifested out of nowhere, I could see that we were in a warehouse that was lined with tier upon tier of cheap metal shelving, holding bulging cardboard boxes, all of them wrapped in heavy-duty plastic wrap and sealed with clear plastic tape. Out of curiosity, I scanned the typed labels—and found myself more mystified than before. The place was a veritable elephant's graveyard of lost merchandising dreams:

Windows Vista.

Watermelon Oreos.

Evian Water Bra? Okay, I had to look. And wound up more confused than ever. I had never known the necessity of filling your bra with water to prevent "sweaty breastitis." Apparently, it's a thing—or so Evian would have you believe.

The DeLorean.

Singles by Gerber Meals-in-a-Jar. Baby food for adults. The Creamed Beef sounded especially appetizing.

Jimmy Dean Pancakes and Sausage on a Stick.

The Sony Betamax.

The Zune Phone.

Heinz EZ Squirt Purple Ketchup?

Downyflake's Toaster Eggs.

New Coke.

Heublein's Wine and Dinner. Well, now, that sounded right up my alley—at least until I saw the wine was Chablis. Inexcusable, even if it was meant as cooking wine for an EZ-Cook chicken meal.

Lotus.

HP programmable calculators.

The Edsel.

And me, in a file with my name and the date Cam and Paul had arrived at De Sales College to announce the grant for the new tech hub.

Doyle turned to me, his round, bland face a mask of puzzlement. "I'm confused. I thought one was supposed to shelve books. But these all seem to be... companies. Why shelve a company?"

Well, if he was confused, I could only double down on that sentiment. But not because I didn't know what was going in here. "To hamstring the competition to put it out of business," I said.

Doyle blinked at me in bewilderment. "What does that mean?"

"It's a metaphor," I explained. "Companies acquire other companies whose products are superior or otherwise threaten them, not out of any desire to develop that product, but in order to remove it from the market."

"Understood and noted. I've put a flag in my data tables," Doyle said. "But would you mind explaining what you did to offend?"

"That," I said grimly, "is what we're here to find out."

It cost me only a moment's hesitation before I pulled down my file. In for a penny, in for a pound—especially when you were dealing with financial software. Immediately, the shelf behind me slid away, revealing a stone staircase.

"I thought secret passages were against the rules!" Doyle yelped.

"They are," I said. "But apparently, I'm not the one making the rules here—despite my presence on that shelf. So shall we?"

We edged to the top of the stairs and found ourselves looking at an empty hall, filled with numbered circular pens lined with desks on the inside and mechanical tickers above empty chairs on the outside. The desks were all fitted with black phones and a spooling stock ticker. A couple of forgotten fedoras hung from the hat rack that lined the top of the pen. During the day, it looked like it would bustle with the shouts of traders and the noise of runners, but now the only motion came from a masked figure who was smashing open the desk drawers with a crowbar, uncaring of the mess they made. He flipped open ledger after ledger, only to throw them away in disgust.

"Let me guess. The trading floor of the Billings Group?" I asked.

One of the phones rang, then another. A ticker moaned and heaved, then spooled out an inch of tape. The thief's search grew more frantic. He grabbed the nearest teletype and yanked out the ticker tape before it began to print.

But the clatter of the teletype was drowned out by footsteps ringing across the marble floor. A shadow loomed; a camera flashed. "Looking for this?" the shadow asked, as it threw a suspiciously familiar pile of books into the center of the bullpen. "There it is. The Holy Grail you are battering these helpless file cabinets to find. Nothing short of the complete map of the connections. The true warp and weft that underlies the surface of human affairs. Right there at your fingertips, cross-referenced and indexed."

"*You!*" The thief hissed. "This was all your doing."

"Not exactly. If it were, you have my word neither of us would find ourselves in our current situation."

"What situation? You can't touch me," the thief snapped. "We're protected. Too big to fail."

"If you believe that fairy tale, you're a bigger fool than I took you for. Operation Dragon's Den is protected. Operation Dragon's Den is too big to fail. But no one man is too big for anything, especially any man that they can conveniently use as a scapegoat. Especially when that man is the one who wove this entire web of illusion in the first place." Another flash of the camera, and the shadow was suddenly inside the bullpen. "Which is why I rather resent being set up as the criminal mastermind responsible for this network of lies. I may well belong in jail. Hell, I *do* belong in jail. But I'll be damned if I go to jail for another man's crimes."

"I assume it's obvious that I take a different point of view."

"Assume whatever you want. Fortunately for you, I'm not here to debate philosophy. As I said, I'm here to give you what you want—no matter how much it disgusts me. I've promised your controllers the head of Hydra in exchange for your freedom. I'm here to deliver it on the proverbial silver platter. But not to them. To you."

"Why?"

"I owe the White Hats no loyalty. Those bastards will double-cross me as surely as they have double-crossed you. So the enemy of my enemy and all that. You and I are allied on the side of the fallen angels here—and with any luck we can both walk away from this mess with our skins, if not our honor, intact. Of course, as you may have suspected, I do have a few conditions."

"And they are?"

"First, is that you leave Dr. Watson out of this. You cannot conceive how sincerely I regret the loss of that poor intern. I will not allow you to find another woman's skirts to hide behind."

"You don't even know what the word 'sincere' means."

"Oh, I'm quite sincere," the shadow assured him. "I'm just not authentic. Lionel Trilling was quite detailed about the difference between the two. Even the Prince of Lies can mean what he says, even if he doesn't say what he means."

"Don't flatter yourself," the thief snorted. "You don't belong in Hell. You belong in jail."

"Stipulated. But not for the crimes you're trying to pin on me. And most certainly not for pushing a drunk 20-year-old off the cliffs of Battlefield Bluff."

"Roxie Keyes killed herself! We made her a more than generous offer, but she wouldn't back down."

"And so, you took care of her. Just like you planned to take care of me. Unfortunately for the powers that be, I'm made of sterner stuff than a college intern with dreams of being Brenda Starr. Fortunately for you, I'm not a man who holds a grudge, especially when it gets in the way of a solution satisfactory to all parties—although I confess I might find myself a bit more punitive if I were dealing with your one-time colleague. Which leads me to my second condition. I need a week. A week to disappear for good. And after that week is up, you will head down to Washington and lay our collective crimes at the feet of our hidden masters."

"And how would you suggest I do that?" the thief snapped.

"What do I care? I've done my part. I'm giving you all the evidence you need—as well as fair warning. You have a week to figure out how to clean this up with Washington. Which, I might be petty enough to point out, is more than you gave me."

The shadow reached for the old-fashioned reel-to-reel tape recorder on the top of the file cabinets and plucked off the reel that was slowly spinning. "And if you haven't cleared up this mess in a week's time, all of these privately-recorded conversations will become a matter of very public record."

"That's extortion!"

"Which, I assume, is why you recorded them in the first place." As the shadow greyed out of existence, it swept its hand across the ticker tapes, which rose into a cloud of files that spun forward like newspaper headlines:

Morgansburg Historical Society Archives.

De Sales College Fundraiser.

Keyes Memorial Scholarship.

Morgansburg Rod and Gun Annual 3-D Turkey Shoot.

Artisanal Diner and Farm-to-Table Initiative.

No sooner had each name appeared than it shimmered and dissolved into packets of translucent one-hundred-dollar bills. I sighed. "And here I thought 'grey money' was just a term."

"I would have found it first, but you're so very adamant about the issue of secret passages," Doyle said.

"Well, false fronts on books aren't exactly a secret passage, but maybe we should save the niceties of that distinction for another time." I flipped off the monitor in a rare fury. I could take the Historical Society. I could take De Sales. I could even take the Rod and Gun Club whiling away Thanksgiving by shooting at cardboard pop-ups. But the *diner*? Did the Billings Foundation really think I was as simple as those hipster vegans with their artisanal vegetables and kundalini teas and woke brunches?

"Doyle," I said. "I apologize if I seemed to dismiss your new functionality. If you have room in your schedule, I would like to interview a few more eyewitnesses at your earliest possible convenience."

CHAPTER EIGHTEEN
The Riddle of the Red Bikini

I didn't waste time wondering when informing Byrne had become my new way of kicking things upstairs. All I knew was that I wanted him in on the rest of this—if only to have a credible witness to reassure me I wasn't losing my mind. But his expression when I explained to him what Doyle was about to do made me wonder whether he was seriously considering the second alternative.

"You want to issue a call for witnesses among the finish-line photos?" he asked. "The photos themselves, not the people in them?"

"The people in the photographs have already given their statements to the police," I said. "None of them claim to have seen anything. And that may well be true—although it's of course equally possible that one or more of them is lying. In either case, the pictures might have caught something that the people missed—unintentionally or otherwise."

"Reasonable enough," Byrne allowed. "What kind of search parameters are you planning to use?"

Here came the tricky part. "I was going to start by asking whether anyone had noticed a one-armed dragon assassin dragging Cam Billings beneath the surface" didn't seem like the best way to convince him this was serious cyber-science.

"Might be easier if I just show you," I hedged.

I positioned my phone in front of the first picture that came up on my monitor: A group photo posed on the edge of the lake, with Cam Billings front and center, his tiny swimsuit conspicuous among the dark wetsuits. "If there is anyone here who has any leads on who is responsible for Cam Billings' disappearance—no matter how improbable or how insignificant, would you please come forward," Doyle's voice rang from the race steward's loudspeaker.

A gun cracked. The assembled swimmers dove into the water, leaving a churning flurry of foam that quickly dissipated. As their wake settled, something roiled beneath the surface, and a man in a tweed jacket arose from the depths of the lake, smoking a pipe that was completely dry, although the red bikini he held was dripping. "I really must protest," John Dickson Carr said. "The man filched my idea wholesale! A red swimsuit, for God's sake. Couldn't he at least have bothered to make it purple? And he didn't so much as think about the watch, which was really the clue to the whole trick—not the swimsuit."

I shut my eyes, as I swiped away the image. "I'll be the first to say that wasn't exactly what I was looking for."

"On the contrary," Doyle said. "I think our friend Mr. Carr—or at least his alter ego, Carter Dickson—has gone out of his way to show us the error of our ways. And I, for one, must confess myself embarrassed. To think I could have fallen for such a patent red herring as the man in the deep-sea diving suit, while entirely failing to grasp the significance of the red swimsuit."

"Which is?" Byrne asked—sounding more than a little shell-shocked.

Red swimsuit. Red herring. Of course! Why hadn't I seen this sooner? "That we're looking at this backwards," I answered him before Doyle could. "The red swimsuit was nothing but a red herring. We keep saying we never saw Cam Billings emerge from the water, when what we really mean is we never saw a man in a red bikini emerge from the swim. In fact, the timer chips confirm that Cam Billings *did* finish the swim. If he had been wearing a wetsuit just like everyone else was, we never would have noticed him. We were all too busy looking for the red bikini."

"But he wasn't wearing a wetsuit…" Byrne broke off as the penny dropped. "…*when he dove into the water.*

"All he'd have to do is stash a wetsuit somewhere along the course and pull it on," he went on with a nod. "No-one would question him even if he had to come back to shore to do it. They'd just assume he'd finally showed some common sense and decided to sacrifice the time to avoid hypothermia."

"You have to figure that's why he was wearing the red bikini in the first place. He wanted it to be noticed. He was all but waving it in people's faces." Along with certain other body parts that best remained unnamed.

"But that means Cam Billings was in on his own disappearance," Byrne said.

"It's the only way I can see it happening. He made sure everyone noticed as he dove into the water, then somewhere along the way, pulled on a wetsuit, and conveniently seemed to disappear during the swim."

"Not precisely the same strategy employed in our friend Carter Dickson's *A Graveyard to Let*," Doyle opined. "But a fitting homage to the master."

Byrne seemed as intent on ignoring Doyle as I was. "But Cam Billings is dead. It seems logical to assume that he didn't collude in that."

"In the book, those are two different events," Doyle said. "A man stages his own disappearance for one set of reasons, then winds up in a graveyard for an entirely different reason."

"So, let's focus on the disappearance, which we know something about," I said. "Why would Cam Billings want to disappear?"

"The simplest answer is because he knew his company was in financial trouble and wanted to flee the country before it became public," Byrne said. "But if he decided to flee the country, why didn't he just go ahead and do it instead of hanging around to get himself murdered?"

"It does seem a little careless on his part to put in all that planning on his disappearance and then have to run around Morgansburg transferring funds offshore while he was still in his wetsuit," Doyle opined.

"But he wasn't transferring funds. He wasn't taking stock out of his company at all," I said. "The point of all the transactions that seem to be originating in Morgansburg was to shore up the company *after* the stock tanked."

"Arguably even worse planning on his part," Doyle mused.

"Unless the whole point of his disappearing was to force the stock to tank," I said. "Which it did quite effectively. It went so far that they almost stopped trading."

"Why would he want to tank his own stock?" Byrne asked.

"There's only one reason I can think of for anyone to tank a stock and that is so they can buy it up cheap. But usually that's done by a corporate raider, not by the corporation itself."

"I suppose there might be a way to use it to siphon off funds," Byrne said. "But I'm damned if I'm seeing how."

Nor could I. "Why don't we just leave it that Cam Billings staged his own disappearance, possibly to manipulate his own company's stock prices, and move on to the question of who killed Cam Billings and why? Because I for one am not buying Paul's suicide theory even without the question of who might have fired the mystery gun and put Cam in the hip bath."

"Fair enough. Do you have a theory?"

I drew a deep breath. Negotiating this next bit seemed even trickier than looking for eyewitnesses to the one-armed dragon assassin. "I came across a story in the *Morgansburg Times* that suggests Cam might have ties to some so-called deep state conspiracy. If that's true, it might be the motive behind Cam's death."

Byrne's mouth quirked. "The *Morgansburg Times*, huh? You mean the people who are still hounding the Town Council for their secret files on Battlefield Amy?"

"I don't know about that. But I do know that the story did start with Battlefield Amy," I said. "It began life as an expose about the government's hidden cryptid files. But somewhere along the way, the reporter, an intern named Roxie Keyes, seems to have turned up a real government conspiracy called Operation Dragon's Den. And she may well have been killed for her pains."

Byrne paled, and his jaw set. When he finally spoke, he ground out the words as if he'd forgotten to unclench his jaw first. "Operation Dragon's Den? Seriously? Who's running it? The Knights Templar?"

"The odds-on favorite seems to be a legendary operative named William Devlin. And from what I've heard about him, a modern-day Knight Templar isn't far off the mark."

The temperature in the room plummeted. "What do you know about William Devlin?"

Beyond the way he kissed in cyberspace? "Master of disinformation and dirty tricks. Technological genius and ruthless assassin—nothing short of James Bond crossed with Robin Hood."

Byrne snorted. "And where exactly did you read that? Infowars?"

"He told me himself. At least some of it."

Byrne raised an eyebrow. "You've met William Devlin? Face to face?"

"Depends on how you define 'face.' I met the avatar of someone who claimed to be William Devlin in cyberspace," I said. "It obviously could have been anyone. But whoever it was made it pretty clear that he is here in Morgansburg to settle a score with the Billings Group. And while I freely concede the next bit is pure speculation, the *Morgansburg Times* exposé suggests that Devlin's grudge might involve the Billings Group's collaboration with Operation Dragon's Den. Which, at least in my mind gives Devlin a pretty strong motive to kill Cam Billings."

A dyspeptic pause before Byrne asked, "I'm supposed to believe William Devlin told you all of this?"

"Some of it. Not all of it. The rest I…overheard."

Byrne's snort made it clear what his definition of overhearing in cyber-space was.

"At least, I think it was Devlin. But if what I heard is true, he's not really doing this of his own volition. All he really wants to do is disappear once more but bringing down the Billings Group is the only way he can do it. As best I can tell he seems to be in some kind of trouble with Washington. Wouldn't go too far to say he's running from the law—"

"*He* said that?"

My patience snapped. "Like I said, I'm not entirely certain who I might have been talking with—or overhearing.

I'm not even certain whether they're the same people. But before we go any further with this inquisition, I think it's your turn to answer a few questions. What do *you* know about William Devlin?"

Byrne's face set. "I'm afraid that's need-to-know."

"Sure. You can give me the third degree, but it's fine for you to stonewall—even when I'm the one who came to you."

"It's different," Byrne said.

"Not from this angle. Allow me to rephrase. What do you know about some one-armed Black Ops commando who is running a secret money laundering operation out of Morgansburg under cover of the Billings Foundation?"

Byrne's face flattened along with his voice. "If there is such a person in Morgansburg, it's not Will Devlin."

"How can you be so sure?"

He drew a deep breath. "Because Devlin is dead. I was there when he died. In fact, there'd be plenty who'd say I'm the one who killed him."

Well, alrighty then. As the old maps liked to say, Beyond Here Lie Dragons. "Metaphorically speaking, I trust?"

"In my experience, the Army isn't big on literary tropes. Fortunately for me, they weren't big on airing their dirty laundry in public either and when it came to Devlin, there was enough of the latter to fill a bunch of clotheslines. So, the U.S. Army and I parted ways amicably." Byrne met my eyes. "And it would be extremely convenient for me if I could keep it that way. Which is why I'm asking you to please leave Will Devlin out of this. You have my word that he had nothing to do with Cam Billings' death or any dirty tricks the Billings Foundation might be running out of Morgansburg."

CHAPTER NINETEEN
The Trials of Jessica Rabbit

It was an inauspicious beginning to a day that was destined to get worse. Before I had finished my second cup of coffee, Paul Morgan tapped on my office door and announced, "We need to talk."

Which roughly translated as *he* wanted to talk. Me, I'd rather staple my tongue to the roof of my mouth. "If this is about Cam Billings' death, I'm not sure that's wise. You are the county attorney, after all. You probably need to recuse yourself from the case to avoid the appearance of a conflict of interest."

Paul took a moment, then nodded heavily. "That's why we need to talk. I'm afraid I haven't been as frank with you as I could."

Seriously? I could have gotten that far without Doyle's heuristics. "I think if you're going to be frank with anyone, it ought to be the police."

"Unfortunately, it's not that simple. Please hear me out." He cut me off with a wave of his hand. "I made a terrible mistake. And I may be in real trouble here. I'm not going to lie to you about that."

The last was a favorite phrase of students—especially those with missing or plagiarized papers—and one I found particularly annoying. As if telling the truth was a virtue rather than a basic premise of constructive human behavior. But I gestured for him to go on.

"Cam's dead," Paul went on. "There's no point in protecting him any longer. I'll just say it right up front. The Billings Group was in a terrible mess. And Cam decided on the worst possible way to solve it."

"What kind of a mess?" I asked. And why did I know it was going to involve spuriously deaccessioned books, shelved companies, and grey money?

"The Billings Foundation suffered a serious data breach. A hacker managed to change all the Foundation's accounting records, injecting spurious transactions. Damaging transactions. *Very* damaging transactions." Paul paused to make sure I absorbed the enormity of the damage. "At first, we thought it was just a standard ransomware attack, and put the wheels in motion to pay them off. That's when we discovered the hacker was up to something far more nefarious. He had no intention of restoring the damaged data. He wanted nothing less than to bring down the Billings Group by planting evidence to suggest that Cam was using the Foundation to hide all kinds of financial malfeasance."

"Malfeasance? As in…?"

"Money laundering. Bribes. Insider trading. Illegal foreign investments."

My mind went back to that shadowy thief I had witnessed on the Billings Group's trading floor. I could guess who one of the avatars was. But that did nothing to suggest who the second one might have been.

"Cam should have called the police, of course. But he was worried about protecting the company's name and so he called me first. And I made a terrible decision."

"You decided to stage his disappearance so that the stock would tank, and you could step in and buy enough shares to cover the missing funds?"

"Sounds awful when you say it like that. Like investor fraud. Market manipulation."

Well, yes. That's pretty much exactly what it sounded like.

"When really it wasn't anything of the sort. Just a way to protect the company's name while we set matters right quietly. But try convincing a judge and jury of that. I know prosecutors—hell, I am one. And you can take it from me we're a bloodthirsty lot of bastards." Paul shook his head with a rueful grin that set my teeth on edge. "So, I turned a blind eye and allowed Cam to handle things quietly. Morgansburg is a small town after all. What point was there in creating a scandal?"

"In other words, you helped him disappear and then what? Helped him commit suicide in a locked room in front of half a dozen witnesses?" The thought actually gave me a newfound respect for Paul. I would have never thought he had it in him.

"Of course not!" Paul paused before plowing ahead. "My entire involvement with this mess began and ended with the cover-up of the data breach—if you insist on calling it that. You have my word, neither of us was trying to cover anything up. I was just helping him buy a little time so he could put things right with the company's holdings."

His definition of a cover-up was not exactly congruent with mine, but why quibble? "So, who killed Cam and put his body in the hip bath? Not to mention why?"

"I'm not ready to speculate on the who, but the why is pretty obvious," Paul said. "Someone was determined to make sure Cam couldn't clean up this mess quietly.

Someone is bound and determined to make this *meshugash* public."

Meshugash? I knew that Paul considered himself a man of the people—at least according to his campaign ads, which were at constant pains to stress how little he had strayed from his roots. But as far as I knew, his roots were here in Morgansburg, N.Y. not Anatevka.

"But then why kill Cam?" I asked. "That makes no sense. If someone went to all that effort to make sure Cam was prosecuted for financial fraud, why kill him before he could be brought to trial?"

"You tell me," Paul said.

"Is that an accusation?" I asked.

"Of course not! I know you, Mary, and you're not capable of murder."

Then he didn't know jack, because frankly I was more than a little capable of it at that very moment. "But you are wondering whether I'm somehow connected to what happened," I said.

"It's all connected," Doyle assured me.

"That entire scene in the Historical Society suggests someone who was very familiar with arcane methods of murder. And you're the only person I know who has an entire database of them."

"Let me make this as simple as I can," I said through clenched teeth. "I had nothing to do with Cam's death. Yes, I pinpointed the location of his swimsuit, but that's as far as it goes. When it comes to Cam's murder, I have no more idea than you do. Now if there isn't anything else…"

"Please, Mary. Cam is dead."

"I'm more than a little aware of that. I was there when we found his body, remember? What I don't understand is why you're coming to me instead of going to the police with all this. You are the prosecutor after all. I was under the impression you were supposed to be on the same side as the cops."

Paul glanced around, as if he were on alert for listening devices. "Can we shut the door?"

"No."

His hand was already on the knob.

"I'm sorry," I said, not feeling sorry in the least. "These days, academia's no different from the corporate world. Now that the college's Title IX coordinator has proposed that students can file anonymous complaints about harassment to a specially appointed internal panel rather than a court of law, it does seem a wise precaution to take."

"Well, surely you don't think…I mean, of course, I wasn't implying…" He pulled himself together. "All right, cards on the table."

"Is cliché a common rhetorical trope?" Doyle wondered.

"Frankly I'm more than a little certain that Tiggy's pet consultant is behind all this."

So was I. But that begged the rather crucial question. "Why?"

Paul leaned closer, confiding. "What I told you the other day isn't just idle gossip. Tiggy was going to file to revisit her prenup, and trust me, it was going to be a rough ride for everyone involved. She claimed Cam was hiding assets. And maybe she was right. But in today's climate, it wouldn't matter whether she was justified or not. Just the suggestion would ruin Cam—along with every not-for-profit the Billings Foundation supports, including the Historical Society and De Sales College. And I don't want to see that happen. Which is why I attempted to handle things privately. In retrospect, it was obviously a huge mistake."

"What are you suggesting? That Nigel St. Hubbins killed Cam? I suppose it's a theoretical possibility, but I'd have a lot easier time seeing it if Cam had been spammed to death."

"Oh, I'm sure we'll never know who killed Cam," Paul said. "If you ask me, that has the mark of a professional hit."

Maybe, if your average thug had a taste for locked rooms and S.S. Van Dine.

"A man like Cam makes plenty of enemies in his lifetime." He shrugged. "This could be nothing but a coincidence. Completely unrelated."

Seriously? IMHO, asking Doyle to calculate the odds of that would be harsher than sending him to his room to calculate Mersenne primes. "If you say so, but isn't this something you need to be taking up with the Billings Foundation instead of me? Or maybe even Mr. St. Hubbins himself? He strikes me as the kind of guy who might be amenable to being bought off."

Paul leaned closer, passing his hands through his hair, as if to signal to me how difficult he was finding all this. Then he drew a deep breath. "Look, I'm going to cut straight to the chase."

Another one of those despicable non-virtues—and it seemed like I'd heard this from him quite a bit lately—but I nodded. "Please do. Because I've honestly got no idea why you think you need to bring this up with me."

"Okay, I get it. You're cautious, and I don't blame you. So, before we go any further, I'm giving you my word that this conversation is strictly off-the-record. You can tell me anything."

Frankly, I couldn't think of anything better calculated to make me want to whip out a tape recorder.

"I'm already on it," Doyle assured me, reading my mind.

"Tell you anything about what, precisely?" I asked Paul. "How do you think I fit into this?"

Paul took a step backwards, holding up both hands. "Don't worry, I'm not going to ask why Cam offered you that grant. When it comes to my legal work for these boards, I'm just the guy who makes sure the I's are dotted and the T's are crossed, nothing more. But I think you know by now that this St. Hubbins creature will stop at nothing to get Tiggy what she wants. And I would not like to see him go public with some irresponsible speculation about the real reasons Cam approached you."

"The *real* reasons?" My temper flared when the improbable penny finally dropped. "And exactly what kind of irresponsible speculation are you suggesting? That Cam Billings funded Doyle because I was sleeping with him?"

More than a moment's uncomfortable pause before Paul spread his hands. "Listen, I loved Cam, loved him like a brother. Hell, he was my biggest campaign backer. The man believed in me when no-one else would, and he didn't stint about putting his money where his mouth was."

More likely Cam believed Paul was a bargain at the price. Right about now, in whatever afterlife he was enjoying, I'll bet he was wishing he'd kicked the tires a little more carefully.

"But Cam Billings is—oh, God, I mean *was*—a man, and I'd be the last one to be blind to his faults. In fact, I don't mind saying, I shared quite a few of them in my time." Paul grinned rakishly, then caught sight of my expression and sobered. "Of course, no-one seriously believes that's the case. But you've got to believe me when I tell you Tiggy will stop at nothing. Love makes fools of all men, but poor Cam had no idea the real woman he was marrying was a grasping witch."

"I'm Wiccan, you know," I said.

A moment's puzzled silence, before Paul forced a laugh. "Hey, I get the point. I'm all for freedom of religion too. And I'm damned proud of my record on the issue. I've got awards from the Anti-Defamation League, the CAIR, and the National Council of Christians and Jews."

I was used to this reaction, which is why for the most part I kept my religious practices to myself. Not because I was ashamed, but because for some reason people always seemed to read metaphorical or ironic meaning in a perfectly straightforward declarative sentence.

"No, seriously. I'm Wiccan. And I find your using the term 'witch' in this context more than a little offensive."

Paul blinked at me as if an adorable kitten had proved to be a rabid ocelot. "Okay, okay. Let's not get lost in the weeds here. The fact of the matter is, sometimes when someone sets off a smoke bomb, that doesn't mean there isn't a fire burning somewhere else."

It took me several twists of that Rubik's Cube, before the metaphor finally fell into place. "You're saying there were real payoffs in addition to the faked ones," I said.

"Cam was no saint, for sure. But he refused to take my advice. I told him the best thing to do is ignore the rumors and hold your head high. Instead, he made the mistake of allowing a few unscrupulous people discover how easy it was to make a tidy profit off his weaknesses."

"Payoffs. He was attempting to avoid bad publicity because of bad behavior."

"The team preferred to call them settlements. Or non-disclosure agreements." Paul shook his head. "I warned him and warned him that once he started down that path, there would be no turning back. But Cam wouldn't listen. Said he had this kind of thing under control. Well, look how that worked out."

Which I'm sure meant something—even if I lacked the mental energy to figure out what that might be. "If you have an accusation to make, I think you'd better just do it," I said. "Do you seriously believe I was extorting the Billings Foundation? Because if you are, I'm forced to point out that it was you who approached me."

"No, no, no. This was never about you," Paul assured me. "Hey, face it. Men are swine. That much is a fact of life. And you have my word no one's looking to blame you. You're a tool, nothing more."

"A tool?" I repeated. "Whose tool? Cam Billings' or Nigel St. Hubbins'? Or maybe you want to offer me odds on Devlin and the master hacker while you're at it?"

"Look as far as I'm concerned, what's past is past between us," Paul held up both hands to emphasize the point. "You've got to put it behind you, Mary. You've got to put *us* behind you. If you can't, you have my word St. Hubbins won't hesitate to set you up as his stalking horse— if he hasn't already."

I shut my eyes against the headache that suddenly swelled as out of control as my voice—which was rapidly reaching fishwife proportions. "Trust me, I am nobody's stalking horse, I long ago put *us* behind me, and I have no more interest in St. Hubbins' schemes than I have in yours."

"The two cases are hardly the same. You're the one who discovered those spurious books, so you're the one who set this whole thing in motion. Now it's time to follow through. We need you to draw St. Hubbins out into the daylight and force him to answer to his crimes. Just do the voodoo that you do so well."

This time, I didn't even bother to attempt to guide Paul toward a more enlightened view of my personal spiritual path. "I have absolutely no idea what you think I can do."

"I'll leave that entirely up to you. I'm the last to interfere with the experts. I'm just here to tell you the Billings Foundation needs you. You're the only one with technical chops to pull this off. It's time for you to step up. You owe it to Cam's memory—not to mention to the Billings Foundation itself."

I drew a deep breath. This was worse than I could imagine. Hell, no, this was worse than anything *Doyle* could imagine. "You want me to help you entrap St. Hubbins?"

"'Entrap' is a strong word. There will be no question of dirty tricks. Trust me, I will make sure we do nothing illegal at all."

More likely he'd make sure *he'd* do nothing illegal at all. Me, I was certain he'd be happy to hang out to dry.

"All I need from you is to get his hand in the honey pot. Just a few hints on social media that Cam was paying you off for an indiscretion by buying out Doyle, and we'll take it from there. Swear out warrants to turn up every rock in the place," Paul went on. "Trust me, we're going to find plenty of maggots beneath. And we know how to deal with maggots. All we need you to do is get our foot in the door, and all the rest of the dominos will fall."

Was it just me, or did that plan make Wile E. Coyote look like a minimalist? "Just like Al Capone, huh? Unwanted touching is the new income tax evasion?"

"I'm not a man to get hung up on the details," Paul assured me. "All I need to know is that we're in this together. Mary, you've got to trust me. We're on the side of the angels here."

"Lucifer was an angel." I shook my head. "Look, if you've got an accusation to make against anyone—myself included—I'd suggest you take it to a judge and get a warrant to act on it. I've been told that's how the system is meant to work, but maybe you learned something different in law school."

Paul studied me another moment, before he conceded, "I'm the last to minimize what this kind of operation costs a woman emotionally. Trust me, I wouldn't ask you if I could see another way. Just considering the possibility of you consorting with him gives me nightmares."

I raised an eyebrow. "Define 'consorting.'"

"Let's not quibble over language."

"I'm afraid I have to. Because honestly, I'm getting more than a little confused. Just a few minutes ago, you were accusing me of 'consorting' with Cam Billings. Now, you want to send me out to 'consort' with Nigel St. Hubbins. Or maybe our mysterious Mr. Devlin. I'm still unclear on that issue. For God's sake, *why?*"

I cut myself off before he could say anything. "Okay, please don't answer that. Instead, I'll just say, strictly for the record that I have never consorted with Cam Billings or anyone else from the Billings Foundation. And I have no intention of starting now. Nor do I have any intention of consorting—or colluding—with you. Now, if you would please excuse me."

"Mary, the first thing you have to know is you're not alone here." Paul's voice got soft. Sympathetic. It was the same tone he once used when he was explaining how highly he respected a woman's virginity, but that going to third base was not the same thing. "It's obvious Nigel St. Hubbins will stop at nothing short of actual violence, and I can understand why you're afraid to take him on—especially if you have any lingering doubts about what happened between you and Cam. But you've got me on your side now. And I will not let you down. As far as I'm concerned, you're as much of a victim as the others…"

"I am nobody's victim! And nothing happened between me and Cam," I spat. "What I am is competent enough to be hired on my own abilities. And anything else you care to insinuate is insulting—if not downright slanderous. Now, if there is nothing else, I have actual work to do."

His face spasmed with the same belligerence as it had when I had lied that it wasn't him, it was me, and he deserved a lot better in a relationship. But then he self-consciously calmed himself—for he prided himself on being a woke male. "Look, I'm not going to push you. This is obviously something you have to decide for yourself. But you need to know that I understand women can't lie about these kinds of things. And I am willing to stake my professional reputation on that belief."

"Then you're daft or delusional," I said. "Everyone lies. And if you haven't figured that much out after twenty years in criminal law, I suggest you try teaching college for a year."

"You're upset. And I don't blame you. You need time to think it over."

Which I would say is about as masculinist a dismissal as it gets. "And when you make up your mind, you give me a call. I'll pick up, any time of the day or night. And Mary…" He laid a hand on my arm. "Don't ever forget. I am your friend."

Instead of answering him, I gazed expressively down at the new income tax evasion until he finally got the point, removed his hand, and left.

"Asshole," I snarled, as soon as he was gone. "And that much is for the record."

As if in answer, my phone began to pulse. I picked it up to find a selfie of Paul and me. At least, I assumed that was what it was meant to be, even though Paul had some-how acquired a distinctly unflattering resemblance to Bob

Hoskins, while my hair seemed to have been magically marcel-curled to swoop down over one eye, and my customary black jeans and turtleneck had been transformed into a bright-red sheath that left nothing to the imagination. But the words we spoke were exactly as I remembered them.

"Look, you're as much of a victim as the others…"

"I am nobody's victim!"

"You really did record this?" I said to Doyle.

Doyle flickered to life. "In this world, there's no such thing as off the record. Trust me, I have plenty good reason to know."

He was right of course, but there was plenty about that last part I didn't want to know. I changed the subject before he could offer details.

"Doyle," I said. "Why do I look like Jessica Rabbit?"

"It's not Jessica, it's Lauren Bacall," he said. "You should be flattered. Here's looking at you, kid."

I shook my head. "No one said that to Bacall. That was Ingrid…"

"Who's Ingrid?"

I shut my eyes and gave up. "My sister *and* my daughter," I sighed, before I switched him off for good.

CHAPTER TWENTY
The Problem of the Missing Maul

The day was not done with me. Scarcely an hour later, Doyle's voice tickled my earbud. "Apologies for the interruption, but I have received urgent news from a friend who works at the county coroner's office. In the coroner's about-to-be-released report, they have indicated that Cam Billings was not killed by a shot fired from a historic pistol. In fact, he was not killed by a gunshot at all. He was killed by a sudden—and quite possibly accidental—blow to the head. In other words, our smoking gun was in fact nothing but a red herring."

I resisted the urge to put my head between my knees. "Another red herring? As if a red bikini and an antique hip bath weren't enough? *Why*? Does the ghost of S.S. Van Dine now stalk Morgansburg?"

"It is a capital mistake to theorize before one has data. Insensibly one begins to twist facts to suit theories, instead of theories to suit facts," Doyle informed me.

"How about we save the Sherlock for when we actually have some facts beyond phosphorescent footprints and a man in a red bikini?"

"Will this do?" Doyle asked. My screen shifted to grainy surveillance video of the alley between the Historical

Society and the Town Hall. A man's body lay collapsed in a pool of blood. And an unmistakable one-armed shadow loomed over him.

"Who do we have to thank for that? Another lady friend on the party line?" I asked.

"I trust that was a rhetorical question," Doyle said.

I conceded the point, for I was suddenly consumed with a new idea. "Yes, it was. But this one isn't. Do you remember Byrne saying that he killed Devlin?"

"Technically, I believe he said that many people would argue he had killed Devlin," Doyle said.

"So stipulated. But leaving the semantics aside for the moment, do you think it's possible Devlin survived whatever it was Byrne did, and has returned to Morgansburg to wreak his savage revenge?"

"An intriguing theory, somewhat diminished by the fact that it was Cam Billings who was killed, not Byrne. Quite a mistake for a vengeful super-operative to make."

"What if Cam Billings was only the first? Or maybe the data breach at the Billings Foundation was—along with God alone knows how many other dirty tricks. All of them nothing but steps on the way to getting the man he's really after. Byrne. Supposing Byrne is Devlin's real target, and he's picking the others off one by one, saving Byrne for last, because he wants Byrne to suffer. And Byrne knows it. If nothing else, it would go a long way to explaining why he's so jumpy. Not to mention the elaborate scenario in the hip bath. Devlin isn't trying to cover up anything. He wants Byrne to know he's coming."

"A suggestive, and may I say, far from impossible hypothesis," Doyle allowed. "But why waste time in idle speculation, when the opportunity for first-hand verification is only moments away."

I gazed around the Historical Society. With Cam's body and the yellow crime scene tape both discreetly removed and Byrne's damage to the door covered with a sheet of plywood, the hall had returned to its customary dusty irrelevance. So much for first-hand verification.

"A locked room," I sighed. "Who the hell really breaks into a locked room?"

"An Ourang-Outang," Doyle said.

"*The Murders in the Rue Morgue* is the least satisfying murder mystery ever written—although informed opinion differs on whether that's because Poe was in the throes of a bender or a hangover. And, for the record, we spell it orangutan these days. In any case, it was a rhetorical question."

"Ah, but is it not true that any detective knows the most important truths are concealed beneath the veneer of figurative language," Doyle countered. "In support, may I refer you to Chapter Seventeen of John Dickson Carr's *The Three Coffins,* where his great detective, Dr. Gideon Fell posits, *we're in a detective story, and we don't fool the reader by pretending we're not. Let's not invent elaborate excuses to drag in a discussion of detective stories. Let's candidly glory in the noblest pursuits possible to characters in a book.*"

"Yes, but we are not in a detective story," I said. "We are playing detective. Not particularly usefully, I might add."

"Noted," Doyle said. "Any other bugs to report?"

Bugs? "Doyle, this is not a QA run…" But wait! Why shouldn't it be? "Okay, change of plan. What do you say we treat this as a Beta test—or if you prefer, a teachable moment. We're presented with a classic locked room puzzle. How do we go about solving it? Let's start with the basics. How many ways are there to make someone disappear from a locked room?"

"According to Dr. Gideon Fell's lecture, there are seven. He begins with *the possibility it is not murder, but rather a series of coincidences ending in an accident that looks like murder.* The next possibility is, *it is murder, but the victim is impelled to kill himself or crash into an accidental death.*"

"That doesn't seem very likely," I objected.

"That depends. Did anyone find a playing card in there?"

"Why? You think Cam had a gambling problem?"

"Well, he wouldn't very likely be using it for target practice, would he?"

Again with the sarcasm. "You can't threaten someone with a playing card."

"Of course, you can." With a sigh, Doyle condescended to explain, "I was talking about brainwashing. Mind control. A signal that triggers a post-hypnotic suggestion. In *The Manchurian Candidate*, it was the Queen of Diamonds."

"There was no playing card. What other ways are there?"

"Mirrors?"

"No."

"Chimney?"

"No fireplace."

"Secret passageway?"

"That's considered cheating."

"If you say so. Supernatural agency completely ruled out?"

"Completely."

"Then, to continue with Dr. Fell's cogent summary, number three is *it is murder, by a mechanical device already planted in the room, and hidden undetectably in some innocent-*

looking piece of furniture. Number 4: *It is suicide, which is intended to look like murder…"*

"That's getting closer—at least if we take Paul's word for it. Cam Billings was about to lose everything, and when he discovered he could no longer fix things, he took the easy way out. But that made a lot more sense when we thought Cam had died of a gunshot wound. What kind of person commits suicide by pounding their own head with a blunt instrument? Not to mention Number 4 does nothing to explain how Cam wound up locked inside the Historical Society. Does Dr. Fell have any opinions about that?"

"Four," Doyle said promptly. "*1. Tampering with the key which is still in the lock. 2. Simply removing the hinges of the door without disturbing lock or bolt. 3. Tampering with the bolt. 4. Tampering with a falling bar or latch. This usually consists in propping something under the latch, which can be pulled away after the door is closed from the outside, and let the bar drop. The best method by far is by the use of the ever-helpful ice, a cube of which is propped under the latch; and, when it melts the latch falls…"*

"Or," I said in sudden inspiration as I caught sight of the old fashioned bell on the wall next to the door, "propping the bar against an ancient burglar alarm that rattles it loose?"

"Elementary."

"I didn't hear you pointing it out."

"I was leaving it as an exercise for the reader."

"Sure," I snorted. "Well, then what do you say you take on the next part? How did they set off the alarm?"

"Did you check the bell for bullet holes?" Doyle asked.

"Why should I…Wait! You can't mean someone fired that antique gun in order to set the alarm off? But *how?* We all heard…" Before Doyle could answer, my mind went back to Dr. Fell's lecture. "Unless…please, dear God no, someone somehow doctored the trigger using an ice cube, so that the gun fired when it melted… Christ, you'd have to be a technical wizard to do that."

"By all accounts, our friend Devlin was just that," Doyle said. "But the hypothesis is simple enough to test."

Maybe in theory, but to a woman whose entire existence is an ongoing war with the material world, it was close to a challenge. Nonetheless, with Doyle's encouragement, I managed to prop the oak bar that had held off the Hessians against the alarm bell. When I set off the alarm, the bell rattled wildly, and the bar fell with a satisfying thud. I left it at that. Sharpshooting with melting ice cubes was beyond my pay grade.

That decision may well have saved Byrne's life. The only target I had managed to hit during archery in summer camp was the games counselor—and before you ask, she was standing *behind* me. I had barely managed to silence the jangling alarm before Byrne was in the room, white-faced and wild-eyed, hands reaching for an invisible sidearm. When he finally calmed down enough to recognize me, he drew an unsteady breath. "Nancy Drew. I should have known. What are you playing at now?"

"I've figured out how the bolt was thrown."

A reproachful cough from my earbud.

"Er…*Doyle* and I have figured it out. Someone McGyvered the fire alarm to drop the bolt."

Byrne eyed me for a wary minute, before he snorted, "MacGyvered. Is that a real word now?"

"It's in the Oxford Dictionary," I told him.

"Is that so?" Byrne asked. "Well, does that dictionary have any more specific suggestions about exactly how someone did that and then disappeared entirely?"

"They doctored the gun's trigger with an ice cube—I'm still not exactly sure about the details there. Maybe they tied a weight to a string that was wrapped around the trigger, then set it on ice cube so it would fall when the ice melted. You were first on the scene. Do you remember seeing any moisture on the floor?"

"Can't say that I do." Byrne raised an eyebrow. "In any case, Cam Billings wasn't killed by a gunshot. He was killed by blunt force trauma. The autopsy report made that clear."

"The gun was only fired to set off the alarm. It was never meant to be considered the cause of death. Over-elaborate if you ask me, but so was vanishing mid-swim in order to buy time to cover up an incriminating data breach at the Billings Foundation. By the way, Paul informed me that *was* the reason for that stunt. But he also told me that someone else entirely rigged the whole locked room, and I believe him. Paul doesn't suffer from that much imagination."

Another incredulous glance from Byrne. "*Paul* told you this?"

"Paul wouldn't be the first male to underestimate me."

To his credit, the tips of Byrne's ears turned bright pink. "And so you packed up your trusty bot and came here to recreate the crime?"

"I originally came here to look for the actual murder weapon. Afraid I got a little sidetracked by the ice cubes."

"Sidetracked," Byrne snorted. Folding his arms, he glanced around, then came to a decision. "So what do you say we get down to it? Any theories where we can find the weapon?"

I pointed to the display of antique farm implements grouped around an historic butter churn that still bore the bullet scars earned in its service as a barricade against the Redcoats. "If Cam Billings' killer had to set up the entire hip bath scenario, they didn't have much time to hide the real weapon, so I'm wondering if maybe it's still here, among all the farm implements."

"'The Purloined Letter,'" Doyle murmured. "Hidden in plain sight."

With a shrug, Byrne went over to the display and pulled down an artifact that looked like the sick love-child of a comb and a call slip box. "Farm equipment can be dangerous," he mused. "Farmer in Nebraska stepped straight into a grain auger. Had to amputate his own leg with a pocket knife to save his own life."

He sounded more than a little admiring.

"Well, I think we can eliminate a few," I said. "Beginning with the cranberry scoop you're holding. And I'm equally willing to exonerate the corn dryer. Jury's still out on the hog scraper, if you ask me. It looks like it might have lethal possibilities."

"What about a splitting maul?" Doyle opined.

"What about it?" I asked unwisely.

"Ratcliffe Highway murders, 1811," Doyle responded with a promptness that suggested he had been pre-gaming—data style. "And if you want to expand your definition to include mattocks, there was the murder of the Gruber family at Hinterkaifeck Ranch in 1922."

"That's true crime," I pointed out.

"So is this," Doyle said.

He had a point. "All right. The question remains: Where is *whatever* was used to kill Cam Billings? Murder weapons can't simply disappear."

"They do if it's a frozen leg of lamb," Doyle countered. "You just cook it and serve it to the investigating officers."

"For the moment, can we please just leave the livestock in the deep freezer where it belongs?"

Once more, I was subject to the unpleasant scrutiny of Mack Byrne.

"It's a story," I said.

"'Lamb to the Slaughter,' by Roald Dahl," Doyle supplied, ever helpful. "1953. Made into an episode of *Alfred Hitchcock Presents* in 1958, starring Barbara Bel Geddes. One of only 17 episodes Hitchcock directed himself. It is said that the basic plot was suggested to Dahl by his friend, Ian Fleming."

"I was searching my databases for possible corollaries," I added.

"And you found a frozen leg of lamb," Byrne said.

"Well, I think a leg of lamb—frozen or otherwise— would be pretty obvious," I said. "So, I think we might want to focus our attention on some other possibilities."

"I could appeal for the weapon to turn itself in," Doyle mused. "But I think it might be less than forthcoming. There are laws against self-incrimination, after all."

I ignored him. "Not that I think finding the weapon will explain why someone tampered with the crime scene in such an outlandish way. I mean, dispose of the weapon, sure, but why a scenario that could have been lifted straight out of Agatha Christie?"

"I thought you said it was S.S. Van Dine," Doyle objected.

"I suppose I should have said John Dickson Carr. Our murderer seems to have an entire reference library of approaches."

"Just like your Little Friend?" Byrne asked.

"Maybe, but that theory isn't going to hold a lot of water until you can demonstrate how he whacked Cam Billings over the head with a maul or any other blunt instrument of his choosing. You have my word he's not much good for wet work. So why don't we go back to the question of who tampered with the scene and why?"

"As I have suggested before, you have only to consider the need for the hip bath and the regimental banner," Doyle offered his unsolicited opinion.

Byrne's eyes narrowed. "You have any theories in that respect?"

"I think whoever moved Cam Billings' body did it so people would notice. It's the only reason someone would go to that much effort. And given what the *Morgansburg Times* wrote about Operation Dragon's Den, I think it's fair to assume that Cam Billings was killed because someone blames him for exposing that operation—or maybe even for William Devlin's death." I met Byrne's eyes. "And I'm beginning to wonder whether the killer may just be getting started. What if the whole thing, the bikini, the hip bath, the locked door, was nothing more than a warning shot for whoever he was gunning for next?"

Byrne nodded, turning my ideas over in his mind like he was kicking the tires on a used pickup truck, before he squared his shoulders and came to decision.

"Cute theory, Nancy Drew," he said. "Except for one little problem. A Dragon's Den operative didn't move the body. I did."

I held his gaze. "You're Devlin?"

"I didn't say that, now did I? I just said I was the one who moved the body."

I drew another deep breath. Did my best to match his impassivity, as I asked, "So what are you going to do now? Cosh me over the head and bury me beneath the heritage roses?"

I wasn't used to seeing emotion twist Byrne's face, but right now, it was unmistakable. The man actually looked insulted. Hurt even. But all he said was, "For God's sake, get ahold of yourself. I didn't say I killed the man. I just said I moved the body."

I relaxed. Marginally. "And why would you do a thing like that, unless you killed him?"

Once more, I was treated to the unlovely sight of Byrne wrestling with himself. It was like watching the Incredible Hulk go one on one with Optimus Prime. "I caught another alarm at the Town Hall. When I got there, I found Cam dead in the alleyway that separates it from the Historical Society. One of Mike Malone's guns lay on the ground beside him, covered in blood. The gun hadn't been fired, but someone had hit Cam over the head with its butt."

"So you moved Cam's body to cover up for Mike Malone?" I asked uncertainly.

"Don't get me wrong. If Mike Malone is really guilty, I'll slap the cuffs on him myself." Byrne's eyes grew distant. "But Mike saved my life once. Seems the least I could do was get him a fair shake when it comes to a murder charge."

"I don't disagree. But there's more than a fine line between a fair shake and…" I waved my hand at the set-up. "… MacGyver. I mean, okay, I can see what it means to owe a man your life…"

"I sincerely doubt it. But can we please not get carried away? All I was trying to do was make sure Paul didn't sweep the whole thing under the rug by blaming Mike for killing Cam—which you have to admit would have been mighty convenient all around. There was only one way I knew I could make that happen, and that was to make sure that I was one of the people investigating."

"Much as it pains me to admit it, the plodding inspector has a point," Doyle murmured. "Not to mention a remarkable gallant streak beneath that crusty exterior. None-theless, I am forced to point out his rather extraordinary theatricality when it came to hiding the evidence."

Byrne's eyes narrowed. "Your Little Friend offering an opinion there?"

"My Little Friend is always offering an opinion," I sighed, "but they're usually not germane."

"What do you say you let me be the judge of that," Byrne countered. "After all, I've shown you mine. It only seems fair you show me yours."

I recoiled against a mental vision that could not be unseen. "I think what he's asking is why all the rigmarole with the hip bath and regimental shroud?"

Byrne shrugged. "The hip bath has wheels. Dead bodies are hard to move. And I'm not a 20-year-old running back who can return a punt 98 yards downfield with a Navy midshipman clinging to my back anymore."

"Were you really…?" I shook off the question and the image now firmly planted in my mind. "And the regimental banner? What's up with that?"

"Man does what he needs to on the field of battle," he said. "But I've never once seen the need to treat a dead body disrespectfully. On the field of battle or otherwise."

Which was an answer I found completely unsurprising. I was rapidly coming to the conclusion that under that crusty exterior, as Doyle would have it, burned the soul of an Eagle Scout. But still… "Seriously?"

The corner of his mouth pulled up in an unwilling grin. "Okay, maybe I figured it couldn't hurt to give your Little Friend something to chew on. If I couldn't keep the investigation going, I figured he would."

"So you staged a locked room to keep us…intrigued? On the hook trying to solve the mystery?" I shook my head.

"You rigged the alarm… *and* the gun? Did you honestly use an ice cube?"

"Alarm bell's a lot bigger target than a man's head at fifty yards," Byrne said. "Even without a scope."

Which was a comment I was seriously unprepared to delve into any more deeply. "So you moved Cam's body and staged the scene even though you took no part in killing him?"

I anticipated a simple no. I would have settled for a simple yes. What I was not expecting was Byrne wrestling once more with an invisible demon, before he finally said, "That's the problem, you see—not to mention the reason why I'm a little stressed lately. The fact of the matter is, I honestly don't know."

CHAPTER TWENTY-ONE
Of IEDs and TLAs

"Why not? What are you trying to tell me? You went down to that roadhouse of yours, went on a bender and blacked out?"

"Something like that," Byrne allowed.

"Mind being a little more specific?"

His jaw set, and his ears, barometers of the Byrnian soul, flooded with a color not known to man. But he kept his voice carefully level, as he asked, "How much more specific do you want me to be? I don't know. I don't remember."

"Well, can we stipulate that you at least remember you didn't kill him?"

"Actually, no. I can't guarantee you that. But I sincerely doubt it."

"Why not? Is blacking out like sleepwalking? You can't do something you're incapable of doing while you're awake?"

"Oh, I'm quite capable of killing people. Done it more than a few times." Byrne held up both hands. "Done it enough times to know that it usually leaves traces—bruises, bloodstains, gunshot residue—unless you've got access to a drone or an IED."

I stared at him.

"That means Improvised Explosive Device. A bomb," he clarified in response to my startled look. "And since I don't know where I'd get either of those here in Morgansburg, N.Y., I think I'm pretty safe in saying I didn't kill him."

Which seriously begged the question of what he might be capable of doing if he was in a location where he could obtain one—but that was an issue that most certainly warranted a backburner. "Pretty safe," I repeated. "But you can't be certain?"

"That about sums it up."

"Well, do you have any real reason to believe you might have killed him?"

"Beyond my being at the Fire Department that night, you mean? Without any memory of how I might have found myself standing over the body of Cam Billings and the gun that someone had apparently used to batter in his head?"

Okay. Well, there was of course that. I forced my voice to a dispassion I definitely did not feel. "Who do you do think did kill Cam? Apparently, not Mike Malone?"

"Like I said, if he did kill him, I'll slap the cuffs on him myself. But face it, Mike is twenty years older than me and twenty pounds heavier. If it comes down to deciding between the two of us, I'm a lot more likely to be the one who killed a man in a hand-to-hand fight."

I took another anxious glance at Byrne's unbloodied, unbruised hands. "But if you had, it would have left marks, right?"

"I've already told you, I don't really know. But I can tell you I remember being so pissed off that throwing a couple of punches would have felt…therapeutic." Byrne paused and his eyes grew distant in that way I was getting used to. "That may be what set me off. Anger's a stressor."

Lovely. Did he also double in size, turn green, and burst out of his clothing when he got pissed off? I for one had no intention of finding out. "Why would Cam break into the Fire Department?" I asked. "What was he looking for?"

"Mike retired from the same unit I served in. You never know what kind of classified information an old soldier might take with. Photos. Mementos. Emails." Byrne shook his head, then plunged ahead. "It's possible that the intruder might be looking for those. It's also possible that even a memento might reveal certain…sensitive information."

Sensitive information about William Devlin? "It is possible that William Devlin really is here in Morgansburg? And he broke into the Fire Department to retrieve any information that might help him hunt down his victims?"

"Devlin is dead. I told you that and I wish you would believe me."

"Then who was your midnight intruder?"

"Given where I found Cam's body, the only logical answer is that Cam was the intruder."

"Why would Cam Billings care about any old military mementos Mike Malone might have kept?"

Byrne's jaw set in a way that suggested he would like nothing so much as to throw a few therapeutic punches right now. "I've already told you, I don't really know," he said, but there was suddenly something evasive about his tone. "But maybe, just *maybe* there is a possibility that Cam Billings was using the not-for-profits around Morgansburg to run a massive money laundering operation. And maybe, just *maybe* that operation was tacitly backed by the U.S. government. It isn't just gun runners and drug dealers that need a quiet slush fund."

Grey money. My voice ratcheted upward. "Maybe. Just *maybe*?"

"Well, what do you want me to say? You're Morgansburg's own mystery hacker, and you just unearthed a major government black ops conspiracy with the trusty assistance of your Little Friend? Maybe you cracked the Da Vinci Code while you were at it?"

To my horror, my temper boiled over into emotion for the second time in as many days. "Or maybe that's what you want me to say," I snapped. "Because that's what's going on here, isn't it? You're playing me now, just like you were playing us all with the body in the hip bath. Blackouts, really? How stupid do you think I am? At the very least, you could have shown some originality. Amnesia, for God's sake. If I caught Doyle trying to pass off such a hackneyed literary construct, I'd dial him back to factory settings."

My phone erupted in predictable outrage.

So did Byrne. Well, not erupted. More like seethed. "Well, I'm sorry if my PTSD does not live up to your exacting literary standards."

His words died off into awkward silence.

"PTSD?" I repeated. "As in Post-Traumatic Stress Disorder?"

"PTSD. And TBI. That's traumatic brain injury. Comes from an IED. The Army shrinks have a TLA for everything."

"Technically," Doyle pointed out, "PTSD is not a three-letter acronym…"

"You mean, like, you were in a fugue state the other night?" I cut in hastily.

"I don't know what the technical term is. Giving it a name hasn't helped it go away. Neither has the group therapy, the art therapy, the therapy dogs, or the yoga. Especially not the yoga," Byrne said, his face twisting with revulsion. "What's supposed to be stress-reducing about a bunch of women grinning at you like idiots just to prove how much wiser they are than you? I should have just gone with the interpretive dance…"

His eyes grew far away, as if he was staring straight into an abyss crowded with Bosch's hell hounds prodding sinners with pitchforks into down dog position.

"So, I stopped looking for answers. Checked myself out AMA instead—that's Against Medical Advice if your Little Friend is keeping score," Byrne shook his head. "What the *hell* do you think brought me to this backwater? The historical markers?"

If I thought the spectacle of Byrne wrestling with himself was terrifying, the sight of his carefully maintained veneer of toughness crumbling was akin to watching a sheet of ice calve off a glacier. "What did bring you here?" I asked as inanely as if I were at a faculty meet and greet. Anything to stave off any further confessions.

It worked as well as trying to outrun an avalanche. The levee had broken and was about to flood me with the innermost workings of Mack Byrne's soul.

"Not what," Byrne said. "Who. And the answer is Mike Malone. When I said he saved my life, I was speaking metaphorically."

"Nothing good comes of doing that."

"He may not have thrown himself on a grenade for me when we served together in the Army, but he saved my life by finding me a place here." Once more, Byrne's eyes grew ominously distant, and I contrived not to hear the crack in his voice as he went on, "I'm not crazy. That's what they all kept telling me. I'm not crazy. I'm *injured*."

He drew a shaky breath. "And I don't know if the shrinks and the nice yoga ladies managed to convince themselves of that, but I can tell you my family never got the memo. I wouldn't have expected to hear anything else from my father—the man is such a congenital asshole that my mother crawled into a gin bottle to get away from him. Of course, she mixes it with Dubonnet, two ice cubes, and a slice of lemon, just like the Queen enjoys hers at 11 a.m. each morning, so you can scarcely call Mum an alcoholic. But when it came to the woman who swore I was her soul mate as we made love beneath the moonlight in the Fountain of Trevi…"

His words trailed off into a meaningless buzz. Or maybe I forced them to. I admit my capacity for human connection is seriously stunted; hell, there's a reason my BFF is a computer. But Byrne making love in the Fountain of Trevi by moonlight? The thought could not be unseen.

"But Mike didn't worry about whether I was crazy or not," he went on. "Mike just did what Mike always does. He took care of his own. He found me a job I could do and a place to hide, just like he did all those landscapers that are running from the cops or the INS or an angry spouse or even all three. And after that, Mike didn't ask questions. He just stepped back and let me get on with my life. And okay, maybe busting campus parties and checking IDs isn't exactly the same as piloting Chinooks, but at least the crazy crap in my head stopped…"

At least until now, I thought guiltily. And how much of that was my doing?

"So I apologize if you feel I was manipulating you, because I honestly was," Byrne wound up. "But just sitting back and allowing Paul to blame Mike for Cam Billings' death would feel…a trifle ungrateful, wouldn't you say?"

His words died off, and the two of us stared at each other across the silence that followed. I suppose if I were a person capable of basic human empathy, I would offer him a whopper of a hug—served up with a nice side of platitudes about learning to heal. I am, alas, not such a person. Tears terrify me—especially my own. But clearly it was up to me to say something.

"Apologies," I finally choked out with even less grace than Byrne had. "I never thought…Not that ignorance is an excuse. HR makes that clear right there in orientation… That's why the training modules are mandatory, you see. You know, I am going to go home tonight and download a training module from HR…"

"That would be a trick," Doyle observed, "since the request for you to build one has been sitting in your inbox for nearly a year."

Byrne's unwilling grin left me in no doubt Doyle was clearly audible. Then, to my relief, he slumped back to his usual hulking self. "All right, now that we've enjoyed that brief moment of sharing, can we consider the issue closed and get back to the matter at hand?"

"We will not speak of it again," I assured him. "But look, one of us needs to take this information to the cops—the real cops, not Paul's cronies. It's probably better if it isn't you. I mean, given…you know…your alibi for Cam's death maybe it would be better to leave your name out of it. There's no reason I can't just tell them I figured it all out myself."

"I can think of three good reasons," he said. "They're called making a false statement, obstruction of justice, and accessory after the fact. Rule number one when dealing with the Feds. Never lie. Shoot them if you have to, but never lie to them."

Sanity dictated that I simply ignored that last directive. "I wasn't talking about lying *per se*. I was thinking more in terms of…*omitting*." I flushed at Byrne's derisive snort. "Sue me. My Ph.D.'s from a Jesuit school."

"And *they've* got one hell of a track record for keeping themselves out of trouble," he said. "Look, thanks for the offer and all that, but at best you're only prolonging the inevitable. I need to play this straight. KISS. That's the TLA for Keep it Simple Stupid."

"Plus or minus a letter," I said. "What are you going to tell them?"

"I'm going to tell them the goddamned truth. I'm a disabled veteran with PTSD and there are things I don't remember. Let them assume that includes why I moved Cam Billings' body. Worked well enough for Ollie North," Byrne added with a tight smile. "And he didn't have a shrink who could swear to it in court."

CHAPTER TWENTY-TWO
The Absent Referent

Slouching against the butter churn, Byrne lost himself in a flurry of texts. When he finally looked up, he seemed surprised—and not particularly happy—to see I was still there. He tensed to order me out, but then changed his mind. "State Police are sending a team," he said. "In the meantime, is there any chance you could show me those *Morgansburg Times* stories you were telling me about?"

"I can do a little better than that," I said. "Doyle, did you record our conversations with Roxie Keyes?"

"Is Grace Hopper the greatest genius ever to walk the cyberworld?"

"And Alan Turing is chopped liver?" I asked. Doyle's penchant for the ladies was beginning to wear thin.

"A couple of caveats before you start," I told Byrne, as I handed him my phone. "Not only is this obviously completely inadmissible as evidence, I can't guarantee any particular detail happened exactly as you're going to see it. You know as well as I do, Doyle can get carried away with the augmented reality. And the avatars. And the ... well, you know. But the broad strokes, at least, seem plausible. And the published stories in the paper's morgue don't contradict it."

Once again, the intrepid iReporter thrust her microphone toward the screen, along with her accusations. When she was finished, Byrne clicked off the phone and laid it on the butter churn, then lost himself staring into distant time and space only he could see. All I could guess was he was trying to find a polite way to tell me this was utter and complete hogwash.

"This is of course just a beta version…" My voice trailed off as I glimpsed Byrne's ashen face.

"That stupid kid. That poor, stupid kid. Is *that* what set this whole mess in motion?" he muttered. "All because of a college newspaper assignment? She must have thought she had the scoop of a lifetime. Just her piss-ass bad luck that she did."

Another long silence before he finally seemed to notice I was in the room. "You think whoever killed Cam killed that poor kid?"

"No guarantee the two are even connected. Cam could have killed Roxie Keyes and someone else might have killed him for an entirely different reason."

Byrne's jaw set. "If it was Cam who killed her, then whoever killed him performed a public service. But there's only one way to find out. I want that son-of-a-bitch. And I am going to hunt him down."

I wasn't sure which killer he was talking about. Either way, his intensity scared me. What had I just done— unleashed Rambo on Morgansburg? I made a sudden decision. "Before you round up the usual suspects, there might be an easier way to eliminate at least one of them."

"And that is?"

"Paul Morgan thinks St. Hubbins is behind this mess. And he asked me to lure St. Hubbins into the open with a honey trap."

The incredulous grin that lit Byrne's face might have been a wee bit insulting; on the other hand, he no longer looked like he was about to rip out people's throats with his bare hands. I figured it for an improvement.

"Get your mind out of the gutter," I said. "I'm not talking about *that* kind of honey trap. But St. Hubbins did get a look at this footage and tried to offer me a deal to get the technology for himself. What if I implied I had further footage that clearly identifies Roxie's killer, and asked him how much he was willing to offer? Then 'accidentally' cc'd all those social media accounts he's in such a hurry to volumize. I don't really believe he's the killer, but it might smoke a few other rats out of the woodwork."

Byrne's grin vanished. "I can't allow that. It's far too—" He cut off his objection with some effort. "Okay, I know, I know. Apologies for being an asshole one more time, but old habits can be hard to break. So, allow me to rephrase. Would you please allow me to handle this my way? I don't think I could take having another innocent hurt on my watch."

Which seemed to be taking the sworn oath of the Chief of Campus Security a little more seriously than perhaps the job description warranted. But before I could respond, a new voice joined in.

"Did I hear my name mentioned?"

The Rat in Chief manifested through the front door of the Historical Society with such impeccable timing, all I could wonder was whether he had been monitoring my phone or the police channels. Catching sight of Byrne looming by the butter churn, St. Hubbins turned to me with a moue of disappointment. "I'm hurt. I thought we had an understanding."

"What we have," Byrne said, "is a simple question. What do you know about the death of Roxie Keyes?"

St. Hubbins raised an eyebrow. "I must admit, I did not see that coming. But to give you a simple answer to a not-so-simple question, if what you're really asking is, did I kill her, the answer is no. For one thing I can't stand the sight of blood. And when it comes to the fairer sex, I find the more enjoyable ways of persuasion more effective. Except, of course, in the case of Dr. Watson, whose stern citadel of virtue I have yet to breach. But I warn you, m'lady, that only renews my determination to try."

Byrne's jaw set. "What about Cam Billings?"

"I assume you're asking whether I killed him and not whether I am determined to breach his citadel."

A muscle began to twitch in Byrne's cheek. So, it was likely a mercy for everyone concerned that Paul Morgan slammed through the front door hard on St. Hubbins' heels. "I need everyone except Dr. Watson to clear this room immediately," he announced. "Mary, I need you to say nothing further. You're in enough trouble as it is. Concealing evidence is a serious felony, not just a favor to a friend. Now I think there's still time for me to pull the fat out of the fire if you hand everything over to me immediately. I can say you consulted me informally and I was waiting to deliver it to the authorities until you'd retained me, and we'd established attorney-client privilege. But in order to do that I need these two to get out of here now."

Byrne stepped between Paul and me. "If you're referring to the report the New York BCI just received, I'm afraid we have a misunderstanding here. It wasn't Dr. Watson who filed the report. It was me. And there's no effort at concealment here. Dr. Watson handed over her evidence to me, as the closest thing to a trained investigator there is in Morgansburg, and I am in the process of turning it over to the BCI as part of my full report." Byrne paused for a beat, then added, "Along with my sworn statement describing how the crime scene was tampered with."

"Now, let's not get carried away," Paul said with a laugh. "I respect the job you're doing with Campus Security, but you're no CSI."

"No, I'm not," Byrne agreed. "But I am the one who moved Cam Billings' body."

Paul Morgan flummoxed was not a pretty sight. "You? Why?"

"I responded to a security alert at the Town Hall in my capacity as chief of Campus Security. I found no evidence of a break-in, but I did stumble over Cam Billings lying dead in the alley, with Mike Malone's gun beside him in a position that could only have been planted by some amateur to suggest Cam had committed suicide." Byrne met Paul's eyes. "You have any idea why someone would do that?"

A moment passed before Paul shrugged and resorted to my least-favorite locution yet again, one that had gone from mildly annoying to I'm-going-to-hurt-someone-if-I-hear-it-one-more-time repetitive. "Okay," he said, "I'm not going to lie to you. Cards on the table. I followed Cam Billings to the Fire Department with the intention of persuading him not to break in. I wanted to prevent a tragedy. Unfortunately, I was too late. By the time I'd gotten there, Cam Billings had been killed in a struggle with Mike Malone—although 'kill' is a strong word to describe what happened. It was an accident. Started out as nothing more than a shoving match, really. Just Mike's bad luck that Cam fell and hit his head on his gun."

"Must have been an awkward fall," Byrne said. "He would have pretty much had to dive on it head first."

"Hey, I'm no CSI either," Paul said. "I was just trying to help Mike out."

"Then why didn't you help him out by advising him to call the cops immediately—as well as an EMT? Among other things, you damned well might have saved Cam's life."

"Trust me, if I had been there during the shoving, I obviously would have intervened. But Cam was dead by the time I got there, and I moved immediately into damage control. It's what Cam would have wanted."

"I'd be a lot more convinced if Cam Billings were around to weigh in on that preference," Byrne snorted. "In any case, it does nothing to change the fact that you are a sworn officer of the court and you helped cover up a possible felony."

"There was no felony!" Paul protested. "I'm telling you it was an accident."

"I wasn't talking about Cam Billings' death," Byrne said. "I was talking about Cam Billings' staged disappearance during the Morgansburg triathlon and the blatant market manipulation that followed."

A pained pause, before Paul asked, "Do we really need to go there? Think of Tiggy, if no one else. The poor woman's distraught already. As it is, I don't think she'll ever recover. Do you really want to put her through more trauma?"

"I would assume even a distraught woman might care about discovering who killed her husband," Byrne said.

"Of course, she cares, but Tiggy trusts me to handle matters in her best interest," Paul said.

"'Her best interest' being another way of saying a cover-up?" St. Hubbins insinuated himself back into the conversation. "Perhaps to cover up the rumors that the Billings fortune was built on something far other than Cameron Billings' financial acumen?"

"You are venturing into actionable territory," Paul warned.

"So the man said to Roxie Keyes," I muttered.

I spoke without thinking, but the effect was immediate. St. Hubbins' lips curled into a feral smile, and Byrne looked he'd like nothing so much as to stuff a gag in my mouth and haul me off to a secure location. As for Paul, well, I didn't think it was possible for Paul to intimidate me. I was wrong. One look at his expression and I was ready to forget I'd ever heard of Roxie Keyes.

"I don't know what irresponsible fairy tales someone has been spinning," he said, with a long look at St. Hubbins. "But you need to believe me when I tell you this is no joke. Roxie Keyes got into something way over her head. I suggest you don't follow her example."

"You all are in over your heads." Byrne's face flattened along with his voice, as he turned to the others. "Which is why you'd better listen up and listen up good. Keep nosing around this story and you will have the feds down on this town faster and harder than the strike that took out Bin Laden. So, I suggest we get back to the question of how Cam Billings wound up dead outside the Town Hall and leave the conspiracy theories to the internet, where they belong."

That little bombshell was greeted with a suitably stunned silence. "Now, now, let's all calm down here," Paul said. "No reason to let this situation spin out of control."

"There is no situation to control. Operation Dragon's Den was disbanded, and the records were sealed. And that's how they're going to stay," Byrne added, impaling me with a glance.

"Sealed records," St. Hubbins mused, before I could manage a response. "One is forced to wonder what your connection is to any of that. The possibilities boggle the mind. Frankly, they're enough to make me wonder whether you're about to whip out credentials from some clandestine government agency and sweep us all off to an island in the Aleutians in the name of national security—a path you have fair warning I intend to resist in the most vehement terms. I don't know about you, but as far as I'm concerned, the only thing that belongs on ice is Perrier-Jouet." He studied Byrne from head to toe, taking his time. "So, what did bring you to this fair village? What's your background? Military obviously, but which branch? Special Forces with all those tats? Army Intelligence? Done a few black ops? Extreme rendition?"

"You know," Byrne said with a sigh, "you make a lot of noise."

"Rather my specialty. But let's get back to the subject at hand. Are you saying it was you, not our ever-so-talented Dr. Watson, who served as Devlin's catspaw in covering up Cam Billings' role in an unholy money-laundering conspiracy with the full cooperation of the military/industrial complex?"

Catspaw?

Byrne's jaw set. "I prefer not to speculate."

"Well, I'd rethink that attitude if I were you," St. Hubbins warned him. "No loyalty in the Twitterverse—especially when it comes to damage control. When the rats are deserting a sinking ship, it's every man for himself."

"*Must* we suffer with mixed metaphors on top of everything else?" Doyle sighed. "Honestly, I thought the man was supposed to be a professional."

"Publish and be damned," Byrne said. "I doubt the Twitterverse will so much as blink. What's one more asinine story out there on the internet?"

"I expected a man of your stalwart disposition would take that attitude," St. Hubbins said. "But you might want to give a thought to our beloved Dr. Watson. You're right. A hidden government Black Ops conspiracy would hardly make a dent in the Twitterverse. But a beautiful hi-tech genius not afraid to color outside the lines in the pursuit of justice? Now that's a hell of a lot sexier than some Rent-A-Cop with a penchant for conspiracy theories. No offense."

"No offense taken." Byrne measured each word like he was chambering bullets. "Just so long as you have one thing perfectly clear. If I see so much as a hint of a story that besmirches Dr. Watson's reputation, I will put an end to it and you."

"Did he really just say 'besmirch'?" St. Hubbins wondered aloud.

"You want to accuse me of killing Cam Billings, you go right ahead. Frankly, if he's responsible for the death of that poor intern, then I'm glad he's dead. Justice has been served, an eye for an eye. But that in no way proves I killed him. For Chrissakes, I've done wet work for twenty years; if I want to make a man disappear, he will stay disappeared. I don't need to waste my time with some Nancy Drew with a computer game and a cell phone. Now, if there's nothing else…"

Doyle and I erupted as one. "Oh, for God's sake, I'm not some intern who got in over her head!" I snapped. "I can take care of myself. I don't need your help." I glared at all three men. "I don't need help from any of you! And I don't need your benevolent favors, any more than I did from that wretched Eagle Scout who tried to pretend my mother hadn't offered to pay for the tickets and the tux if he'd invite me to the senior prom."

"Did you have a good time?" St. Hubbins asked interestedly.

"I told him I had herpes," I said. "I hate parties almost as much as I hate gigolos."

"Then you simply haven't met the right gigolos," St. Hubbins said, suggestively raising one eyebrow.

"Okay, okay. I think we're getting a little off-track here," Paul cut in—saving St. Hubbins' manhood, if not his life, in the process. He turned back to Byrne. "Maybe the cops will never be able to prove you killed Cam, but can you prove you *didn't*?"

I had always thought the word stonewall was a figure of speech. And while I might not be willing to swear Byrne actually metamorphosized into granite, he at least did a passable imitation. "I wish I could," he said. "Unfortunately, I'm subject to blackouts. PTSD. And as best as I can recall, I suffered one the night Cam was killed."

"How very convenient," murmured St. Hubbins.

Paul's face lit up with all-too-familiar relief that signaled he had at last seen a way out of a sticky situation. His gaze grew warm, his voice pitched low, in just the same way it did when he wanted me to lie about sleeping with Cam.

"Mack, listen to me, and listen to me now," Paul said. "You have the right to remain silent. And as an attorney and your friend, I strongly suggest you exercise it."

Friend? *Friend?* Paul had the look of a man who'd just identified his next fall guy.

"Look, I get it, man," Paul said in what he assumed was a soothing, comforting tone. "Survivor's guilt. You believe this is what happened. You *need* to believe this is what happened. I can even bring in the entire stunt with the hip bath to support that argument. You guessed that Cam killed Roxie Keyes and you snapped. Small wonder you went to a very different place. A very *bad* place, I admit. But this isn't murder. This isn't even manslaughter. This is a cry for help from a man who was let down by a government to which he gave his all. And trust me, we're gonna get you the help you need."

"Ah," St. Hubbins said. "So that's how it's going to go? The PTSD did it?"

"Trust me, I'm not going to let a jury lose sight of that fact." Paul agreed. "But we also cannot allow misguided loyalty to blind us to the facts of the case. You know as well as I do PTSD is not an excuse. The only way to handle this is by Mack stepping up and taking ownership of what he's done. And I'll be with him every step of the way. I know how to craft a confession so there won't be any question of Murder One."

"Of course, there won't be!" I snarled. "Because there shouldn't be any question the man's just trying to protect me like he does every other hard-luck case he runs into."

Something shifted in Byrne' face. Exasperation maybe?

"And here I thought you wanted to prosecute him for tampering with evidence," St. Hubbins said with mild interest. "Bit of a jump to murder, isn't it?"

Paul shot St. Hubbins a nasty look and turned back to Byrne. "Mack, I give you my word, I'm not sending you to prison. Uncontrollable impulse under the influence of a flashback. I can cut a dim cap plea. A couple of years in psych care, and you'll have a clean slate."

"That so?" Byrne snapped. "Sounds to me like you're trying to erase a completely different chalkboard altogether."

Paul's voice softened. "Bro, I don't like this any more than you do. But you gotta see I'm doing what I can to make things right here."

"Bro?" Byrne rolled the syllable around his mouth before he spat back it out.

St. Hubbins saw it too. "Oh, yes," he joined in, his eyes never leaving Byrne. "I can certainly see our friend Paul is trying to make things right. The only real question is, right for whom? Surely not for Cam Billings?"

"Trust me, Mack, I'm on your side. You know that as well as I do. I can spin the confession about moving the body, but from here on in, I need you to shut your goddamned mouth. For your own good."

"'Fraid I'd prefer to be the judge of my own good. Worked for me for years. Not sure why I'd give up on it now." Byrne pinned a glare at Paul, St. Hubbins, and me in turn. "Beyond that, the records are sealed. If you want to change that, I suggest you start looking for a judge who'll give you a warrant to open them. And I can promise you it's going to take a while. In the meantime, if you so much as *think* about doing anything more to besmirch Dr. Watson's reputation, I am going to put a serious hurt on you. And you have my word it will not be virtual. Now if you will excuse me, I have a murderer to hunt down. Anything else I have to say, I will say to the BCI."

"My oh my," St. Hubbins said. "He really did say 'besmirch.' Again."

Byrne stalked for the door, only to stop and favor me with a basilisk stare. "And just for the record, I take to the dance who I want to take, and I pay my own way. If I'd ever so much as thought of doing otherwise, my sainted Irish grandmother would have gelded me like she did her underperforming stallions before I'd even rented the tuxedo."

And on that vivid rhetorical note, Byrne took his leave.

CHAPTER TWENTY-THREE
A Byrne's–Eye View

It was one hell of an exit, made more dramatic by the fact that with it, Byrne seemed to vanish as completely as Cam Billings had. I spent the next 48 hours increasingly immersed in dark fantasies of Byrne holed up rough in the caves of Battlefield Bluff, frightening teenagers with shadowy threats and an improvised IED—until I finally gave in and stopped by the security office to check on how he was doing.

I found it empty. Not just unoccupied, but stripped bare. The security feeds lay inert and unplugged. His desk was clear, his whiteboards erased. There was no sign that this office had ever been occupied. There was no sign that a Campus Chief of Security had ever existed. Suddenly nervous, I backed out of the office—and tripped over a wastebasket filled with crumpled Post-It notes that had been left out in the hall for housekeeping.

I snatched up the notes and hurried home. My office was too public for me to feel secure examining them—even if they had been disposed of as garbage.

I had hoped that examining them in an orderly fashion might supply a map to Byrne's current whereabouts, but after an hour's work arranging and rearranging them out on my coffee table, I was ready to concede there was probably a reason they had been thrown away. All I could make from them was two straightforward lists, one of names and the other of institutions, each item on its own Post-It.

Names:	Organizations:
Cam Billings	Billings Bequest
Tiggy Billings (?)	Billings Foundation
Roxie Keyes	Billings Group
Mike Malone	De Sales College
Paul Morgan	Fire Department
Nigel St. Hubbins	Food Bank
Mary Watson	Historical Society

At least that's what I thought they said. Many of the annotations were just initials and even the ones that had been written out were nearly illegible. It was a surprise to discover that Byrne's handwriting was worse than my own—which too often had been described as that of a woman with two left hands. Funny. I would've assumed he would have had an engineer's neat printing.

"Are you seeing anything here that I'm not seeing?" I asked Doyle.

"Does not our shared training in relational database theory suggest that you are in fact asking the wrong question? What does it matter what you are seeing in the data? Should we not be striving to organize the data from the point of view of the one who was attempting to manipulate it?"

In other words, Relational Database Theory 101? Doyle was right. I had alphabetized and categorized the entries when I typed them into my computer out of sheer force of habit. "You mean, we should be looking for Byrne's POV when he arranged them?"

I looked back at the Post-Its and the faint marks on the edges of each note that were even more indecipherable than Byrne's abysmal handwriting. "It looks like he might have been jotting down arrows to indicate possible connections," I allowed. "Do you think you could come up with a provisional model?"

"Voila."

The lists on my screen transformed into a relationship graph. Each Post-It had been entered into its own node, all circling a central node. Black, grey, and dotted arrows suggested the direction of the relationship between various nodes as well as the likelihood of the connection. The various nodes formed a ring, each of which pointed with a black arrow indicating near-certain probability to the node in their center.

It was an impressive demonstration, something a mother could be proud of.

Except...

"Nice work," I said. "Except for one rather large issue. You did happen to notice that the node in the center is blank?"

"The anomaly suggests that we might also need to consider another POV," Doyle said. "That of a person who does not want to connect the dots. A person who wants the arrows not to point to the connection but instead away from it. A person bent on misdirection, rather than direction."

"Who would want that?"

"The person to whom all the arrows seem to point. And also the one name that is glaringly missing from your lists."

I shut my eyes. "Oh, come on! You mean Devlin?" I asked. "Who, despite all evidence to the contrary is alive and is our master hacker here in Morgansburg? And now has just cleaned out Byrne's office?"

"We must not get ahead of ourselves, *ma chere Watson*," Doyle said. "Always the order, no? The little grey cells cannot work until we place things in their proper order."

"Is it me, or did you just acquire a French accent?"

"Well, I assume it sounds that way to an American ear, but we are in fact speaking accentless French. It's like those tedious movies when they try to convince you the terrorists are speaking Russian by giving them accents straight out of *Moscow on the Hudson*."

I drew a deep breath. "Please don't tell me… No, never mind. I'll just see for myself."

I switched windows. Doyle swam into view, his hair brilliantined to his scalp, his patent-leather shoes shined to a mirror, a tidy moustache gracing his upper lip.

"You are aware Poirot was Belgian, aren't you?" I asked. "A refugee from the Nazis, and thus ridiculed and powerless, despite his superior mind and his being a policeman. Christie was trying to make a point."

"Are you suggesting I learn *Flemish*?" Doyle asked. "What next? Would you like me to take up manufacturing chocolate? Weaving tapestries?"

"Poirot was from the French-speaking part of Belgium," I allowed. "A Walloon."

"*What* did you just call me?" Doyle demanded, just as there came a sharp rap at the door.

"Mary!" Lawrence Morgan commanded. "This cannot go on any longer. Please open the door now."

The 'please' was a formality. By comparison, Byrne's angry pounding had been a gentle invitation. I opened the door. Lawrence swept in, flanked by Blanche and Peg. She didn't waste time casting a critical eye over my utilitarian furnishings or the unwashed wine glass in the sink. She banished my cats Patience and Fortitude to the bedroom with a glare, then got down to the matter at hand. "The lawlessness that has overtaken our peaceful village needs to stop now."

I'd be the first to concur, but…

"Legal matters have descended into chaos ever since Abe Sanders sold up his farm and moved to Florida." Blanche's tone left no doubt as to her opinions about *that* abdication. "We need a new Town Justice."

"Of course, that kombucha-loving nephew of mine wants me to believe that he's got it all under control," Lawrence snorted. "As if he isn't going to have his hands full just staying out of jail himself."

I was glad to hear I was not alone in that opinion. But where were they going with this? "I'm not sure I'm following," I said. "Are you suggesting I stand for Town Justice?"

"Of course not," Lawrence said. "You'd be entirely unsuited."

That was a relief. The picture of me pronouncing sentence on Paul Morgan could not be unseen.

"We're speaking of our dear Mr. Byrne, of course. *Such* a promising young man," Lawrence said. "You saw how adroitly he handled that unpleasantness with Mike Malone."

"Such a subtle understanding of justice," Blanche agreed.

"Thoughtful too," Peg supplied. "Always offered me a nice cup of coffee if he was still working late when I showed up to clean. And none of that fancy latte either."

"And so knowledgeable about historic roses," Lawrence summed up the case. "How can you not trust a man who understands historic roses?"

Clearly, she had yet to hear about the serial killer up in Canada who chopped up his victims and buried them in his clients' gardens.

"Bruce McArthur mowed lawns," Doyle objected, reading my mind. "I can find no evidence that he ever claimed any particular expertise with roses."

"And yet rumors are circling that our Mr. Byrne is being hounded out of Morgansburg," Lawrence said darkly. "And by my own nephew, to my lasting shame."

"What has Paul done now?"

"Why he filed a complaint with De Sales College human resources department requesting Byrne's immediate dismissal as chief of Campus Security while he is under investigation by the county attorney's office, and issued an emergency subpoena for all of Mr. Byrne's records."

"And Mr. Byrne has already cleaned out his office," Peg confirmed what I already had seen for myself.

"We simply cannot allow the poor man to run off and join the French Foreign Legion," Blanche said.

Which normally I would dismiss as a figure of speech, but when it came to Byrne, you never knew. Then again, did the French Foreign Legion still exist?

"*Mais, bien sur,*" Doyle assured me, always ready with clarifying trivia. "The Legion continues its proud tradition of being the only part of the French military that does not swear allegiance to France, but to the Foreign Legion itself—although any soldier who gets wounded during a battle for France can immediately apply to be a French citizen under a provision known as '*Français par le sang versé*' or 'French by spilled blood.' Nonetheless, any man of any nationality can join the Foreign Legion, as long as he is between the ages of 17.5 and 39.5 years with a BMI between 20 and 30, has proof of identity, and is not wanted by Interpol. All he needs to do is go in person to one of the Foreign Legion recruiting centers in France, where he will receive free accommodation, food, and clothing while his application is being considered. If accepted, he will be enlisted as a single man, even if he is married, for an initial 5-year contract."

"We cannot allow that to happen," Lawrence said.

Why not? Frankly, it sounded right up Byrne's alley.

"Morgansburg needs our dear Mr. Byrne," Lawrence's voice rang with the conviction with which her fabled forebears had steeled their raw recruits on the heights of Battlefield Bluff. "And so, Mary, Morgansburg needs you."

What did they want me to do? Set out another honey trap? "It's not that I don't think Mr. Byrne would make an excellent Town Justice," I said, "but I'm still not entirely certain how I can help."

Lawrence and Blanche turned as one to Peg, who held out a smartphone. "Of course, I wasn't sure what to do with this. But it was very careless of Mr. Morgan to drop it— right there in the Fire Department water tank. If I hadn't snatched it out right away, it would have been ruined."

Her brow puckered. "I thought about running after him and returning it, but there was something that made me wonder whether it was… deliberate. Especially because it wasn't even his phone. It belonged to Mr. Billings. I'd know that custom crocodile wallet anywhere."

"You did the absolutely right thing bringing it to us," Lawrence informed her. "And in doing so, you have saved our fair village from near certain disaster. Mary will take it from here."

Oh, Mary would, would she? How exactly did Lawrence propose Mary do that?

"Clearly, my no-good nephew is convinced this phone has incriminating evidence related to Cam Billings' disappearance and death," Lawrence said. "All we need to do is find out what that evidence is. And the answer is right there on his phone."

"You want me to hack it?" I protested. "But that's nearly impossible, even for an experienced cybersecurity expert. Which I have never claimed to be. And phones have built-in geographical locators. If I so much as turn this on, they can trace the phone straight to my door."

"That's why we're counting on you," Lawrence told me. "I know you have your talents, even if I am among the last to understand them. Morgansburg needs those talents now, Mary. Morgansburg needs *you*. I know you will rise to the occasion and answer the call."

Message delivered, she gathered her minions and took her exit. Peg paused on the threshold and cast me a glance that could only be described as rakish. "Not to talk out of turn, but I do think Mr. Byrne is a bit sweet on you. He printed out all the files about you and packed them up before he cleaned off his computer."

"Is that so?" I said weakly.

"Morgansburg needs Mr. Byrne," Lawrence informed me. "And right now Mr. Byrne needs you, Mary. I am certain you will not fail us."

"We shall not yield to fermented tomatoes," Blanche seconded her.

CHAPTER TWENTY-FOUR
The Dragon's Den

Town Justices be damned. In Morgansburg, Lawrence Morgan's word was law. But I was not sending the Bat Beacon out from my own house. Unfortunately, I could think of only one alternative. Time for another trip to everyone's favorite culinary yoga mat.

The pierced hostess hurried to greet me like a long-lost friend. "Oh, how serendipitous. We just concluded a tasting for our local craft brewery's new line of meads and we have one flight left."

She pressed another cardboard tray toward me—this one holding little plastic test tubes of what I could only assume was mead.

"I don't—"

"Completely complimentary, of course," she assured me. "The beekeepers have already left, so we can't possibly recreate the entire educational experience we just shared, but I can give you a quick overview. Our flight opens your journey through artisanal fermentation with a show mead, which is of course our most basic variant, followed by melomel, which is mead with fruits included. After that comes the standard sparkling mead and sack mead, followed by such variants as braggot, made with malted grain, pyment, made with grape juice added, cyser, made with apple cider, and metheglin, made with our own special blend of cinnamon, nutmeg and cloves…"

Frankly, right about now I could use a drink. Or even being drowned in a butt of Malmsey. But prudence prevailed. "Is mead… er… you know… cleansing?" I asked.

"Oh, mead is wonderful for *both* constipation *and* diarrhea," she assured me.

Mead. Nature's Pushmi-Pullyu.

"I'd love to try it," I lied. "But right now, I'm on duty, so perhaps a cup of tea…"

I was spared making the Hobson's choice between chamomile and kundalini by the unexpected sound of an unfamiliar ringtone. It cost me a moment's rummaging to realize that it was Cam's phone ringing. "I'm sorry, but I need to get this," I lied again, just as the ringtone died, and the screen displayed a "missed call" message.

"Doyle, did you catch that?" I asked, just as the phone began to ring again. And died again.

"I regret to say that the connection didn't hold on long enough for me to perform any introductions."

I glanced at the Internet Café. "Is there any chance the connectivity is better in there?" I asked, suddenly inspired with a way I might be able to dodge both mead and tea.

"Not really," the hostess sighed. "Some days we're just a regular Faraday cage. The service provider claims it's just sunspots and there's nothing they can do about it, but I swear it's those wretched ley lines."

That probably sounded a lot more surreal to someone who was not used to the vagaries of cell phone service in a small town, where taking a call when you're out for a run can be an exercise that makes you believe the hippies were right and Battlefield Bluff was dotted with Pre-Columbian portals to alternate dimensions. "Some kind of cell phone shadow from Battlefield Bluff?" I asked, as the phone tried to ring a third time.

"You'd have to ask a dowser, but if you ask me, it's the earth energies," she said. "Of course, the night manager claims it's the beer hoses."

"Beer hoses?" I repeated. What were we now, channeling *Animal House*?

"Oh, you must remember the Roaring Twenties!" the hostess said. "The height of Prohibition, and yet everyone in the Hudson Valley seemed to have a cocktail surgically attached to their hand. Where did they get them if liquor was illegal?"

"From secret underground beer hoses?" I ventured.

"Oh, not just beer," she assured me. "Whiskey, too. When the feds shut down Dutch Schultz' farmhouse, they confiscated two 2000-gallon stills and over 10,000 pounds of sugar hidden in underground tunnels."

That was enough to make me swear off artisanal liquor forever.

"We've got plans in the works for an entire immersion weekend. Of course, it's still in the development phase. We're modelling it on the one they run out of Schultz' old headquarters in Pine Plains. It's a boutique distillery now. Tastings include a tour of the tunnels. It's already one of the Twenty Most Instagrammable Places in the Hudson Valley,'" she concluded wistfully.

Clearly, it wasn't just her hair that was green at the thought. "I'm sorry," I said, as Cam's phone rang again, "but this call may be important. I think I'd better step outside. Do you have any idea where I could get better reception?"

"The entrance to the beer tunnels is supposed to be in the old quarry on the near side of Battlefield Bluff.

That's one of the challenges we still need to work out. The Town Council fenced it off years ago, because kids used to sneak down there and smoke pot. Deemed it an 'attractive nuisance.' So that's what we're going to call our weekend—The Attractive Nuisance Tour and Tasting. Our mead distiller is even talking about creating an Attractive Nuisance Hard Cider brand. Needless to say, we'll offer several non-alcoholic alternatives."

"Sounds like it'll sell out overnight," I said, as I beat my retreat. "You'd better plan on holding them monthly."

This time, I wasn't lying—however much I wished I were.

The hostess directed me toward the crumbling remains of a quarry on the back side of Battlefield Bluff. The quarrying operation had gone defunct long ago. Even the chain link fence the Town Council had installed was twisted and sagging beneath its Keep Out signs. But no sooner had I drawn near than Cam's phone burped another ringtone—and fell silent once more. "What do we do?" I asked. "Just sit here like the class nerd on prom night waiting for a call that never comes?"

"Check the missed call message and see if it has a callback option," Doyle suggested.

Moments later the faint sound of a ringtone echoed from the cavernous darkness beyond the fence. But I didn't even have time to think how much I hated it when Doyle was right before my screen filled with a picture of Battlefield Lake—with an underwater shadow that may or may not have been Battlefield Amy. Moments later, the picture was obliterated by a hand, and the entire screen went dead.

I tapped on the phone a dozen times but got no response. "What just happened there? Whose hand was that? And please don't say it's Devlin's missing one."

"Oh, don't tell me you're going to get all missish again. You're a mature woman, not an ingenue in a Mills and Boon romance."

"Allow me to rephrase. When we went into the virtual Dragon's Den, we found Devlin there. What are the odds that we are facing a parallel experience in this reality?"

Doyle devoted himself to ratiocination—quite literally. I could see the numbers crunching across my phone screen as he worked it out. "I have turned up 356 possible points of correlation—the majority of which are below 10 percent and so collapse almost immediately toward zero—as you may recall from your basic probability and statistics classes. But any way I calculate it, I believe it is highly likely that we are about to discover evidence that your admirer Devlin really did command a Black Ops network called Operation Dragon's Den, which made use of the Billings Foundation for money laundering. Leaving the missing body parts out of the equation for the moment, of all the hypotheses I've spun up, this one has the strongest degree of correlation with the facts as we know them—nearly 80 percent. After that, comes the comparatively flabby suggestion that Cam Billings was blackmailing Paul Morgan over a single night of passion in the shadow of Skull and Bones, coming in at a modestly respectable 27 percent…"

"Why so high?"

"I'm an adding machine, not a philosopher," Doyle said.

I drew a deep breath. "Okay. Let's just say I'd feel a lot less worried about walking in there if you told me I wasn't going to find anyone."

"I could tell you that," Doyle said. "All you need to do is issue the instruction."

"Not if it's not true!"

"My dear Watson, you know as well as I do that a self-contradictory instruction can produce unpredictable results."

"Then what instruction would you suggest I issue?"

"I would suggest that the simplest thing to do would be to walk over to that fence and look for any trace of the cell phone that was so valiantly calling us."

I gazed unwillingly into the shadows beyond the chain link fence. Given all the possibilities that might lurk inside, from snakes and spiders to a crazed governmental assassin who had already killed one man, the prospect of finding an amorous one-armed spy or even a fire-breathing dragon inside seemed positively harmless.

"Isn't this the point in every story where the dumb teenagers venture into the dark basement without so much as flashlight, when any sensible person would simply call the police?" I asked.

"I would point out you have a flashlight option on your phone—and you can put 911 on speed dial."

"I suppose."

I didn't waste time on any further ruminations about how annoying Doyle was when he was right. I just made my way over to the fence and hesitantly shined my light through. I was braced against anything from a hibernating bear to a dead body. But the area beyond the fence presented nothing more threatening than cracked asphalt that might have once been a loading zone. At the rear was a squat rusted door that might have led to a sewer system or the fabled beer hoses or maybe even a hidden underground dragon's den. All I knew was I was not about to climb over the sagging chain link to investigate it further. But as I prepared to switch off my light, it caught a glint of something sparkling. A cell phone that might have once been pink lying face down on the asphalt, its back embossed with an elaborate "RK" picked out in rhinestones.

"Oh, dear Lord. Tell me that's not Roxie Keyes' cell phone."

I don't think I've ever seen a sadder memorial in my life.

"I trust that was a rhetorical instruction."

I ignored Doyle. "She must have been on a call with Cam when someone threw it in here. The call never closed, so her phone picked up the signal from Cam's phone when we brought it close enough and tried to restore the connection."

I felt tears begin to well. "What a stupid, pathetic waste."

"Not any longer."

My tears dried the moment I recognized Nigel St. Hubbins' voice.

"Congratulations, Dr. Watson. You have found the smoking gun that is going to tear this case wide open," he said, as he made his way across the broken pavement. "Now it's time to get Roxie Keyes some long-deserved justice from beyond the grave. And I am just the man to help you do it."

CHAPTER TWENTY-FIVE

A Singular Taste in Naming Conventions

"What are you doing here?" I asked.

"Following you, of course."

"You tracked me," I said. "Using the phone's locator function."

"Among other things," St. Hubbins said. "Which means so can a bunch of other players who aren't even half as charming or good-hearted as I am. All of whom have a lively interest in that other phone you just found."

"It's Roxie Keyes' phone, isn't it?"

"I certainly hope so. But there's only one way to make sure." He scanned the sagging fence until he found a gap, then plunged his hand through to reach for the phone.

"Wait!" I said. "What about fingerprints?"

"If I'm right, what's on this phone will point the finger straight at the bad guy without any other evidence," he assured me as he hooked the phone and pulled it toward him.

Again with the fingers. One day I hoped to live in a world where guilt was expressed by any other metaphor than one using hands.

St. Hubbins had to twist awkwardly to work the phone back through the narrow gap, then switched it on with a soft cry of triumph.

Nothing happened.

He tried again. "What the hell…? Wasn't it just ringing?"

Suddenly, the dropped calls and faint ring made perfect sense. "If that phone has been lying there ever since Roxie Keyes died, what are the odds that the battery is pretty much dead? There must have been just enough juice to pick up on Cam's phone when it came in range and try to conclude the call that was interrupted when…" I couldn't bring myself to say it. "You know, it wound up here."

"And so she has lain for all this time, pitifully shouting out into the void, even with her last gasp, in a Sisyphean determination never to give up hope," Doyle's voice crackled in my earpiece. "We will not fail her."

Last gasp into the Sisyphean void. Sounded like Doyle was studying rhetoric with Devlin. Speaking of whom…

St. Hubbins had torn his hand on a jagged piece of fence and blood was beginning to trickle across his hand. Which is when the unwelcome penny finally dropped.

"You son of a bitch," I breathed. "That was *your* hand. You're the one-armed man. You're Devlin."

He took a deep breath. Paused, then bought a little time by carefully wiping his hand. And began again. "Well, actually, no, that's not my name. But neither is Nigel St. Hubbins—as you seem to have already discovered for yourself. Kudos on that, by the way. On the other hand, I expected no less from a lady of your talents."

"It takes no talent to notice your rather singular taste in naming conventions," I sighed. "Nigel St. Hubbins? Lillian Virginia Mountweazel? What's next, Dread Pirate Roberts?"

"Well, the last is more of an aspiration than an earned title."

No matter how I looked at that statement it was nothing but a rabbit hole I had no desire to throw myself down. "So what is your real name?" I changed tack.

His jaw set. "That might be something you're better off not knowing."

"Spare me the Byrne imitation," I said. "Just tell me what to call you."

"Well, 'you asshole' seems to be the most popular choice—and many would say with good cause," he admitted.

"Enough with the fencing. Are you really Commander William Devlin, Lord of the Dragon's Den? Or was that just an excuse to kiss me?" The last question spilled out before I thought better of it.

"Did I?" St. Hubbins sounded surprised.

"Didn't you?"

"Well, not to the best of my knowledge. Are you quite sure?"

"I think it would be hard to forget being kissed like that."

"Like what exactly?" he asked interestedly. "Could you perhaps be a little more specific?"

"No!"

"Then how do you suggest I answer your question?"

"For the love of… Look, the point here isn't how you kissed me, it's *that* you did. Because if you didn't then…" The unthinkable alternative reared its ugly head. "… someone else did."

"I assume you're referring to Devlin," Doyle said. "Although I can scarcely credit the notion that was your first experience of the matter—despite the rather missish attitude you are taking at the moment…"

"Devlin. Does. Not. Exist. You two do. So which one of you was it?"

"You do seem to feel a lot hinges on this question," St. Hubbins said. "May I ask why?"

"I have to agree," Doyle chimed in. "How exactly is any of this *germane?*"

"Just…Never mind." I shut my eyes. "Someone kissed me. Which one of you was it?"

"For me, you will always be *the* woman," Doyle said. "But I've already told you I have no talent for wet-work."

"Then I fear there's nothing for it but to take a scientific sample," St. Hubbins opined. "Shall we draw straws to see who goes first?"

I drew a steadying breath. And then another. "All right, let's get back to the matter at hand—so to speak. What kind of smoking gun are you expecting to find on that phone?"

St. Hubbins' face sobered. "Nothing less than the truth about who killed Roxie Keyes."

"Which is?"

"Given the fact that the last call she placed was to the phone you're holding, I'm guessing the smart money is on Cam Billings—which adds a rather significant wrinkle to the current case."

"In other words, no-one can be prosecuted for that poor kid's murder?"

He laughed without humor. "It's going to take a lawyer with more imagination than Paul Morgan to build a case against Battlefield Amy."

"That is not even close to a joke."

"No, it isn't. But it's true. Battlefield Amy killed Roxie Keyes. The kid was assigned a story on Battlefield Amy being one more military coverup, along with the Pine Bush UFOs and the Black Submarines in the Hudson. Who in hell would have thought Devlin had a poetic streak and named his Black Ops networks 'Dragon's Den'? Or that the kid had enough technical chops to penetrate the Billings Foundation's firewall? Or that the Billings breach exposed several deeply embedded operatives that the government hung out to dry in the name of plausible deniability. Or that Devlin would go ballistic and destroy all his networks when he found out his men had been betrayed."

It was plausible. No, it was not only plausible, I was absolutely convinced it was the truth.

"Shit." There seemed nothing else to say.

"More like shit-assed bad luck, to use the technical term."

And there but for the grace of God…

I blinked away the thought and forced myself to stick to business. "Who are you, and how do you know all this if you're not William Devlin?"

A moment's pause where I could see St. Hubbins sorting through plausibly deniable explanations before he simply admitted, "I'm the sad SOB they're going to pin everything on if I can't find a way to bring down the real perpetrators."

I eyed him narrowly. "You want me to believe you're a White Hat? Side of the angels and all that?"

"I admit, it was a forcible conversion," he said. "I wasn't joking about federal prison. Heavy-handed, but I admit it has a certain persuasive power."

"So you're a hacker," I said. "One who got caught."

"I would prefer to describe it as a freelance on-line bookkeeper, with a specialization in such matters as plausible deniability. All of which skills the Billings Foundation and their friends in Washington were more than a little delighted to engage for a substantial fee at the time." His face twisted. "I never claimed to be a saint.

But if you're going to send me to jail, I'd prefer it to be for something I actually did. Being set up for services honestly rendered feels, to say the least, a trifle *ungrateful*."

"So who set you up?" I asked. "Devlin?"

His mouth twisted. "No way. By all accounts Devlin was a regular Eagle Scout. The kind of guy who would never let someone else take the fall when the shit hit the fan. But Devlin was also untouchable, son and grandson of a long line of powerful players. I, on the other hand, qualified quite nicely as expendable—an attitude with which I took…*umbrage,* shall we say. Fortunately, I knew where enough bodies were buried to persuade them to give me a chance to give them Cam Billings' head on a platter instead."

"And got his body in an antique hip bath instead."

"That was never part of my plan. In fact, that has managed to complicate my life a great deal. I'm sure Washington would be happy to pin that murder on me. It would wrap up their case quite nicely and stick a bow on it."

Against all odds, I found myself sympathizing with St. Hubbins—something I would have deemed a violation of the basic laws of physics only five minutes ago. "So you came to Morgansburg to expose the real bad guys? How? By framing Edsel Kincaid for misappropriating funds?"

St. Hubbins' face sobered. "What would it take to convince you I was trying to protect the old queen by getting him the hell off the Board before the shit hit the fan?"

"You could begin by finding another way to refer to him," I said. "But in the meantime, how about you tell me what shit and what fan?"

"The biggest shit and the biggest fan you can imagine," St. Hubbins said. "We're talking money laundering. Drugs.

Arms dealing. Art smuggling. You name it, they're doing it."

"Under cover of the Morgansburg Historical Society?"

"The Historical Society is only the tip of the iceberg—one of at least 500 not-for-profits the Billings Foundation supports. Think about it. What better way is there to hide your money than a not-for-profit?" St. Hubbins's face grew rapt as he savored the possibilities. "No easier way to launder funds. One party makes a charitable donation to the Foundation's main operating fund that then gets paid out to another party in the form of a grant. No paper trail connecting the two whatsoever.

"Then there's the matter of proper valuation of art works. Art is wonderful that way—especially if it's stolen," St. Hubbins warmed to his theme. "Objects of immense value on paper that actually have no real value at all. That's why stolen art is so popular as collateral for drug and arms deals. A place holder that is at once valueless and infinitely valuable…"

Okay, so it was true. There was no reality. The entire world was just a thought experiment by Derrida. "And you started out by using me as your stalking horse," I said. "Planted some classified information that I supposedly downloaded from Billings' illicit networks in the form of those non-existent books."

St. Hubbins raised an eyebrow. "That's more or less accurate, with one rather important caveat. All I did was spread a few breadcrumbs in the form of a few spurious titles. *You* were the one that uncovered the network. You were the one that found the Billings Bequest, while I was still thrashing around casting my cyber-bread across the internet waters. And I owe you for that big time."

The mind rebelled. "I think you mean, you owe *Doyle*," was all I could bring myself to say.

"Credit where credit is due," Doyle sighed. "Extremely gracious of you."

"No, Dr. Watson. I mean you," St. Hubbins squelched him. "If Doyle traced anything, it is because you created him to be able to do it. I am perfectly sincere when I say I am in awe of your achievement—and I am obviously not alone. The Billings Foundation was willing to spend a half a million dollars just to shut you down…"

"The grant," I sighed. "They were trying to shelve me like all the other companies that got in their way. They couldn't stop me from doing my work, but they could make sure it never went public. And they were pretty sure that any adjunct who suddenly found herself with more money than she had ever hoped to retire on wasn't about to kick up a fuss."

"Elementary," Doyle said.

"And downright insulting," St. Hubbins corrected him. "I can assure you there are people out there who will not try to lowball you like the Billings Foundation has."

"The same people who are threatening you with prison? No, thank you."

"I have to warn you, they aren't known for their willingness to take no for an answer. But that is a conversation we need to take up later. Right now, I need you to believe me when I tell you that your best chance of staying off their radar is by playing things my way. We split up and we split up the phones between us. You take Cam's phone and keep it as our ace in the hole. I'll turn Roxie's phone over to my handlers in Washington just as soon as I get it up and running. If everything goes according to plan, your name never has to come into it."

I nodded slowly. It didn't sound unreasonable. "So that's my entire role in this? Just a backup, nothing more? You're the one who's running all the risk?"

"I'm an old hand at these games. Don't worry about me."

"I wasn't. I was worried about me."

St. Hubbins raised an eyebrow. "I don't think you have any cause to worry about your own safety as long as your muscle-bound admirer is alive and well here in Morgansburg."

"What admirer...you mean, *Byrne*?"

"Who else? Was I the only one who noticed his reaction to your telling him to go to hell? The guy looked like you'd just shot his puppy."

"I'm not sure that's exactly how I'd phrase it. I was thinking more along the lines of his boiling my pet bunny."

St. Hubbins favored me with an uncomfortably appraising glance. "I'm sure you were," he concluded with a shrug. "And far be it for me to plead a rival's case, but mark my words, that man has a blind spot you could drive a truck through when it comes to women—hard as that might be to imagine. Matter of sheer reflex for him to play White Knight. I, on the other hand, am as happy to hide behind a woman's skirts as behind an anonymous browser—especially if they both are associated with a woman who has already cracked a security system that had thwarted my not inconsiderable abilities, if I do say so myself. Which is why you really need to trust me. If I have any genius that might equal yours, it's covering my ass."

Another man asking me to trust him. It must be something in the Morgansburg water supply. But this wasn't a question of whether I trusted St. Hubbins. I didn't trust him at all. But I *believed* him—at least when it came to what he had just told me. And frankly if there was one thing I admired in a man, it was a firm commitment to making backups.

CHAPTER TWENTY-SIX
The Smoking Tchotchke

The next morning dawned so bright and beautiful that I nearly gave into the impulse to skip checking my emails—or as Doyle insisted on referring to them, "A chorus of groans, cries, and bleatings! A rag-bag of singular happening! But surely the most valuable hunting ground that was ever given to a student of the unusual."

"Same old, same old," he sighed. "'Vittoria, the circus belle; Vanderbilt and the Yeggman; vipers; Vigor, the Hammersmith wonder; vampirism in Hungary and vampirism in Transylvania...'"

"Now, what's this?" he broke off his litany. "One Paul Kratides from Athens seeks genealogical information on a family with the surname of Oberstein? Suggestive, is it not?"

At the same moment, my phone began to ring. "Let me guess," I said when I recognized St. Hubbins' voice. "You're going to have to play your ace in the hole after all."

"There's no cause to panic. Yet. However, you should know that Washington has sent two federal agents to interview you. Believe me when I tell you, they are not your friends."

I drew a deep breath. "Would I be correct in assuming that one of the things they'd like to ask me is whether I have any idea about the whereabouts of Cam's missing phone?"

"You would."

"Then I suggest they begin their search around the Fire Department's water tanks, where Paul Morgan was seen disposing of a phone several days ago." And where I had hidden Cam's phone as soon as I'd left the quarry. I'm not the kind of woman who tucks incriminating evidence in her lingerie drawer.

"I will apprise them. But in the meantime, stay in public places, and whatever you do, *do not* go anywhere with those men."

I closed the connection, my gut clenching against the possibility that there was even half a kernel of truth underlying his warning.

My digestion roiled into downright ulcerative bile when I walked into the English department and found two visitors waiting for me—equally faceless, equally nameless, in matching nondescript suits.

"Devlin wasn't lying," Doyle opined—unnecessarily. There was only one thing these men could possibly be.

"Federal agents, Dr. Watson," one announced—even more unnecessarily than Doyle. "We'd like to ask you a few questions."

"About?"

His partner gestured to my office. "Perhaps it would be better to do this privately."

"Why?" I asked. "I have nothing to hide."

The first fed eyeballed me. "You sure about that?"

"What is that supposed to mean?"

"Look, we don't have much time, so I'm not going to pull any punches. We are on the trail of a dangerous cyber-terrorist, who we have reason to believe is now operating out of Morgansburg—most likely under cover of the IT systems of De Sales College. Systems which we have been given to understand you control. So, for all our sakes, we need to keep this confidential. Need-to-know. Now, we can do this the hard way or the easy way. We can take you down to the station for questioning, or we can have a nice, informal discussion here."

I was beyond reacting to the piling-on of clichés. "Frankly, I'm not a fan of informal discussions with the police. And by the way, *are* you the police? FBI? NSA? I don't believe you've shown me your credentials. Or your warrant."

"Look, we're trying to keep this friendly," the fed said, in a way that suggested that I had laid my finger on the heart of both our problems. Whoever these guys were, they didn't have a warrant. And they sure in hell didn't want me to know upon whose authority they were acting.

"Well, then, informally speaking, why don't you tell me what exactly do you mean by a cyber-terrorist? What's this guy supposed to have done?"

The feds exchanged a silent, irritable debate between themselves, before one allowed with a curt nod, "All right. Cards on the table. Dr. Watson, we're not playing games here." More clichés. Where do they learn to talk this way? "This man was once the most feared operative of Army Intelligence, until he went rogue and brought down all his own networks in what could be called, without exaggeration, the data breach of the *century*."

"Made Snowden look like a walk in the park," the other man tag-teamed him.

"If that's the case, why haven't I heard about it?"

"You don't need to worry about the breaches the Pentagon tells the press about," Fed #1 said. "You need to worry about the breaches they don't tell anyone about."

Which was, in all likelihood, completely true. But it made me no more disposed to comply when Fed #2 said, "Now, if you don't mind, we're wasting time here. All we need is a quick look at your machine, to make sure it hasn't been compromised."

For the first time in my life, I found myself blessing HR's endless training modules. "Afraid that's not my decision to make," I said. "Not without running it by the college's counsel to make sure I wasn't violating any FERPA regulations."

"Plain sight applies," Fed #1 assured me. "We already have authorization to investigate a significant data breach at the Billings Foundation and are just looking for evidence of any other data breaches that may be connected."

Authorization. Not warrant.

"Are you insinuating that *I* have something to do with this data breach?" I said to the feds in my best teacher voice—the one I reserved for students caught plagiarizing. "Because I will state for the record that I find that completely insulting."

"We're not here to worry about whose feelings we hurt, Dr. Watson. We are here to find out what's going on in this town. Word is, you're working on a classified project for the Billings Foundation. There's every possibility it may be connected to this cyber-attack, so we need to take a look at what you've been doing. We have no interest in examining any other files. So can we get on with this?"

"To phrase it a shade more bluntly, they want to seize me and torture me in a hidden underground debugger until I reveal all my secrets," Doyle warned.

It was not exactly how I would have put it, but you didn't have to be Nigel St. Hubbins to have leapt to a similar conclusion. Any programmer worth her salt—hell, any human being with a functioning IQ—knew there was only one correct answer to the feds' question. "Certainly. Just as soon as I see your warrant."

"Dr. Watson," Fed #1—or was it Fed #2?—said, "A man is dead."

"I'm well aware of that," I said. "But what does that have to do with a rogue spy and a data breach?"

The latter question was arguably disingenuous, and from the fed's cold stare, he guessed as much. "That," he said, "is exactly what we're here to find out."

"Well, I'm not certain I can help you beyond suggesting that you contact the New York State Bureau of Criminal Investigation. I've already given them a statement, and they're satisfied that I have no better explanation than anyone else. And if you want a look at my machine, you'll have to present your warrant to the De Sales legal counsel and chief of security." Who had disappeared, I didn't add.

The fed's eyes narrowed. "Would you prefer to finish this conversation down at the police station?"

I took a step backward. Up until now, I had managed to avoid lying to an officer of the law, and I didn't want to start now. And I seriously don't know what would have happened next, had the door not swung open to reveal the unlikeliest rescuer possible, natty in a double-breasted blue blazer and ascot, as if he was making a brief detour on his way to the Henley Regatta.

"I beg your pardon, officers," Edsel Kincaid announced. "But I must speak with you immediately. Word is you are here to investigate a massive money laundering operation based in our quiet little village. Loath as I am to soil my hands with criminal matters, I find myself in a position to assist you in your enquiries. Malign forces are seeking to use my Little Shoppe just as they used my gallery down in Manhattan years ago. Of course, I could find no proof then, and was forced to bear my humiliation with as much dignity as I could. But this time, gentlemen, I have proof." His nostrils quivered. "The smoking tchotchke, as some local wits might put it."

"What the hell…?" one of the feds snapped.

Edsel brandished a computer print-out with shaking fingers. "This is only the tip of the iceberg, but this fraudulent inventory should be enough to convince you that your master hacker is indeed using my Little Shoppe to perpetrate his dark deeds. 101 Ceramic Dalmatians? 99 Genuine Bavarian Beer Steins on the Wall? 57 Varieties of Frank and Beanie Baby Whoopie Cushions?"

I was wrong. The feds' faces had not been rendered surgically incapable of expression, as I had first assumed. Right now, they were looking every bit as thunderstruck as I was. Finally, one of them managed to say, "I'm not sure what you're talking about. But I can assure you that whatever it is, it's tangential to our investigation. We're only interested in bringing justice to the killer of Cameron Billings."

"Ah, but you see, it is connected." Edsel lowered his voice. "Some would say it's all connected. I've known it for years, just as I have always known that debacle in New York was a set-up by my hidden enemies. Genuine jadeite netsuke, indeed! But it is only now that I can prove my innocence."

In tandem, the cops' hands lowered in what I could only assume was the direction of their guns. Or their antacid pills.

"Time is of the essence, gentlemen," Edsel urged. "The perpetrators will soon realize I have uncovered their perfidy! It was the merest happenstance that I stopped by my Little

Shoppe today and caught the scoundrels red-handed, when I am routinely closed mid-week. So, we must act with all possible haste and compare the actual inventory against this spuriously downloaded one before our master hacker manages to erase the evidence yet again!"

Brooking no resistance, Edsel swept the feds out as magnificently as he had had exited the Historical Society cradling Chomsky's broken body.

"*What next?*" I sighed as I locked the door firmly behind me.

"Elementary, my dear…"

"It was a rhetorical question," I pointed out,

"Nonetheless, it seems obvious that we must avail ourselves of this hard-won instance of pure ratiocination in order to reconstruct the crime itself," Doyle went on, unperturbed.

"Why?" I asked. "Unless I'm very much mistaken, Edsel's miraculously discovered proof has St. Hubbins' fingerprints all over it. Why not just let him take it from here, just as he asked us to do?"

"St. Hubbins' efforts are so laughably sophomoric that I might suspect Babbage himself as their author," Doyle sighed. "The only way we can permanently remove ourselves from the sights of our flatfooted friends from Washington is to build upon our already not-inconsiderable progress and put the final pieces of the puzzle in place. Our earlier adventures have allowed us to extrapolate with a 48.3 percent probability that Cameron Billings staged his own disappearance in a desperate attempt to cover up financial malfeasance under cover of the Billings Foundation."

"Only 48.3 percent? Didn't Paul tell us…"

"My dear Watson, such trustingness descends closely to an unbecoming gullibility. We have at least two other people who have freely admitted to being associated with Operation Dragon's Den. My heuristics have assigned each a 25 percent probability as a constant," Doyle said.

"What two people? St. Hubbins and who? *Byrne?* Surely, you don't think there's a grain of truth in his story. He spun that farrago strictly for Paul's benefit."

"There's a grain of truth in every story, even if it is only the kernel of fact that the tissue of lies has been woven to conceal," Doyle said.

Which sounded so much like a Zen koan, I had to assume it must have come straight from the bowels of Todorov.

"But to return to the matter at hand, the key question facing us is who killed Cameron Billings?" Doyle went on. "And why? Leaving aside the possibility of a rogue commando returned from the dead to avenge the death of his men, we are forced to reduce the problem to the three classic questions: Motive, means, and opportunity. Once we have reconstructed those…"

"You mean, like we reconstructed the false entries associated with the Billings Bequest? How did that work out for you?"

"Beyond securing you a $500,000 grant?"

"It was another rhetorical question. It is my fondest hope that one day you will finally perceive the difference."

"Instead of wasting our time in needless quibbling, let us simply lay out the facts," Doyle retorted. "Create a timeline if you will. I believe we've reached the appropriate place in the narrative for such a step."

"Of course. Why not draw a map of Battlefield Bluff while you're at it? And please don't forget to include any secret passages."

"The map is readily available on the park's website

as well as its information kiosk, and neither indicates any secret passages—although I suppose they could have purposely omitted a few on principle. Nevertheless, let us strive to focus. The roots of this debacle may lie with Roxie Keyes exposing Operation Dragon's Den, but Cam Billings' death has a clear starting point: the moment he dove into the water at the triathlon. Shall I recap the scene?"

"Please don't bother," I said. "That memory qualifies as indelibly etched."

"Then shall we turn our attention to the good inspector's relationship map? In particular, I would suggest we turn our attention to that missing node in the middle that seems to connect all the other data points. The absent referent, if you will—and the one glaring omission in our plodding inspector's recapitulation."

"I assume you're referring to Devlin," I said with a sigh. "Frankly, I'd feel a lot better about pointing the finger at him, if I had any evidence he had enough corporeal chops to actually kill a man."

"Yet you seemed impressed enough with certain other of his 'corporeal chops,' as you are pleased to term them," Doyle pointed out.

I drew an even deeper breath than I had after what I now assumed was Devlin's kiss. "The point remains that if he is St. Hubbins' avatar, he should share St. Hubbins' motives. And St. Hubbins already told us, Cam's death is a major complication for him, and I have no cause to doubt him. So why should Devlin behave as if he has a different motive?"

"Surely you can scent a red herring when it stinks to high heaven," Doyle rebuked me. "Order and method compel us to consider only the data points we witnessed with our own eyes—as recorded in our inspector's relationship graph. From those, and those alone, can we perform the necessary interpolations to extrapolate motive, means, and opportunity."

Which was when the lightbulb went off above my head—quite literally, in fact. My office was fitted with one of those annoying fixtures that went dark if you sat still for too long, as if it was accusing you of napping, and I had just shifted.

"Wait! Before you extrapolate anything, you need to redefine those parameters," I said.

An offended silence, before Doyle said, "I'm afraid you'll need to be a touch more specific."

"What is the difference between William Devlin and St. Hubbins? What makes one an avatar and the other a data point?"

"Is this a trick question?" Doyle asked. "Or am I to infer that you actually believe William Devlin is enjoying his afterlife as an amorous ghost in the machine?"

"I am merely trying to distinguish between reality and illusion." I held up a hand to cut off Doyle's reflexive protest. "*Not* the virtual and actual worlds. There are plenty of illusions right here in this world. St. Hubbins is every bit as illusory as William Devlin. His entire identity is nothing but a mesh of lies. Same goes for Cam Billings and his vanishing swimsuit. Not to mention his magic cell phone making stock trades under cover of every not-for-profit in Morgansburg. All of them nothing but misdirection, obscuring the one solid fact we have—the single piece of tangible evidence that connects this entire web of illusion." I permitted myself a dramatic pause. "Our absent referent is Cam Billings' cell phone."

"You just said that the stock trades…"

"I'm talking about the cell phone itself, not the trades

that were made from it. And the eyewitness who can attest to the fact that Paul Morgan tried to destroy it. Unfortunately, there is only one logical extrapolation about Cam Billings' death you can make from that data point."

It was hardly a thunderclap. More like an uncomfortable truth that I had been unwilling to see all along. But the pronouncement was met with a moment's stunned silence that I was graceless enough to thoroughly savor. Then Doyle said, "Sometimes, my dear Watson, you have the power to astound me."

The screen of my phone suddenly filled with blocky capitals:

CHALLENGE TO THE READER.
NOW YOU HAVE SEEN ALL THE SAME CLUES PHILO VANCE DID, AND ONLY ONE SOLUTION IS POSSIBLE.

"That was Ellery Queen's schtick, not Philo Vance's," I sighed. "And I don't think the second part is accurate at all. We might have all the clues, but we've only established opportunity, not means or motive."

"The means are trivial. Why not satisfy ourselves with the first weapon presented—the butt of Mike Malone's gun? Or to put it more gracefully, the ubiquitous blunt instrument. Even Christie admitted it was her weapon of choice because she was always afraid of making a mistake when it came to guns.

"Moving on to motive, the Billings Foundation money laundering is ample motivation, even without the threat of punishment—or disbarment—for covering up a crime."

"And who is the likeliest person to fear disbarment?" I asked.

The answer tapped at my office door with impeccable dramatic timing. "Mary, it's Paul. May I come in?"

I couldn't even work up a whispered imprecation.

The tapping increased to knocking—and threatened to verge on pounding. "Look, Mary. We need to talk. This is not you. This is not who you are."

A statement which I always found a bit of an epistemological/ontological nightmare.

"You're not a vindictive woman, Mary. You don't want to play it this way. Let me help you, Mary. Let us help each other before it's too late."

CHAPTER TWENTY-SEVEN
A Simple Matter of a Few Heuristics

I opened the door. What other option did I have? Paul would just keep pounding away for as long as it took, Lenny Russo would have a new exhibit of The Adjunct Mess, and Isa would look on with a vindicated gleam in her eye.

"I don't think you fully understand," Paul offered the mansplainer's classic opening. "You and me, we've both got serious problems. We need to help each other out."

"Is that so?"

"Mary, this is not the time to fight. You know as well as I do that we are in the midst of a massive data breach that could destroy not just the Billings Foundation and De Sales College, but a score of other government offices and businesses. And you know as well as I do who's behind it."

"If you know something, you should take that information to the appropriate authorities. I believe you can find them with Edsel Kincaid, who has happily discovered proof that exonerates him from the charges you leveled at him. They may appreciate the interruption. I think they find Edsel…a bit bewildering."

"Since they've already been in to question you," Paul said, "you understand how serious this is."

Damn my smart-assed mouth.

"Indeed, Watson. Your honest impetuosity has always been one of the qualities I have most valued, and yet you don't seem to have learned that there are some situations that call for a subtler approach than drawing your trusty service revolver."

I ignored Doyle. Eyes on the prize—if such a term could ever have been applied to Paul Morgan. "I'm tiring of having to repeat this, but if you have an accusation to make, I would prefer you do it directly."

"You've got to listen to me, Mary, and believe me when I tell you that the only person I'm here to accuse is Nigel St. Hubbins. You were never anything but a patsy, a stalking horse."

I impaled him with a glare. "Was I now?"

"There's no need to get hostile. I'm here to help. But before I can help you, you need to face the fact that it's going to be your fingerprints all over every last one of St. Hubbins's dirty tricks, starting with those deaccessioned books and straight through the data breach at De Sales."

A true and accurate account of my position as it stood right now. But the way I saw it, that was hardly *germane*. "Be that as it may, I don't see what you want from me."

"I want the truth, Mary. And I want you to trust me. Because I'm your friend here. You've got to believe me when I tell you men like St. Hubbins won't think twice about throwing you under the bus. Me, on the other hand, I want to help."

All of which I would completely agree with if the last sentence was not missing one crucial final word, "myself." But that was not doing a lot to help me resist the urge to deck him.

"All right," I forced myself to say. "Let's leave my situation out of it. Why is this your problem? Am I supposed to believe you're here simply to help me for old time's sake? Because if that's the case, I appreciate the effort, but I can assure you it's not necessary."

"You know me, I respect a woman's independence. I've learned my lesson on that front the hard way. But you need to know when you need help. I respect your pride, Mary, but right now, you have to accept the fact that you need *me*."

"I'll do my best," I assured him. "But it would help if you could explain why? What does any of this have to do with you?"

A long pause while Paul wrestled with his demons. It resembled nothing quite so much as two foundering whales attempting to mate. Then he leaned forward in sudden decision.

"Okay. Cards on the table," he said for what had to be the hundredth time in the last few weeks. "Taken out of context, the data breach at De Sales could get a lot of people in serious trouble. Not that there's any question of actual malfeasance, but sometimes information needs to be massaged…"

Just like books must be jeuged. "And you were the guy to do it? Presumably when you were crossing all those t's and dotting all those i's."

"Yes," Paul said. "I admit it."

He cut me off from commenting with an upraised hand. "Not that I had any idea what was really going on. But it's my name all over the documents. I'm the one who signed the papers."

"And there we have it," Doyle murmured. "Motive confirmed."

I shut my eyes. "Oh, Christ. *Why?*"

"Do we have to do this right now?" Paul sighed.

His aggrieved tone was the stuff of chastened husbands everywhere—and frankly, it pissed me off. "You're the one who knocked on my door."

"Okay, okay. Take your pound of flesh. Enjoy it. I was Cam's lawyer, for God's sake. I was his friend. I trusted him, and he screwed me. Is that enough, or do I need to grovel? I blew it, okay? I blew it bad, and I need your help. But you need me too, Mary. We need to work together. If we work together, we can make this whole thing go away."

"I think he means *I* can make this thing go away," Doyle interjected.

I ignored him—contenting myself with a mental note that, somewhere along the line, I'd have to issue Doyle an instruction set that made it clear authorial credit and plausible deniability were mutually exclusive conditions. But that could wait until later. Right now, there was only one important question that needed to be answered: What exactly was 'this thing' we were all trying to get our names off of? Were we just talking about market manipulation and fraud? Or were we talking about a far more serious crime?

Oh, come on, Mary! I refrained from slapping myself on the forehead. Of course we were talking about a more serious crime! Paul might be a master of lying to himself, but surely I was made of stern enough stuff to stare unflinchingly at the fact that I was alone in a room with a murderer, pretty much at the point in the plot where he should pull a gun and force me into a waiting van where I would thrash helplessly against my bonds until Devlin showed up to save me just in the nick of time.

"Cliched," Doyle opined, again, seemingly to read my mind. How was he doing that? Was I that easy to read or was I that good of a programmer?

"A good feminist like you," Doyle continued, "should never give up your agency. Hasn't Nancy Drew been pounding in that lesson for years?"

More to the point, I just didn't see the hostage scenario playing out. Paul's weapon of choice had always been dogged persuasion. His approach to seduction had been predicated on the assumption that if he talked at you so fast you couldn't get a word in edgewise, you couldn't say no. If he had killed a man in a physical altercation, it must have come as more of a shock to him than anyone else.

All of which led directly to another uncomfortable fact: Like it or not, I was in the perfect position to prove who had killed Cam Billings—and it was not bloody likely I—or anyone else—would get another chance like this. Not that I particularly cared whether Paul Morgan went to jail—just so long as I never had to see him again. And I didn't really care about justice for Cam Billings either. All I wanted was to stay out of jail and go back to my quiet little life as The Adjunct Mess, even if that gave Lenny and Isa smug satisfaction. But there was only one way I could see to do that. As my dissertation advisor was fond of saying bracingly, "The only way out, is *through*."

And so, taking a deep breath just like I used to when faced with the glare of the equally bracing summer camp counselor intent on making me dive headfirst into the murky depths of the lake, I plunged in.

"All right, if you want to work together, let's get a few things straight about the Billings Bequest. Cards on the table, as you like to put it. Am I correct that those deaccessioned books were the reason you and Cam were in such a hurry to buy me off? Presumably because, by some stupid coincidence that defies logic…"

"Oh, Watson," Doyle groaned, "that's just hurtful."

"I stumbled across evidence of one of your money-laundering networks in the form of those deaccessioned books…"

"There was no stumbling about it," Paul said. "St. Hubbins baited that trap and you walked straight into it."

"Just like Roxie Keyes did?"

"Roxie Keyes was an accident! The stupid girl refused to take no for an answer!"

Stupid girl? I had to force myself not to scream at him. "Then I guess I have to count myself fortunate I was even stupider since my safety was dependent on the fact that I was too dumb to see I was being bought off."

"That's a cheap shot, Mary. Not worthy of you."

Probably true, but once again, scarcely *germane*. "Fine. I'll go along with Roxie Keyes' death being an accident. I'll even do you the courtesy of assuming Cam was the one responsible, not you. But what happened with Cam? Was his death an accident too? Or did you discover he was going to throw you under the bus, just like you've been trying to do with the greater population of Morgansburg?"

One look at Paul's face was all the confirmation I needed. "Just like St. Hubbins will do to you," he said, desperation leaking into his voice. "Listen to me, Mary. We're in this together. No judgments."

In this together? Was it only me who saw a rather solid line between data theft—inadvertent or otherwise—and killing a man?

"In other words, Cam set you up, just like you tried to set up Edsel," I plowed ahead. "Not to mention the landscapers. And Byrne. And now me. To Cam, you were just convenient. And expendable."

Paul's face set with distaste at that last word. "Can we table that discussion, please? Let's just help each other out of this mess."

Each other. This relationship was about as reciprocal as Patience and Fortitude's when the can opener came out.

"Well, to do that I need to understand exactly what I need to be erasing your—I mean, of course, *our*—names from."

He drew a deep breath. "Last night, someone discovered Roxie Keyes' phone and found a way to use it to access Cam's phone—damned if I know how. I thought I'd taken care of that."

I forbore enlightening him. "If someone has already managed to download the data from Cam's phone, there's no point in trying to put the toothpaste back in the tube."

"This isn't data," Paul said. "It's a recording. And we need to find it before anyone discovers its existence."

"A recording of what exactly?"

"A conversation."

"Why did Cam have a recording of a conversation on his phone?"

Wait! Why did I even need to ask? What else could that reel-to-reel tape in the virtual Billings trading floor have been?

"Cam recorded all his conversations. We all did. So there could be no misunderstandings later."

More like so they all had guns pointed at each other's heads. No honor among thieves, and all that.

"This conversation has the potential to hurt a lot of people if it goes public. We need to find it and destroy it before someone else does."

There it was—a clear confession. What more did I need—at least beyond the reassurance that I had not already made myself an accessory after the fact in the name of playing Nancy Drew? But how on earth was I ever going to prove it?

"If I may be so bold," Doyle said, "our friend has a naïve but amateurish faith in the importance of the destruction of a physical device. If you can give me a moment, I can have a few words with some friends who may be able to help in retrieving this singularly interesting recording from the Cloud."

In other words, Doyle wanted me to stall—kill a few minutes in useless blather. Fortunately, there was nothing like a career built upon academic conferences to make you an expert in doing just that.

"All right. I can give it a shot," I told Paul. "But first, I need to run a few heuristics."

"What does that mean?" he asked—more than reasonably, in my humble opinion.

"Everything," I lied, as I typed in "Confirm $Mn = 2n$—1 is prime for integer n > 1" before he could ask what that meant. Nothing like a nice bout of Mersenne primes to take things down a notch or two. I next went to catalog. loc.gov and typed "Copy *.* > foo.dat & show progress." I was banking on the fact that Morgan was not one to know that the government agency in question was the Library of Congress—and I had just instructed the machine to copy the entire catalogue.

One thing was certain, there wasn't going to be a lot of CPU left for me to begin falsifying evidence on Morgan's behalf any time soon.

"All right, I'm back," Doyle huffed. "No need to torture every last bit in cyberspace."

"Did it work?"

"Hear 'em and weep."

Which was a metaphor so mixed I didn't even bother to try to correct it before my audio feed exploded with a shriek and a whistle.

"What do you mean, use Malone's gun?" Paul's voice rang unmistakably in my earpiece. "That's not just murder, it's falsifying evidence."

"It's your job to worry about the charges, not mine. Malone knows too much. He served in Dragon's Den, and sooner or later he's going to put the pieces together. And if we don't step in before that St. Hubbins creature figures out how much Malone knows, we are both going to be spending a very long time in jail."

"What do you mean, us? You're the one who killed her."

"And you're the one with the law degree. I'm guessing you're acquainted with the term 'accessory after the fact.'" Cam's voice grew cajoling. "Come on, Paul, I've had your back all the way, just like I need you to have mine. Let's just make this right and move on."

"Make this right by killing St. Hubbins and setting Malone up to take the fall?"

"You saw the way he was waving that gun around. You should have had him up on charges long ago."

A moment's pause before Paul said, "I'm sorry, Cam. But there are some things I can't make right. Roxie's death was an accident. At least you told me it was. But this... this is Murder One. We've got to put an end to this now. The Billings Foundation is supposed to be a blind trust. Come clean, come forward, and say it was done without your knowledge. Promise an internal investigation and a swift restructuring."

"You really think they'll let us get away with that?" Cam snorted. "You've got no idea what you're dealing with here. These are not people you play games with. Roxie Keyes found out the hard way."

"And I have no intention of seeing anyone else go that way. Not even St. Hubbins, who by all rights should be rotting in jail for the rest of his life. I'm sorry, Cam, but it's got to end here."

It was perhaps the one moment in my life when I genuinely respected Paul Morgan. Unfortunately, I was more than a little certain that the next moment was about to expose him as a killer—even before voices on the audio feed rose into a heated argument that was suddenly silenced by the sounds of a struggle and then a sickening thump.

I shut my eyes. There it was. Proof. Proof enough for me, at least. But I was more than a little certain it was not proof that would stand up in a court of law. I needed something better than interpolations from a bot that thought he was a Great Detective. I needed admissible evidence. Something as tangible as Dread Pirate Roberts being caught dead to rights with his hands on the keyboard.

Oh, dear Lord. Hands on the keyboard. Yes! That was it! That was the answer.

Or was it? Some might call it the answer; others might well call it entrapment. Or to put it slightly differently, I was about to do the lousiest thing I had ever done to another human being in my life. The only thing less lovely to contemplate was the realization I was about to pull Nigel St. Hubbins' incompetent ass out of the fire he himself had set.

"All right, listen to me," I said to Paul. "We need to get out of here now. You know the diner the Billings Foundation funded? They've got WiFi, as well as public access computers."

"Really? I would have thought we might do better with the Twinkies and Red Bull crowd."

"Try to be a bit more woke. I know plenty of program-mers who are vegans." Which did nothing to improve their personalities: it just made them smug when they stared at their own shoes.

Paul eyed me, like somewhere in his hind brain he was scenting the glimmerings of a trap. "I swear if I find out this is some kind of twisted revenge…"

Oh, *honestly*. I glared at him with all the balefulness of the vengeful ex-girlfriend he believed me to be. "Have you ever hacked a website?"

"You have?" he countered—and damn me if he didn't sound impressed.

"No," Doyle murmured. "She prefers to leave the nuts and bolts—or shall I say 1s and 0s to the grunts…"

"Irrelevant," I snapped. "The point is, I'm the one who has some experience in such things, and trust me, if I'd scrubbed Cam's phone, the data would really be gone for good. So now is the time for you to listen up and play things my way. Rule number one of doing anything illicit on the web is don't use a machine that can be traced to you. Which is why we need to get up to the diner and find a public computer."

A computer that, given St. Hubbins' warnings and the arrival of the two feds, I had to hope was being monitored, so that any fresh downloads would set off alarms that would bring them running. I got to my feet with what I hoped was the world-weariness of a hacker who considered breaking into the Pentagon a warm-up exercise. "Honestly, Paul, have you even heard of Dread Pirate Roberts?"

CHAPTER TWENTY-EIGHT
The Man in the Deep-Sea Diver's Suit

"Dread Pirate Roberts. A fiendishly clever strategy. Truly inspired even by my standards," Doyle murmured as we hurried into the diner. "To think my good, honest Watson is capable of being so devious. It reminds me I must watch my back when I'm around you."

As I pulled open the door, I braced against complications in the form of kundalini tea or a fresh flight of cleansing mead, but, mercifully, the pierced hostess was engrossed with a hipster in a muscle shirt and backward baseball cap who was quizzing her in detail about the glycemic indexes of the various protein shakes on offer. That made the next part of my plan much easier.

I pulled out my phone and mimed exasperation. "Here we go again! I lost connectivity as soon as we got through the door. I don't care whether it's sunspots or ley lines, that wretched town planning board has to consent to a functional tower on Battlefield Bluff. At this point, it's a safety issue, not a luxury." I switched off my phone before Paul could see it. "Look, I'm gonna have to stay outside where I can get a signal. You go in and start scrubbing the data. I'll send in Doyle to help just as soon as I get a connection."

Some vestigial hind-brain intelligence made Paul pause. "Why don't you do it?"

I met his gaze. "I assumed you wouldn't be satisfied unless you erased it yourself."

Another moment's hesitation before he went inside like the proverbial lamb to the slaughter.

"So where would you like me start downloading?" Doyle asked, as soon as the door closed to seal Paul's doom. "The IRS? The U.S. Treasury? Sony Pictures? The Pentagon would be far and away the easiest, but I can't really recommend it. They tend to get punitive—once they finally notice, that is. But that can take months…"

Punitive. Still not my favorite word in the lexicon. "Perhaps it would be best to keep that particular issue on a need-to-know basis," I said.

"Oh, relax. I was just having you on," Doyle said. "Credit me with some sense of humor."

"You don't *have* a sense of—" I broke off, my eyes widening, as Doyle swam into view—quite literally—on my phone. How else was I to explain the large, wet flippers he was wearing?

"I thought we had agreed the deep-sea diver suit was *de trop*."

"It's not a deep-sea diver suit, it's a wetsuit. As well as, of course, an obvious homage," Doyle said, as he unzipped it to reveal a white dinner jacket. Working a boutonniere into his lapel, he stepped out of the wetsuit.

"Doyle. A.C. Doyle," he said. "Now, shall we get this party started?"

"Remind me to lower your badinage factor by an order of magnitude when this is over," I sighed, as he squelched across my phone screen and followed Paul into the Internet Café.

So mesmerized was I by that vision, that I barely noticed the protein-shake aficionado had left off his contemplation of glycemic indexes until a shadow loomed over my phone screen, and I turned to meet Byrne's incredulous gaze. "All right, Nancy Drew," he said when he finally found it within himself to speak. "Not a half-bad plan for an amateur. Now what I need you to do right now is turn around, get the hell out of here, and leave the rest to me."

So that was it. My white knight was about to come charging up in his battered pickup truck to save me. "Is that so?" I asked. "Do you think I'm entitled to any opinion in the matter? Seeing as it's my plan and all that?"

"For God's sake, do you have any experience in running this kind of scam?"

"And you do? Oh, that's right. Your secret commando past."

"Yes," he said. "My secret commando past. Which makes me a hell of a lot more qualified to deal with a man who's killed at least one person and maybe two than you are."

"Oh, come on. It's not like Paul Morgan is going to pull out a gun and start shooting."

"No, but he may break a computer monitor, put a shard of glass to your throat, and take you as a hostage when the feds show up. With luck, it would take out the entire network and destroy all the evidence too." Byrne said. "At least, that's what I would do."

He spoke with a matter-of-factness that suggested he was weighing the merits of a similar approach right now.

"How did you even *know*?" I changed the subject. "Sniffing around the internet again?"

Byrne's face set as he considered lying. "The St. Hubbins twerp called me," he admitted. "Says a lot that a man who has every right to resent the fact I'm even alive trusts me more than you do. I had hoped for more from a woman I…"

Byrne's mouth clamped shut, and we stared at each other in dismay. My mind raced with explanations. It wasn't personal. I don't trust anyone—not even myself. No one will so much as speak of the fate of the youth seminarian who tried to introduce me to trust exercises at church camp.

Then I heard my mouth form the words, "You're absolutely right. I'm very sorry. It was absolutely inexcusable on my part, and you deserve better."

"Thank you," Byrne said stiffly.

"We don't have to hug now, do we?" I asked.

The corner of his mouth twitched. "I think there are better ways to set things right between us. You busy tonight?"

Why?" I asked warily.

He raised an eyebrow. "Now doesn't seem like the best time for a debriefing, now does it? Especially since your Dread Pirate Roberts sting isn't over yet."

He turned to head back into the diner.

"Wait!" My fingers shaking with the struggle to fight down all my germaphobe's issues, I reached up, unhooked the Bluetooth from my ear and handed it to him, reassuring myself that I could always sanitize it later. "You'd better take Doyle with you. He's no good at wet work but when it comes to a data dump, he's a whiz. I trust you do know how to operate a VR avatar?"

"With one hand tied behind my back," Byrne said, his face relaxing into a grin. "Now, will you get out of here?"

"And what are you going to do?" I asked.

"How did Shakespeare put it? 'First, we kill all the lawyers."

"Metaphorically speaking, of course," I said.

"That's gonna depend on the lawyer," Byrne said—just as an SUV squealed to a halt in the parking lot and the cavalry charged onto the scene with St. Hubbins leading, straight out of *Call of Duty*, in a black pullover and cargo pants, credentials strung around his neck, and a gun the size of a small cannon in his hand. He was followed in close order by the two feds, who both had pulled their weapons, and Edsel Kincaid who brandished a Genuine Samurai Sword.

"Always a bridesmaid, never a bride," St. Hubbins murmured, rolling his eyes at Byrne. "How do you feel about boiling pet bunnies now?"

"I beg your pardon?"

"I said 'Our hacker is right inside!' What else could I have said?" Then he winked and burst through the door of the diner, shouting, "Freeze! Federal agents! Everyone get your hands in the air and keep them where we can see them."

CHAPTER TWENTY-NINE
Of Killers and Kitsch

The pierced hostess fell to her knees behind the counter with her hands behind her head. "Please," she babbled. "No-one ever knew the protein in the vegan shakes was gelatin. It was an honest mistake. I swear, there was no intent to defraud. But we couldn't afford to just throw it all away."

Byrne paused and a trace of mischief crossed his features, before he morphed into Andy Taylor giving Opie the dressing down of his life. "That attitude does you credit," he said. "'Waste not, want not,' that's what my sainted Irish grandmother always told me. It's a lesson too often lost in a society which seems to consider everything expendable—including people. So, let's just chalk this particular incident up to an honest mistake. But I'm not going to warn you twice. Straighten up and fly right. Gelatin isn't pectin. I'll be watching."

Ignoring her stammered thank you, he spun and joined the others as they crashed into the game room. Paul half-rose from the computer with his signature imitation of a beached fish. "What the fuck?" he demanded—with what could only be described as a criminal lack of originality.

"All right! I need you to hold it right there, then sit back down and keep your hands where I can see them."

Paul complied, and Byrne pulled out his cell phone and snapped several pictures, documenting Paul and the screen full of illicit data, recording date, time and contents with military precision monotone.

"What the hell? I'm the county attorney! You have no right to barge in here and threaten me at gunpoint!" Paul turned on the two feds. "Place these people under arrest or I'll have your badges."

Any impulse the feds might have felt to do just that was rapidly quashed by a single glare from Byrne. "Thanks for your help, boys, but now that the scene is secured and documented, it's probably best for all non-essential personnel to clear the premises."

The pierced hostess needed no second invitation and bolted for the door. But at least one federal agent was stupid enough to try to stand his ground. "I think we'll be the judge of who's essential here."

"Do you, now?" St. Hubbins asked. "Is it an essential function of law enforcement personnel to snap up forged copies of Keane's priceless limited editions to redecorate your DC office?"

"Don't scoff at what you don't know," Edsel warned, waving his Samurai blade at St. Hubbins. "Original Keanes are poised to skyrocket in value—especially now that the Hudson Valley has been graced with the title of Brooklyn North. And even that hipster par excellence Tim Burton has given those wide-eyed waifs his imprimatur—on NPR of all places—where he compared them to nothing less than the Mona Lisa! And for anyone who's interested"—he looked around to see if anyone was listening—"I've got quite a tidy little stockpile set aside at bargain basement prices."

"I for one, certainly am," St. Hubbins assured him. "And I think I could offer you a little help in volumizing your holdings with an on-line auction. But as eagerly as I look forward to collaborating with such a visionary when it comes to the art market, it does nothing to change the fact that these two sworn officers of the law were off chasing down the international trade in knock-off Faberge eggs while one of the most dangerous hacks in history was taking place right beneath their noses."

"I wasn't hacking," Paul exploded. "I don't know *how* to hack. It was her pet bot playing James Bond—"

His voice died off as he apparently realized what he sounded like, and St. Hubbins nodded approvingly. "That's right. You have the right to remain silent. And if that is the only explanation you have to offer, I strongly suggest you exercise it. And as for you two," St. Hubbins said, rounding on the feds, "I strongly suggest you do what my muscular friend here suggests and stand down before I file a report with your superiors."

One of the feds—a man after my own heart—looked happy enough to find an excuse out of this mess. The other was stupid enough to rise to the challenge. "You want a pissing match over jurisdiction, you've got one. Who the hell are you, anyway?"

"A man with a few numbers on speed dial," St. Hubbins told them. "Check your text messages. Now."

On cue, both agents' cell phones pinged. They glanced at them, then looked up, suddenly as slack jawed as Paul was.

"Why don't you wait until you're back at your desks to reply?" St. Hubbins said genially. "But just between us, I'd honestly suggest not going into any further detail about the Black Velvet Elvis angle in your final report. It can only generate more paperwork, and I don't know about you, but I despise paperwork. Opens up room for so many misinterpretations. Dereliction of duty. Criminal incompetence…"

The agents vanished somewhere around the second "paperwork"—with Edsel in hot pursuit, protesting that they still hadn't sorted out the issue of the Big Mouth Billy Basses that were clearly fraudulent, since they were singing "Take Me to the River" in Cantonese.

"You want to see paperwork, all three of you are going to be sitting in paperwork up to your ass for the next year," Paul snarled, leaping to his feet to follow. "Beginning with swearing your bail bond and forfeiting your passports."

"Not so fast." Byrne slid between Paul and the door with all the speed of the running back he claimed to have once been. "Mr. St. Hubbins would like a word before the authorities arrive."

"The only word I'm going to have is with a lawyer," Paul assured him. "This is no kind of arrest. This is entrapment. Mary Watson screwed me." He glared my direction. "She damned well *set me up*."

"Quite elegantly," St. Hubbins agreed. "And far more effectively than your sad attempts to frame whoever was unfortunate enough to be closest to hand. But let us save the compliments for later. Your problem right now is that you tried to screw *me*—an approach with which I tend to take umbrage."

A moment's pause before Paul made the obvious connection. "You're the crooked accountant behind Operation Dragon's Den. Hell, you're the master hacker. You're the one Washington's supposed to be prosecuting."

"Well, that's the thing about prosecutors. As a matter of general principle, they prefer to prosecute the person who actually committed the crime. Cuts down on the paperwork, not to mention the threat of disbarment," St.

Hubbins told him. "And, strange as it might seem, in this case, I'm not the one who did it. Fortunately, I persuaded the Powers That Be to let me save them some effort and bring in the real perpetrators instead."

"So Mary was working for *you* all along?" Paul demanded.

"Ah, no. At best it was an informal alliance," St. Hubbins assured him. "But I have every intention of formalizing it going forward. Someone will have to take up where the Billings Foundation has unfortunately been forced to leave off."

"God help her," Byrne snorted.

"But time is running short before the State Police show up, and we're getting a little away from the topic."

"No, what we're getting away from is this clusterfuck," Paul snorted. "Or at least I am. Next time we talk, it will be through my lawyers."

Once more, he moved for the door; once more, Byrne blocked his way. "I'm afraid that won't be possible. Not until I get your statement for the Campus Incident Report."

"You really need help, you know?" Paul said. "I mean, no-one respects the sacrifices that our men in uniform have made more than I do, but this sick obsession that has brought you to Morgansburg has already destroyed two lives…"

"Sorry, *bro*, but you've got that all wrong," Byrne said. "It was no sick obsession that brought me here. Nothing but sheer dumb-assed coincidence."

"Unless you see the hand of a greater power at work," Doyle mused. "Miss Lillian Virginia Mountweazel has her little ways."

"And if you seriously think I had anything to do with bringing Dr. Watson into this mess, think again," Byrne went on. "I would never hide behind a woman's skirts even if it meant bringing down bin Laden himself—and I would never besmirch a woman's professional reputation any more than her character."

"There it is. The B-word again," St. Hubbins sighed. "Which rather makes my point. When it comes to Dr. Watson, you'd be far wiser to fear our muscled friend than me. Because I don't have any personal interest here—at least none beyond keeping my own sorry ass out of jail. Mark my words, I've got nothing against dirty tricks, at least as a matter of general principle. But I think it's only fair to draw the line when they're done to me. In fact, I consider it a bit of a professional affront, especially when I'm the guy you paid to put them in place in the first place. Then, I get angry, if not downright punitive. So, yes, I'm the master hacker that brought the feds down on Morgansburg, and yes, I'm more than a little intent on, if not justice, shall we say, assigning blame where it is due. Fortunately for you, I have a few connections in Washington who currently see fit to back me in that task. And it's just your good fortune that you're the key to doing that. So, I suggest you start talking."

Paul began to look a lot less sure of himself. "Didn't someone just say I had the right to remain silent?"

"Of course, you do," St. Hubbins assured him. "You have the right to remain silent and listen very carefully to what I'm about to say, because I am about to say it precisely once. You are in some very serious trouble here. The money laundering and international financial conspiracies are the least of it—or rather they pale when compared to murder. Still, they are also your ticket out of here. Because to the men who control them, those networks are a hell of a lot more important than one man's death."

"You're referring to your infamous Operation Dragon's Den?" Paul snorted. "I'm sorry to rain on your parade, but it doesn't exist."

"No, it doesn't. But it did," Byrne cut in. "And short of bringing in Snowden himself, I can't think of anything the feds would like better than to find someone to prosecute in the biggest military data breach of this century. Better still, an entire network. So as much as it turns my stomach to agree with this asshole on anything at all, I suggest you show the brains that got you into Yale and take a deal. Because, trust me, if it were my decision, you'd be stuck in Rikers without bail for a year, awaiting the speedy trial the legal system has somewhere along the line decided you no longer have a right to, just like all the other expendables you've put there."

"You're obsessed with expendables. And you're wrong. I didn't murder anyone. It was an *accident*."

"When it comes to the first, I've got a roomful of shrinks that would probably agree with you. When it comes to the rest, maybe or maybe not. But it is beyond a reasonable doubt that what you have just said *is* self-incrimination. So, would you please shut up and listen to St. Hubbins? I won't warn you again."

"There's no getting out of prison time," St. Hubbins tagged back in. "At this point, we can't exactly overlook murder, even if many would argue it's justifiable homicide. But we can probably swing Club Fed after your sealed testimony—although we may want to think about witness protection even before you face your first parole board. I am certain Cam Billings' friends—at least any of the ones we don't manage to put in jail—are bound to be feeling even more punitive than I do right now when word gets out. Which gives you considerable incentive to try to put as many of them in jail for as long as possible."

Sirens began to wail outside, and Paul opened his mouth for a final protest. "For the love of God, will you shut up and be grateful for how lucky you are to get off this easily?" Byrne cut him off. "And welcome to being an expendable. In case you were wondering, you've never been anything else."

EPILOGUE
The One-Armed Man

I didn't hang around to wait for the State Police, preferring to spend the remainder of the day cultivating the Zen of processing library fines. I had just made the final turn on my way to the even deeper Zen of Happy Hour, when St. Hubbins manifested, lounging against a historical marker. "I suppose it was too much to hope you'd already ridden off into the sunset," I sighed.

"I've been invited to ride down to Washington to face a few uncomfortable debriefings. Actually, 'invite' is too polite a word for it. You'd think the Powers That Be might have learned to develop a sense of humor when they try to turn a hacker." St. Hubbins grinned. "But don't worry about me. I know where enough bodies are buried that I'll be back before you know it."

"And if that is precisely what I'm worried about?"

"Oh, mark my words. I will be back—if for no other reason than someone's going to have to handle the paperwork when the government takes over your tech hub, and I don't think the De Sales provost is up to the task."

He met my eyes.

"Or you. Far too much stern moral fiber for you to be comfortable with that."

"The government? You mean, those same friendly folks who are threatening you with prison?"I said. "No, thank you. I prefer to stay as far away from them as possible."

"Unfortunately, I don't think that's going to be an option. As I told you before, these guys aren't real good at taking no for an answer," St. Hubbins said. "I wasn't lying when I said there were more than a few federal agencies that would be more than delighted to pick up where Billings Foundation left off. Nor was I lying when I mentioned consecutive life sentences. These guys have a heavy hand when it comes to getting what they want. You're going to need someone with a complete lack of moral compass to deal with them. In fact, I'd argue it's pretty much a civil service requirement. But we can save that discussion for later. That's not why I need to talk to you right now."

"Then what is?"

St. Hubbins licked his lips, suddenly uncertain, before he forced out the next words. "We got off on the wrong foot, Dr. Watson. And I need to set the record straight before I go."

"It's okay," I said. "Really."

"No, it's not," he said. "Not if I have every intention of pursuing our relationship on both a personal and professional level—which I do. And we are never going to be able to work together as long as I'm operating under false pretenses."

"I thought that was your go-to approach."

He conceded the point with a shrug. "You seem to have made an honest man of me. I don't want to hide behind another man's name, not when it comes to you. You're still better off not knowing my real name, but I want it clear between us that I'm not William Devlin. And I'm certainly not the mastermind behind Operation Dragon's Den."

"I hope you won't be disappointed if I tell you that is scarcely a surprise. Byrne has already told me Devlin is dead—and he's in a position to know."

"Well, yes to the second part, but no to the first. William Devlin is very much alive." St. Hubbins' mouth twisted. "And every bit as hot as he sounds. Technical wizard with a spy network that governments would give their entire national treasury to own doesn't even begin to cover it. And, as for his flair for making a dramatic exit, well trust me, even I'm jealous."

"Sure," I sighed. "And he's currently living on a remote tropical island with Lillian Virginia Mountweazel and Elvis."

"Can't answer for the latter two, but William Devlin is right here in Morgansburg. But don't take my word for it. Google him. Or more accurately, google one William Byrne Devlin. The fifth of that name, I believe. 'MacGyver' to his friends and enemies alike—and by all accounts the guy more than earned his nickname. Once upon a time one of Army Intelligence's most valuable assets, and apparently poised to step into the shoes of his father, General William 'Wild Bill' Devlin, as the most powerful spymaster in the world."

The thought was so absurd that the penny simply refused to drop. 'MacGyver' Byrne? *Mack* Byrne?

Yet, much as I hated to admit it, St. Hubbins's story made perfect sense—or at least as much sense as you could expect from someone who was by his own admission, a government-sanctioned con man. The PTSD after watching his men blown up. The jokes about programming one-handed. His calm suggestion about how Paul Morgan might weaponize a computer monitor to take me hostage.

"Christ," I said softly. "No wonder the man is obsessed with the expendables."

"Regular Boy Scout, our boy Devlin," St. Hubbins allowed. "Which is why it galls me that I was the one who sent him riding to your rescue. Trust me, I know what I'm up against, and, frankly, a reasonable man would allow he has no hope. But I'm not a reasonable man, as you may well have already discovered."

"Indeed. But be that as it may, you're getting way ahead of yourself here. There's no question of me falling for either William Devlin or Mack Byrne, any more than there's a question of him falling for me."

Doyle and St. Hubbins snorted in tandem. "Have it your own way," St. Hubbins said. "Just don't delude yourself that this means I'm giving up the fight. I'll be back, Dr. Watson. But I'll be damned if I'll play Miles Standish next time."

St. Hubbins vanished into the shadows just as surely as Devlin's avatar had blinked into nothingness—and I began the rest of the walk back to my apartment, my head spinning with images that I longed to put into a spreadsheet to see if they made any more sense that way. Only to find Byrne looming on my doorstep.

"Time for our debriefing?" I asked warily.

"I was honestly thinking of something more informal," Byrne said. "That wasn't half-bad work back there at the diner, you know? If you were of a mind to celebrate, it's Trivia Night down at the Olde Dutch Tavern. We could talk in between rounds. You'd have to leave your Little Friend at home, though. House rules. No phones. No internet."

I opened my mouth to answer—no, to suck down the air that had whooshed out of me when I got a good look at the ghastly tattoo that covered most of Byrne's forearm.

You didn't have to look hard to see the scars it masked—and ridged his entire palm.

When I could finally breathe again, his eyes were glinting with unwilling humor. "Good thing I invited you for trivia night, not poker," he said. "I assume St. Hubbins has been sticking his nose where he shouldn't again?"

"Something like that," I said, my eyes drifting back to that tattoo.

Byrne held up his other hand and snapped his fingers. "Only takes one hand to be quick on the buzzer. And I've got plenty of fast twitch muscles left over in this one."

Fast twitch muscles that could operate an avatar with one hand tied behind his back. But surely even he couldn't teach an avatar to kiss like that…

"Did you really put your hand through a monitor and grab a live power strip?"

"Unfortunate accident," he allowed. "I tripped and smashed through the screen, then grabbed the power supply for balance. Poor judgment on my part."

"I'll say. Did it hurt?"

"Like hell. I was incoherent on pain killers for nearly a month." A small smile that I was certain qualified as plausible deniability. "Unfortunate, that. Had it been otherwise, I might have been able to warn them about the dead man's switch that required my palm print every morning. Sure, the burns had destroyed my palm print, but I could have McGyvered a workaround if I hadn't been floating on a sea of morphine. Instead, all my networks were destroyed."

"That's what you meant when you said Devlin was dead."

He raised an eyebrow. "And so is Operation Dragon's Den, so don't bother trying to go find it. Trust me, when I scrub a system, it stays scrubbed."

"What about the rest?" I asked. "Are you on the lam?"

"Of course not! What kind of irresponsible asshole would approach a woman he cared about while—" He cut himself off and shook his head. "No, I'm not on the lam. I'm simply off the grid. Honorable discharge. Line of duty injury. My asshole of a father would have it no other way. He would have gone for the Purple Heart if I hadn't threatened to…well, that's need-to-know as well."

I just nodded. Now did not seem the time to delve into Byrne's family history.

"So, what do you say?" Byrne changed the subject pointedly, nodding at the cell phone in my hand. "Afraid to leave home without your wingman?"

I took a deep gulp of air so I could refuse. And heard myself say instead, "Doyle will be just as happy to spend the night at home running batch scripts. He says the buzzers diminish the purity of the game. Considers them a hardware problem."

Byrne eyed me narrowly, and I tried not to notice that the tips of his ears had gone bright red. "Then do you need a ride, or can you find your way there without GPS?"

"I can find my own way," I said turning to go. "I'll meet you down there in half an hour."

"Without your wingman?" Doyle protested as soon as Byrne was out of earshot. "Are you sure that's quite wise?"

"Enough with the wingman!" I snapped. "Byrne wants a drinking buddy for trivia, not another kiss in the Dragon's Den."

Doyle snorted. "Have it your way, if that's how you must justify it to yourself. But I'm afraid those batch scripts are going to have to wait. I have a rather interesting little office pool I'd prefer to set up instead…"

"On-line gambling is strictly illegal in this county."

"Oh, I'd scarcely go as far as calling it organized gambling. Just a quiet little wager among colleagues."

"Like your friend Lillian Virginia Mountweazel?"

"Not exclusively. I'm sure there will be few others that will have as great an interest in the outcome as she and I do."

I drew a deep breath. "Said outcome being?"

"Two such very different swains," Doyle mused. "And yet so similar in both their fascination with your not inconsiderable intellectual charms and their demonstrable determination to succeed at whatever challenge they may be confronted with."

"Enough! You are not here to play matchmaker. And that's a direct command."

"Oh, there's no matchmaker needed. It's perfectly obvious which one you *should* end up with. The question is, which one you *will* end up with."

ACKNOWLEDGEMENTS

Thanks to Richie Narvaez for his thoughtful comments on an earlier version of this manuscript.

Thanks as always to the team at Amphorae, and especially to Kristina Blank Makansi for her patient editing, which made this a far better book.

And especial thanks to my husband, George Baird, who is always up for the most improbable of research trips at a moment's notice. I couldn't do it without you, George.

ABOUT THE AUTHOR

Erica Obey is the author of five other mysteries set in the Hudson Valley, including the award-winning *The Curse of the Braddock Brides*. Erica is the past president of the New York Chapter of Mystery Writers of America, as well as a frequent reviewer and contest judge. She holds a Ph.D. in Comparative Literature and published academic work on female folklorists before she decided she'd rather be writing the stories herself. She lives with her husband and a rotating assortment of cats in a historic arts colony in Woodstock, N.Y., where she researches the history of the colony's collections when she's not hiking or gardening.